I0732875

PRAISE FOR FREYA BARKER

Freya Barker writes a mean romance, I tell you! A REAL romance, with real characters and real conflict.

~*Author M. Lynne Cunning*

I've said it before and I'll say it again and again, Freya Barker is one of the BEST storytellers out there.

~*Turning Pages At MidnightBook Blog*

God, Freya Barker gets me every time I read one of her books. She's a master at creating a beautiful story that you lose yourself in the moment you start reading.

~*Britt Red Hatter Book Blog*

Freya Barker has woven a delicate balance of honest emotions and well-formed characters into a tale that is as unique as it is gripping.

~*Ginger Scott, bestselling young and new adult author and Goodreads Choice Awards finalist*

Such a truly beautiful story! The writing is gorgeous, the scenery is beautiful...

~*Author Tia Louise*

From Dust by Freya Barker is one of those special books. One of those whose plotline and characters remain with you for days after you finished it.

~*Jeri's Book Attic*

No amount of words could describe how this story made me feel, I think this is one I will remember forever, absolutely freaking awesome is not even close to how I felt about it.

~Lilian's Book Blog

Still Air was insightful, eye-opening, and I paused numerous times to think about my relationships with my own children. Anytime a book can evoke a myriad of emotions while teaching life lessons you'll continue to carry with you, it's a 5-star read.

~ Bestselling Author CP Smith

In my opinion, there is nothing better than a Freya Barker book. With her final installment in her Portland, ME series, Still Air, she does not disappoint. From start to finish I was completely captivated by Pam, Dino, and the entire Portland family.

~ Author RB Hilliard

The one thing you can always be sure of with Freya's writing is that it will pull on ALL of your emotions; it's expressive, meaningful, sarcastic, so very true to life, real, hard-hitting and heartbreaking at times and, as is the case with this series especially, the story is at points raw, painful and occasionally fugly BUT it is also sweet, hopeful, uplifting, humorous and heart-warming.

~ Book Loving Pixies

ALSO BY FREYA BARKER

ON CALL SERIES:

BURNING FOR AUTUMN

COVERING OLLIE (May 14, 2019)

ROCK POINT SERIES:

KEEPING 6

CABIN 12

HWY 550

10-CODE (Coming soon!)

NORTHERN LIGHTS COLLECTION:

A CHANGE OF TIDE

A CHANGE OF VIEW

A CHANGE OF PACE

SNAPSHOT SERIES:

SHUTTER SPEED

FREEZE FRAME

IDEAL IMAGE

PICTURE PERFECT (coming soon!)

La Plata County FBI
ROCK POINT SERIES 3

HWY 550

FREYA BARKER

ISBN: 978-1-988733-36-4

Cover Design:
RE&D - Margreet Asselbergs

Editing:
Karen Hrdlicka

Proofing:
Joanne Thompson

Interior Design:
CP Smith

DEDICATION

To the most amazing group of friends
a girl could ask for.

"I do not wish to treat friendships daintily, but with the roughest courage. When they are real, they are not glass threads or frost-work, but the solidest thing we know." - Ralph Waldo Emerson

HWY 550

CHAPTER 1

Luna

"Just picked up some interesting chatter on the scanner. There was another one last night."

I look up as Jasper saunters into the office, carrying a bag of sandwiches from the small deli a block over. Starved, since I never really got around to breakfast this morning, I snatch up my order and have my mouth full with the first giant bite before I respond.

"Where?"

Jasper wipes the crumbs I accidentally sent airborne off his shirt.

"Jesus, Luna. Feeding you requires a hazmat suit."

"Sorry," I mumble, this time behind my hand. "Hungry."

"So I gather. You really need to start eating like normal people, you know…Anyway, yes, a store in

Silverton. Mostly the same MO—maybe ten minutes before closing, two masked guys, both armed—but this time they left a calling card." He takes a bite of his own sandwich and leaves me hanging.

I wipe my mouth before talking this time. "And?"

"As before, one covered employees while the other ransacked the place, but apparently he dropped his gun and never picked it up."

I have to think on that for a bit. Seems strange that after pulling off a string of robberies with near perfection, these guys would suddenly do something so stupid.

"Seems out of character," I observe.

"Maybe they were spooked. I'm pulling the full report now." He shoves half his lunch in his mouth and turns to his computer screen.

Jasper is our resident techie slash hacker, and although I can hold my own in a pinch, I have nowhere near the practiced ease with which he extrapolates information from the web. Especially information not meant for the public eye.

We first heard of these robberies about a week ago, when we received an internal memo from David Aiken, head honcho of the main FBI office in Denver, to keep an eye out for any similar cases popping up in our backyard. In our case that backyard constitutes the southwest corner of Colorado: Archuleta, Dolores, La Plata, Mineral, Montezuma, and San Juan counties. Bordering three other states, our field office is generally a busy place, but luckily we have a good relationship with local law enforcement. Much easier to work with friends than with adversaries.

SAC Damian Gomez, my boss, immediately got in touch with Durango PD and the various sheriffs' offices to give them a heads up and to see if there'd been any reports that would fit the bill. So far nothing. At least not in the past month or two, and nothing quite as professional as these recent robberies. From all accounts, these guys made off with not only a good haul of cash, but enough marijuana bud to set up a respectable distribution network of their own.

"Apparently they pistol-whipped one of the employees without much provocation, according to other staff, dropped the gun, and hightailed it out of there," Jasper paraphrases from the report he's reading off his computer.

Crumpling up my napkin and tossing it in the trash on passing, I walk up and lean down to read over his shoulder. "Holy shit! Fifteen grand and another ten in high-grade product in one take? Nice haul, Silverton isn't as big as some of the previous ones they hit."

"That's well over a hundred grand cash in total, on top of at least eighty-five thousand street value in product," Damian announces, coming out of his office. "They're making their way through Colorado in a highly profitable way, and geographically, guess what's next on the map?"

"Right here." I knew that when I heard Silverton. These guys look to be making their way south, and even though there are some dispensaries between there and Durango, nothing that would net a decent return. They could score big in Durango.

"Exactly, so let's see if we can get ahead of these guys. Start contacting every last dispensary in town, see what their security measures are, and encourage them to upgrade. Make a list from most vulnerable to least. Jas, work on those with cameras and do what you need so we can tap into those directly."

It's past seven by the time I get out of the office after spending all afternoon cold-calling pot stores. On my best day, I'm not the most sociable person, and this afternoon required me to use up my quota of nice for the week. People are stupid, on the whole. They don't heed warnings, because they think shit will pass them by. Well, I have news for them, shit doesn't pick and choose, it just hits randomly. I should know. Not only from personal experience, but also from what I've seen in my years with the Bureau. Bad stuff happens to good people all the damn time.

I'm about to turn left to go home, to a hot shower, my eclectic collection of brews, and an unhealthy addiction to Netflix—all of which are meant to help me get to sleep, but won't—when I spot the sign for a yoga studio I've been eyeing for months.

I actually laughed at my therapist the first time he suggested yoga to help me relax. My attempts to accomplish that usually involve a good session at the shooting range, where I visualize faces on my targets, or a good romp with Jasper or Dylan, my other teammate, in the ring at the gym, but nothing quite as noncombative as yoga. Maybe it's worth a try.

Without thinking too hard, I turn right instead.

Joomba Yoga Studio. What the fuck kind of name is that? More like something you'd see on a daycare center. The more obscure boxing gym adjoining looks to be more my speed. The building looks to be an industrial warehouse. Its only redeeming feature: the large garage doors I can just see around the back when I park, open to the Animas River running by.

The promise of sleep and the draw of the river stronger than the urge to run, I grab the sports bag I always have at the ready in the back of my Jeep and aim for the entrance marked as the yoga studio.

"Can I help you?"

The tall, svelte—and damn her—stacked woman behind the counter when I enter, greets me with a wide smile.

"Yeah, maybe. Do you have a class I could try out? This is my first time here." I hate feeling like a newbie, but I doubt I can pass for seasoned in this place. Next door I could probably hold my own, but yoga is alien to me.

The woman checks the clock before turning back to me. "I have a novice class starting in five minutes, if you're looking for something right away. Can I sign you up for a membership, or would you prefer to pay as you go?"

"Pay as I go," I answer quickly. Memberships make me nervous. Any kind of commitment other than my job has me break out in hives. I don't like predictability, it can be dangerous, which is why I don't live in one place longer than maybe six months at a time, and I rarely share where I live.

I pay the woman the amount she quotes, and follow her directions to a locker room, where I quickly change into bike shorts and a fitted tank top. It never occurred to me most of the people joining this class would be women. In fact, the only man in the group appears to be the instructor. It's fine by me, I'm used to working with men, I've learned how to read them much better than I do women.

I'm told to grab a loaner mat from a rack on the wall—most people have brought their own it appears—and roll it out in a spot to the right of a woman who looks like she's done this before. I follow her suit and lie down on my mat, waiting for further instructions.

This is not comfortable for me: I feel vulnerable, I can't see everything from this vantage point, and lying on my back, I'm at a distinct advantage in case of an attack. Of course I'm not quite sure who'd have any interest in launching an offense on a bunch of women in tights, but still.

Then the instructor starts talking about breathing and how it has to be the center of our focus. Through the nose and on a long steady loop, in and out without interruption. When the class starts collectively humming, I'm about ready to make a run for it. Not one thing about this is particularly relaxing. It's just… weird.

I'm glad when we're told we can sit up, I can see the whole space in the mirrors.

"Stretch your legs out in front of you, your arms over your head, hands reaching for the sky, and breathe in through the tips of your fingers, all the way down to your toes."

The fuck?

Last time I checked, my lungs weren't attached to either my fingers or my toes, so I'm not sure what to do with that.

The last straw comes when I'm trying to copy the woman next to me on something called Balasana, on my knees with my upper body bent forward, hands spread and flat down on the mat. I'm concentrating so hard on my neighbor, trying to get all the mechanics right, I don't hear the instructor approach until I feel hands pressing down on my shoulders. In one move I have the man on his stomach on the floor, his arms pinned under my knees and his head torqued back in an uncomfortable chokehold.

Needless to say, that doesn't go over too well.

Mumbling apologies, I slink back to the locker room, shove my feet in my boots, and grabbing my bag walk out with my head high, throwing what I hope is a casual wave at the woman behind the counter.

Ramped up on adrenaline I need to get rid of, I push through the door of the boxing gym next door, hoping for release on a punching bag or on a training partner in the ring.

I don't even notice the motorcycles parked out front.

Ouray

"Paco, Rowtag, you two are with me. Kaga, take Lusio with you and check on the apartments. Rest of you, head home—Momma probably has a massive pot of something waiting."

I just pulled the crew off the road before the turnoff up the mountain. We've been on the road for a couple of days, coming back from a bike rally in Morrison, just outside Denver. That event is usually the first of a number of rallies we annually attend, and every year these long rides seem to get harder on the body. Since we've been gone for a good week—only Nosh, Momma and the younger cubs staying behind—we need to check in on a couple of our properties in town.

I wait until my second-in-command takes off with Lusio, wave the rest of them up the mountain, and lead the other two guys straight across the road to the gym.

"Do we got time for a quick workout?" Rowtag asks when we park our bikes.

"Half an hour, and I'm not waiting for your ass," I bark, annoyed at the kid for keeping us waiting a few times on this trip, while he was out doing fuck knows what. I throw Paco a look he receives with a chin lift. He'll be on the kid.

I take a minute, stretching my legs and getting feeling back in my ass, before I follow the younger men inside. Instead of going into the gym, I slip into Bubba's office. Bubba Williams is the gym's manager, a former pro boxer turned MMA trainer and in high demand with some of the young kids dreaming of making it big in the sport. He's a decent manager too, keeping track of the day-to-day running and administration for the gym, the only drawback is he's totally computer illiterate and does everything by hand.

That means I have to go in and physically scan the books, instead of taking a quick look on my laptop back at the compound. I do that with the other businesses, including the yoga studio next door. Happy as fuck about that too, I'll avoid taking a step in there at any cost. Last time I did, I got suckered into something that took for fucking ever to get out of.

Bubba is on the phone and waves me to the visitor chair by his desk. Of course, before I can sit, I have to move a box of protein powder. Bubba's office is a hoarder's paradise. The one time he and I got into it was when I hired a girl to help him with filing and shit. He almost walked out on the spot. I've never messed with his management style or his office since, and as long as he's bringing in the numbers, I never will.

Still yapping on the phone, he shoves his thick

ledger across the desk at me, and I start flipping through the entries for the past two weeks. I have an issue with trust, something all of our managers know about me. If they can't handle me keeping a tight rein on the wallet, I'm happy to show them the door.

Ten years ago, when I took over the gavel, and proceeded to move the Arrow's Edge MC toward more legit business ventures, I promised the guys they wouldn't lose out on income. The process hasn't been without significant discord in the club at times, and we've had members leave because of it. But when pot was legalized four years ago, it justified my move away from the stuff. It doesn't mean the pressure is any less to bring home the bacon another way, which is why I stay on top of the books.

"So how was Morrison?" Bubba finally asks after ending his call. His big frame bends the desk chair back farther than it was built to go, and he folds his hands behind his head.

"Good. Music was good, guys had fun. Can't complain."

"You know what you're not saying is loud, right?" Bubba chuckles at my expense. "Getting old, my man."

"Shit." I run a hand over my face. "You're not lyin'. I fucking feel every bone in my body. And the drinkin', Jesus, I can barely keep up. Even that kid out there holds his liquor better'n I do." I point through the dirt-covered window looking out on the gym. Rowtag is climbing into the ring where some other young punk is already waiting, getting ready for a spar. "What the fuck kind gear is that?" I'm referring to the tight shorts and top, the guy is…"Is that a girl?"

Bubba sits forward in his chair and the two of us watch Rowtag get the snot beat out of him by some girl, a head shorter than him.

"Sheeeeeit, that dumpling's putting a hurting on your boy, Chief."

There's something familiar about the tightly controlled moves of Rowtag's opponent. I walk out of the office and into the gym to get a closer look. Just in time to see Rowtag try to avoid the sharp snap of her gloves by folding her in a bear hug and trying to take her to the mat. That apparently wasn't a good choice on his part either, because now she twists in his hold, grabs the back of his head, throws her hip into it, and flips him—easy as pie—on his damn back. The hooting and hollering is not going to go over well, as every set of eyes in the gym is focused on the bout in the ring. Although you can barely call it a bout, the feisty little thing is wiping the goddamn floor with him.

"Rowtag! Get your ass out of the ring," I call out, walking toward them.

The girl backs off him, and the kid scrambles to his feet, ripping off his gloves and the protective gear from his head, flinging them into the gym. Bubba's gonna have something to say about that, but Rowtag's too pissed to care as he storms off.

Up close I can tell the woman in the ring is not as

young as I thought she was. I watch her slowly turn to me as she pulls the headgear off. Dayum.

"Well," I drawl, with a shit-eating grin on my face. "If it isn't my favorite FBI agent. How are you doin', darlin'?"

Her blue eyes squint at me as she shakes out her blonde shoulder-length curls, before she answers, a little smirk on her face.

"Fuck of a lot better now I got to take down that punk of yours."

She slips between the ropes, throws her gear in the duffle bag, and stuffs her feet in a pair of cowboy boots that look ridiculous with the tight athletic outfit she's wearing. With a toss of her hair, she flings the bag over her shoulder and marches right past me out the door, head held high.

Fuck if another taste of that feisty sprite of an FBI agent's attitude doesn't give me an instant hard-on.

CHAPTER 2

OURAY

Damn, my bed feels good after way too many nights on cheap, lumpy mattresses in second-rate motel rooms.

I'm generally an early riser, but the past couple of mornings—since coming back from our ten-day trip—I've had a hard time hauling my ass out of bed in the morning. My phone alarm goes off again, and this time, instead of silencing it, I swing my legs out of bed first. If I want to get to Cortez by ten, I'd better hustle.

The call came in last night from a buddy who runs a tattoo place in Cortez. He'd been watching this kid going through the dumpsters in the alley behind his shop for a couple of days, and last night he caught him trying to get into his van parked out back. The boy, only about twelve or thirteen, looked like he'd been on the street for a good long time. Dirty, smelling like he'd not seen water in weeks, and attitude too big for his scrawny, skin-over-bone body, Al hauled him to his apartment over the shop. He stuck him in the shower, and washed the kid's dirt-caked clothes while the boy ate half the contents of Al's fridge.

He hadn't been able to get much out of the boy last night. Kid was tight-lipped and wouldn't even share his name, but he fell asleep on the couch. Al called me right away.

We pick up strays. Lost boys. Kids who should be hitting their pillow every night, safe in knowing there are adults who will watch over them, but instead have to sleep in places that require keeping one eye open at all times to see danger coming. I grew up like that. On the streets, living off the dregs other people threw out, and leery of every single person who even looked at me. You learn that real fast.

I hop in the shower and quickly get dressed. No time for a leisurely coffee on my deck this morning, but a quick run up to the compound to pick up Paco and the truck. Momma is waiting with a fresh pot.

"You're a lifesaver this morning," I tell her with a kiss on her cheek. Everyone calls her Momma, but to me she is the only mother I've known.

"I'm a lifesaver every damn morning, and you well know it. Now go and bring me that boy back." Crusty as always, but with a heart so big it can hold the world.

Momma is good with the boys. She's usually the

first one they open up to. Sometimes they're simple runaways, wanting to get away from a home with too many rules for their liking. Those kids often just need someone to listen, and in most cases are willingly returned to the care of their parents. A lot of them escape the foster system, which is still far from perfect and places kids in homes where all they care about is the small check they get each month. More kids than you'd think take off out of self-preservation. Whether it be violence, abuse, or neglect, some are kids so desperate that living out of dumpsters, without any basic life comforts, is preferable to staying in that situation.

"You drive, Paco." I hop in the passenger seat of the extended cab Silverado. Paco is the only guy I'll ever be passenger to. He's a good driver. The rest of them are fucking kamikaze pilots. I wouldn't even trust my right-hand man, Kaga, to drive me to the corner of the street. Fucking wannabe NASCAR drivers—the lot of them.

"Tell me about the boy," Paco says in his quiet voice when we leave Durango behind us.

"Don't know much. Kid doesn't talk—at all. Only sounds Al says he made, were when he was scarfing down whatever he could get his hands on."

"Any signs of violence on the kid?"

"Some scars, but nothing recent as far as he could tell."

"Age?"

"Very young teens."

Paco nods, keeping his focus on the road. He's what you'd call our shaman. He's the one who homeschools the kids, although we haven't had one this young in quite some time. Quiet, unassuming, and for all appearances a pacifist—until you threaten to hurt one of his *family*—then he becomes lethal. I've seen it happen.

"We'll have to stop at Walmart on the way home," he points out. "We've got a few clean things for older kids, but nothing for one this young."

"That's fine."

This is what we do, we catch the kids who are threatening to slip through the cracks. It's what Arrow's Edge has done since its inception back in the seventies, under Nosh's guidance. We'll drive anywhere, but only bring back boys, since law enforcement would be all up our ass if we started taking on girls. It's hard enough staying mostly under the radar as it is. Any girls we encounter we call in a shelter working out of Grand Junction. The boys who have nothing and nowhere to go back to can stay with us. We feed them, guide them, even homeschool them, and we keep them safe. If they stay with the MC, they can opt to become cubs, or prospects, when they turn eighteen.

Al's shop, Skin Art, is still closed, but when we pull in around the back, we can see him out on the fire escape behind his apartment, having a smoke.

"Christ, I'm glad you're here," he says when we make our way up the stairs. "Kid locked himself inside the bathroom when I tried to ruffle his hair this morning, and he won't come out." He flicks his cigarette in the alley below and grabs me in a one-armed man hug.

"Guess you are happy to see us," I joke when he gives a very uncomfortable Paco the same treatment. "Get anything out of him?"

"Not a peep. Damn kid looks at me like I'm some fucking pervert. Y'all know I don't roll like that." Al walks ahead into the apartment and points at tools lying in front of the closed bathroom door. "I was gonna take the door off, but thought I'd wait for you guys instead."

In the next five minutes we have the door leaning against the wall, revealing a skinny kid pressed into the corner between the tub and the toilet, no more than a scant five feet tall with dirty-blond hair. The shirt he's wearing has seen better days, and is about two sizes too small, as are the threadbare track pants he has on.

"We'd like to help you out, kid, but we're gonna need a name," I try, studying as he tilts his head slightly, watching my mouth move but doesn't say a word. "Give me a few with him, will ya?" I ask the other two on a hunch. When they move into the small kitchen, I slide on the floor, with my back against the wall facing the door.

I'm getting too old to sit on the damn floor. I just move my mouth without making a sound, and the kid reacts the same way: a slight tilt to the head and eyes on the movement of my lips. Damn kid's deaf.

My name is Ouray. I spell my name with my fingers, and note his eyes shift from my lips to my hands. *Al, the man who lives here, is a good friend. He called me because he knows I help kids in trouble.* This time I only use sign language and he seems to follow along.

It's clear that at some point in this kid's life he learned ASL.

What's your name?

The wait is long, in reality probably no more than a minute or two, but it fucking feels like an eternity. I almost miss the hesitant movement of his fingers as he spells out *C O D Y.*

Nice to meet you, Cody. I know you have no reason to trust me, and there's not a lot I can do about that. All I can do is tell you why I'm here, sitting on a floor outside a bathroom, talking to you.

For the next ten minutes I give the kid a hint at my own history, and a description of the club. Occasionally he motions for me to stop and I have to spell out certain words for him. It's a lot like taming a wild animal when dealing with some of these kids. And this boy in particular—since he is deaf—feels more threatened than most.

It takes another ten to coax him out of the bathroom and into the kitchen, where Paco and Al are waiting. Al can't sign, but Paco can, and he quickly introduces himself.

You all know sign language? the kid asks.

The former president of our club is deaf. Most of us have learned ASL because of him.

The sight of the slimmest of smiles breaking through on that boy's face slices my gut. I'll be damned if I won't teach him how to laugh again.

LUNA

"Did you see this?"

I toss the memo that just came in from the Denver office on Damian's desk and wait for him to scan its contents.

"No shit."

"Yeah, the gun was registered to one Mark Strongbow. A local guy. Never heard the name though, have you?"

Damian looks up at me with a smirk on his face. "I know the guy. Not so sure I like him for these robberies, though. Still, guess we should have a chat with him. Why don't you take Dylan?"

I turn to look at Dylan Barnes, the youngest member of our team, who seems engrossed in whatever he's doing with the filing cabinet.

"I can handle it," I respond under my breath, wondering if I've given Damian reason to doubt my abilities.

"Rein it in, Roosberg," my boss cautions, his voice low and an eyebrow raised. "That was not a question so much as an order. Furthermore, I know damn well you can handle it, but aside from the fact Dylan needs to get out of the office before he starts reorganizing my desk from sheer boredom as well, I think you'll appreciate having some backup once you get up there."

It's true, things have been slow. Other than backing up the Durango PD on a few of their cases, we've seen little action this summer. Just a couple of cyber security cases I've been assisting Jasper with.

Something about what Damian says nags at me. "Where's 'up there'?"

"County Road 205. The Arrow's Edge compound."

"Arrow's Edge? What am I doing there?" I ask, even though I can guess the answer. First time I was up there I was investigating a weapon as well. They run a decent outdoor shooting range, there aren't that many around.

"That's where you'll find Mark Strongbow."

"How can you be so sure he's there?"

"Pretty positive they know him up there, just ask at the gate."

Can't say I particularly look forward to heading into the gated compound again and running the risk of bumping into the club's fearless leader. I just did that two nights ago at the gym.

The man gets under my damn skin every time I run into him. Misogynistic pig. Looks at me like I'm some alien specimen under a microscope. I'm likely an anomaly in his world, being a strong, capable woman. Felt damn good though to teach that young punk a lesson in the ring. The kid's attitude is even worse than his boss's. Foulmouthed little miscreant.

"Barnes!" I call out, as I walk to the door. "You're coming with."

I hear the scrape of his desk chair on the floor, and next thing I know the heavy fall of his boots is right behind me on the stairs. The guy's like a coiled spring, ready to jump into action.

"Where to?" he asks when we get to the bureau-issued Expedition. He tries to round the SUV to the driver's side, but I just throw him a dirty look. I was the rookie in the office for the longest time until Dylan joined, it's my time to reap some seniority perks. He doesn't argue and gets into the passenger seat.

"Name came up on the weapon left at the scene of that last robbery in Silverton. According to Damian, we can find the guy at the Arrow's Edge compound."

"Sweet."

I glance sideways at him as I drive off the parking lot. Not an expression I would've expected from the mostly quiet man. Guess it's inevitable, MCs seem to have that effect on men of any age. It's a fantasy: bikes, brotherhood, the lure of the open road, freedom. Although if I'm honest, I have to admit the lifestyle has its appeal. There have been times I've been sitting on the porch of my small home, drinking my morning coffee, listening to those bikes rumble by, when I've wondered what that life would be like. Living outside of any kind of established structure, away from society's expectations.

I use the drive up the mountain to update Dylan on the latest in the case. The weapon, left at the Silverton scene, is a Smith & Wesson M&P series, nine millimeter rounds, all accounted for. So far, other than a few of the less compliant employees who were pistol-whipped, no weapons have been fired at any of the robberies.

Just my luck, the gate is manned by a familiar lanky figure, who is not going to be happy to see me.

"The fuck do you want now, bitch?"

Yup, as expected, the young man's attitude hasn't improved one bit. I'm tempted to go another round with him, but since this is a professional call, I shall have to restrain myself.

"Dylan." I turn to my partner, who is grinding his teeth and glaring at the kid. One wrong move will undoubtedly set him off. My curse to be saddled with men intent on defending my virtue. "I don't believe you've been properly introduced to this delightful creature. Meet Rowtag, gatekeeper extraordinaire, but unfortunately his false sense of power doesn't do much for him in hand-to-hand combat."

The kid may not have two brain cells to rub together, but he knows a taunt when he hears one. This is confirmed when I hear the sound of a safety catch releasing right by my ear. I watch Dylan's eyes flick to mine before they narrow over my shoulder. Taking in a deep breath, on my exhale, I swing my elbow around through the open window, catching the kid off guard. Before he knows what's coming, I have the gun knocked out of his grip, his hand twisted in an unnatural position, and his body pulled through the window. My face is inches from his, and I work hard not to flinch at the unwashed stench wafting off him.

"A little slow on the uptake, are we?" I ignore the hate-filled eyes directed at me. Not making any friends today. "Let's try this the polite way. I am looking for an individual by the name of Mark Strongbow. I've been told I can find him here. I suspect he might be a member of the shooting range? Could you please find out for me?"

"Let the boy go."

I should've expected that too. Fate would not be so kind as to let me off the hook today. I turn my head and watch Ouray's leisurely approach.

"Would love to, but he wanted to play with guns, and I wasn't in the mood today. I'd rather not let go until the gun is secured, if you don't mind." The kid is trying to twist out of my hold, which isn't getting him anywhere. It's amazing how easy it is to control someone's movements, without exerting a whole lot of strength, by simply manipulating a few small parts. It's the first thing I was taught in my old self-defense training: eyes, nose, fingers, and my personal favorite, balls.

Ouray slowly shakes his head, that perpetual toothpick hanging from the lopsided grin on his lips. He momentarily disappears from view when he bends down to collect the weapon, holding it up for me to see as he resets the safety, and tucks the gun behind his back.

The moment I release the kid, his other hand, curled in a fist, comes flying through the window, but falls a fraction of an inch short of the bridge of my nose. Courtesy of Ouray, who has his paw around the kid's fist, doing some manipulating of his own, judging from the kid's face.

"Lesson I thought you would've learned at the gym, Rowtag: brute force rarely ever wins out over dexterity and cunning. Now open the fuckin' gate and let 'em through. I'm keeping your gun for now."

Like I said, I doubt I'm making any friends today, Ouray may have well asked the kid to hand over his dick.

"So, Agent Roosberg," the man drawls when I park the Expedition and he pulls open my door. "To what do we owe the pleasure?"

"Knock off the theatrics, Ouray. We need to speak to someone by the name of Mark Strongbow." I turn to include Dylan, but he's already off ogling the collection of bikes parked on the other side. Figures. "We were told we could find him here."

Ouray tilts his head to one side, giving me that semi-amused, semi-inquisitive look again. "Who told you that?"

"SAC Gomez." My response seems to be funny, since it elicits an amused chuckle. "Don't see what's so amusing," I snap, already bristling at the man.

"Funny part is, SAC Gomez apparently left some

information out," he says lazily, chewing on the end of that damn toothpick.

"And what would that be?"

I hate my short stature, especially when I have to look up and squint into the sun to see the man in front of me.

"I'm Mark Strongbow."

CHAPTER 3

OURAY

I leave her standing with her mouth hanging open and walk inside, straight through to my office, in the assumption she'll eventually follow.

To say her use of my legal name has thrown me is an understatement. Other than Nosh, Momma, and the guys who've been here long enough, it's not widely known. Granted, I'm forced to use it on official paperwork, banking, driver's license and such, but since I'm only addressed by my road name here, most people in my circle don't know me as anything else. It's always been my way to keep a little bit of privacy from the club.

An unsettled feeling enters my office with me. I have a sense this may have something to do with the theft I reported Friday night in Morrison. I dismissed it at the time—this kind of shit often happens at rallies—things get stolen from saddlebags and motel rooms often. That's why I carry most anything worthwhile on my body.

"You are Mark Strongbow?"

I knew she would follow. Stepping around her, I shut the door, closing out any nosy fucks out there.

"Not something I advertise, but yes, that's me."

"You don't want it known?" She seems curious, sitting down across from my desk when a knock sounds on the door. "That's probably Dylan," she explains, getting up again to let in her partner. "Have you guys met? Special Agent Barnes, meet Mark Strongbow."

I have to say, the guy has an impressive poker face. The small flicker of surprise is gone as fast as it appeared. I remember him from last summer when Gomez's sister got snatched. I shake his offered hand and wave him to a chair.

"To answer your question, no, I don't really feel the need to advertise my name."

"Guess it would kill the mystique, wouldn't it?" Her sarcasm is loud and clear, and for some reason I feel compelled to explain.

"Doesn't have fuck to do with mystique and everything with wanting to keep some part of my life just for me."

"Oh, so lack of trust then?"

Goddammit, the woman seems intent on pushing all my buttons, and I catch myself before I bite again.

"What can I do for you, darlin'?" I purposely use

my drawl and do a bit of poking myself. I know damn well she hates to be addressed like that, which is why I like doing it. The chip on this woman's shoulder is visible from outer space. She does all she can to be seen as one of the guys, and everything to hide the fact she's a woman. A mighty attractive one at that.

I watch as she presses her lips together and takes a deep inhale before she leans forward to address me.

"Do you own a nine millimeter Smith & Wesson?"

"More than one." I shrug, lean back in my chair, and plop my boots on the desk. "Most of them are up at the shooting range in the gun locker."

"Can you tell me your whereabouts for the past two weeks?"

That sense of unease suddenly turns cold in my veins. She's fishing for something and I'm at the fucking receiving end. I pretend to look at the calendar on my desk, just to get my bearings while my mind spins at warp speed.

"We were in Morrison for a rally. We left the Tuesday before, to do the Million Dollar Highway ride like we do every year with a couple of other clubs. Got to Morrison Friday the seventeenth—you can check with the local PD because I filed a report that night for stolen property. Left Monday for the second leg of our ride, staying in Pueblo for a night, stopped in Crested Butte the next day, and spent that night in Montrose. Wednesday Ouray, and Thursday we got back to town"

"What stolen property?" Of course she would

zoom in on that.

"Smith & Wesson. From my saddlebags. Fuckers slit the locked buckle."

"Really?" I'm not liking the smug smirk on the sprite's face. "How coincidental."

"Mind tellin' me what this is about, darlin'?"

Before she has a chance to respond, the other agent, Barnes or whatever, clarifies. "Series of armed robberies, Glenwood Springs, Avon, two in Denver, Pueblo, and Silverton, all dispensaries, all in the past two weeks. Your gun was found on the scene in Silverton."

That has me drop my boots to the floor and sit up straight. "No shit." Seeing the expression on both their faces, I can tell they're dead serious. *Motherfucker.* "I'm gonna need a smoke," I announce, walking past them out of the office, ignoring everyone in the common room.

"Chief?" Momma calls from the kitchen doorway. "Got a minute?"

"Not now, Momma. Can it wait?"

"Depends," she says. "Cody here has a knife at Nosh's throat, I'm suggesting you hold off on whatever you're running out to do to deal with this situation first."

Jesus fucking Christ. If it rains it pours.

"Hey, kiddo," I say, walking into the kitchen where Nosh is calmly sitting at the table, with a freaked-out kid behind him, holding Momma's favorite chef's knife against his throat. I know the kid can't hear me, but I also know he reads lips, and his panicked eyes are plastered to mine.

Without breaking stride, I walk up to the table, pull out the chair across from Nosh, and give the old man a nod.

Care to tell me what happened? The question is intended for Nosh, but I know Cody is watching too.

Kid got up without cleaning up his plate. I grabbed his arm. He doesn't seem to like that.

I snort, trust Nosh to be absolutely unmoved by the precarious situation he finds himself in. The man is cool as a cucumber, even with a trickle of blood running into the hollow of his throat. Kid must've nicked him.

I snap my fingers to get the boy's attention. *We have rules here. Momma does the cooking, but we all clean up after ourselves. That's what the old man was trying to tell you. He didn't know you don't like being touched. Nosh didn't mean anything by it. Put down the knife.*

The only response I get is a sharp shake of the head before his eyes flit over my shoulder. I assume others have entered the kitchen, but I keep my eyes on the boy. I hear hushed talking and rustling behind me; seeing panic grow on the boy's face, I quickly start signing, drawing his attention.

The man I told you about this morning, the one who took me in when I was living on the streets? I get a hesitant nod. *Same man you're holding a knife to. Nosh won't hurt you. I know that because I was you many years ago, and he never hurt me either. Put down the knife, Cody.*

His eyes dart behind me again, and from the corner of my eye I see the FBI sprite move closer, her hands furiously signing. *No one is angry with you. You can put down the knife and I promise nothing will happen to you. I sent everyone else away. If you want, you can hold onto the knife, but let Nosh go. He's a good man, I promise.*

Suddenly the kid moves the knife away from Nosh's throat and scurries into the corner by the fridge, holding the weapon out in front of him defensively. The damn fool woman moves to put herself between the knife and Nosh, who calmly drains his coffee, gets up, and sets his cup in the sink before sauntering out of the kitchen as if having a knife to his throat is an everyday occurrence. When he passes by me, he touches my shoulder and tilts his head to the door.

No fucking way, I sign, not about to leave her in the kitchen alone with the freaked-out kid.

She's got this.

I'm not sure where the hell the old man gets that insight from, but I'm not budging.

"You can go," she says without turning around. Just fucking great, we've got two mind readers now. "I'll be fine. I know what I'm doing."

Damn Nosh almost yanks me out of my chair by the back of my shirt. "Fine. But I'm staying right outside the door."

"Do what you have to, just give the kid some

space, will ya?"

For some reason that last remark reminds me what it's like to be in the kid's shoes. On the streets you learn fast that every action has consequences, and there is no one around to shield you from those. The boy freaked out, took action, and is simply waiting for those consequences to hit. It's what he's learned to expect. He may have trusted me earlier, but I'm still a fucking threat. Reluctantly I get up and follow Nosh out the door.

LUNA

Not sure what the kid is doing here, in the kitchen of an MC compound, but what I am sure of is he's scared out of his mind. The less people in here, the better it is.

When I hear both men exit the room, I turn my full focus back on the boy.

"My name is Luna. Do you want to come sit down at the table? You can keep the knife if you like." I'm actually talking out loud as I'm signing, for the benefit of whoever is outside the door listening in. I turn my back, my Spidey-sense on full alert in case he makes a move, and sit down at the table. I wait, maybe a few minutes, but finally I hear the shuffle of his feet on the linoleum as he rounds the table, sits down opposite me, and lays the knife down in front of him.

Who are you?

It's the first thing I've seen him sign. I clued in pretty much immediately the kid's deaf when I walked in and saw Ouray signing to him.

"FBI," I spell out, noting the jerk of surprise. "I needed Ouray's help on a case."

A girl agent?

"Sure, why not a girl agent?" I try not to grin.

You're small.

"True, I'm a little short," I confirm, "but I can kick the ass of a man twice my size."

He looks like he's not buying into it.

"Don't believe me? Ask Ouray, he's seen me fight." I'm hoping the man in question is listening, because this would be his cue to return, very calm like.

With him?

This time I don't hide the grin. *No, one of his guys, but I could kick his butt too.*

"I wouldn't count on it." Ouray appears to ignore the boy, whose hand shoots out and grabs the knife from the table, but he doesn't get up when Ouray pulls out a chair and sits down himself.

With one hand tied behind my back, I tell the kid with a smile, and I finally get a shadow of one back. *I may not be big, but I'm fast and I'm twice as smart.*

Can you teach me? he asks with innocent eagerness.

Christ. The boy kills me. Still not sure where Ouray picked this stray up, but the scars of a hard life shadow the light in the young kid's eyes.

Absolutely, I can, I promise, mentally scrambling to figure out how and where I might be able to do that with my unpredictable schedule, but one look at his face and I vow to make the time.

By the time I walk out of the kitchen, Cody and Nosh are communicating again, Momma is overseeing things from behind the stove, and Ouray took off a few minutes before me, claiming to need a 'goddamn smoke.' I find him at the front of the building, standing with a virtually drooling Dylan beside the parked bikes.

"Can we get back on track?" Both guys turn around at the sharp tone of my voice.

"All yours, darlin'."

I grind my teeth at Ouray's prod and try hard not to react. It's what he's looking for with what I'm sure he considers his charming side, and I'm determined not to give it to him.

"We were discussing the involvement of *your* gun in a string of robberies that coincidentally all occurred along a route *you* apparently traveled around the same time," I remind him with a saccharine smile.

I watch with some satisfaction as he closes his eyes, grinds the butt of his cigarette under the heel of his boot, and takes a deep breath in, trying to collect himself. Then he walks over to the bike at the end, flips open a saddlebag and pulls out a folded piece of paper.

"Here," he growls, shoving it in my hand. It's

a copy of a police report from the Morrison Police Department, dated August seventeenth, eleven forty-five at night.

"Those the saddlebags you say were cut?" He doesn't answer, just invites me to see for myself with a tilt of his chin.

I take a good look at the one on the opposite side with the cut edges and missing buckle. It's easy to see it's a relatively fresh cut, the saddlebags are old and beaten up, but the ends of the strap are clean. To be honest, my gut tells me Mark Strongbow, aka Ouray, would never leave a weapon behind at the scene of a crime. The man is too sharp for that. I'm not sure why, but I don't even really get the vibe he has anything to do with it.

"Talk to me about the circumstances. How did you discover the gun missing?"

He leans his ass on the closest bike and folds his bulky arms over his chest. "A bunch of clubs stay at the same motel every year. We catch up, usually hanging around the parking lot or the pool, drinking, partying. I headed for bed around eleven. Did a check of my bike, and saw it was fuckin' tampered with. Called the cops."

"Do you usually check your bike before you go to bed?" I realize I sound incredulous, but it seems a little strange to me. It's clear I embarrass him with the question, which is not something I would've associated with Ouray.

"Every fucking night." This comes from one of

the bikers as he passes by. "Can't sleep if he don't."

"No one fucking asked you, Yuma."

"Always happy to help law enforcement, Chief, you know that." With a big shit-eating grin on his face, the vaguely familiar looking man walks off.

"Do I know him?" I ask, looking after the guy.

"He's Nosh and Momma's son."

I manage to get a timeline from him for the Friday night, dragged out a few names of some of the other clubs, but he wasn't playing when I asked if he had any idea who might've stolen his gun.

He shrugs. "Coulda been anyone. Parties are loud, everyone's got their doors open, people going in and out of rooms. No way to tell."

Dylan's phone rings and he takes the call, walking off toward the Expedition, leaving me alone with Ouray.

"Look, I've got no idea who's behind this, but it ain't me or my brothers."

He looks at me with what appears to be a sincere look on his face. Intense blue eyes, looking straight into my own. Damn. It would've been nice and tidy to have him be involved, but I'm not really feeling it.

Might've cured the unhealthy preoccupation I have with this guy.

CHAPTER 4

LUNA

"How many clubs join for this annual ride?"

James Aiken, the FBI bigwig in Denver, is on speakerphone in the small boardroom.

"Five altogether," I answer. "Mesa Riders, Shiprock, and Amontinados all meet up at the Arrow's Edge compound. The Moab Reds join them in Ridgeway. The route is basically the same every year, just as I've described in my report. The same clubs will be back here this coming weekend for the Four Corners Rally."

"And all those groups are in Durango now?"

This time it's Damian who takes the question. "According to Strongbow, just the Amontinados and Moab Reds are. The other two outfits are supposed to rejoin them on Friday."

"How sure are you Arrow's Edge, or at least this

Mark Strongbow, is not involved?"

"I can't vouch for every individual," Damian offers. "But in the last decade they seem to have kept their noses clean, they've established several legal businesses in town. I'm solid on Strongbow, he's a straight shooter. Luna checked with the Morrison PD yesterday and they confirm the theft report. The officer she spoke to also mentioned that in all the years they've had maybe three other encounters with his club. Two fights and one DUI. He couldn't say the same for some of the other clubs."

"I assume you've done criminal backgrounds on the other outfits?"

Damian nods at Jasper, who starts outlining the laundry list of crimes accredited to some of these clubs, up to and including murder. Two of them are currently under investigation in open cases.

Aiken is quiet for a moment, seeming to process the information when his voice comes back on. "I'm thinking chances are good Durango is next. I suggest putting a bug in the ear of local dispensaries. Tell them to increase security."

"Already done," Damian responds. "We've been in close contact with Durango PD. They've called in all the manpower for the upcoming weekend. Not just to monitor the rally, but for extra patrols out there."

"Good. Tough when there are so many goddamn suspects."

"Close-lipped bunch too," Jasper agrees.

"Except maybe that Strongbow guy. Say…how

willing do you figure he'd be to help us out?"

"What are you thinking?" Damian wants to know.

"Well, I don't know about you, but it's giving me hives sitting on my ass waiting for something to happen. What if we could get behind the eight ball on this?"

"How do you figure?" This from me. I don't know why my senses are suddenly on sharp. Call it intuition.

"Would Strongbow agree if we had one of our guys cover as a club member? You've got Barnes there, right? Scuff him up a bit and stick him on a bike. He could pass."

Dylan sits up straight, a fat grin on his face. Every boy's dream.

"Possibly." Damian looks around the table. "Only problem is, we've got days left. Inserting a guy into a club and having everyone buy into it takes a fuck of a lot longer than that. They're generally not the most trusting bunch." His eyes land on me and a small smirk tugs at the corner of his mouth. "However, no one would question a new pretty face on the back of one of the bikes."

—

"Are you nuts?"

I stomp after Damian into his office the moment the conference call ends.

"It's perfect," he says, sitting down behind his desk, raising an arrogant eyebrow. "We'll talk to

Ouray, get you hooked up with one of his guys, and—"

"Have you looked at me? How the hell am I supposed to pull off a biker babe?"

Seriously, I'm as bland as they come, and from what I've seen of those women hanging off the back of a bike, they're anything but bland.

"Selling yourself short, Roosberg. I bet with a bit of makeup and the right clothes, you'd make a knockout biker babe." Disgruntled, I'm about to launch into a long list of arguments again, when Damian adds, "Besides, we'd need someone with your intuition and skills, and those aren't easy to find."

Trust him to take the wind out of my sails with professional flattery. As a woman in what still is predominantly a man's world—a fairly diminutive woman at that—being seen as valuable is an ongoing struggle. Not so much by my team, these guys treat me as equal, but there are many—also in the ranks of the Bureau—who continue to believe women have no place in this line of work.

Damian is playing me. He knows it, and I know it. I would never refuse an order, especially one that's dressed up as a challenge.

"Fine," is my less than gracious answer.

"Let's see if Mr. Strongbow is willing to meet with us here. Best for us to keep a low professional profile at the compound from here on in if we want this to be believable."

OURAY

That's a first.

I have to admit it's mostly out of curiosity that I agreed to meet with Gomez at the FBI office. Can't say I've ever been invited before, nor have I been interested to be, but discovering my gun looks to have been used in a chain of violent robberies has left me with a bad taste in my mouth. The whole sequence of events leaves me irked. Not like guns are too hard to find, but it seems fucking suspicious that my weapon gets swiped and immediately is used in a string of crimes which seems to have followed my club on a path through Colorado. Gets my blood pressure up.

And I'm not going to deny the prospect of going toe to toe with that blonde fireball has the same damn effect.

I know where the field office is, I've just never actually been up here. Perched on the edge of a cliff, the solitary building at the end of Rock Point Drive has views of a large chunk of Durango. I park my bike and walk to the edge of the parking lot, overlooking downtown. Fuck, this would've been a nice place for the Arrow's Edge clubhouse, like some impenetrable fortress, although a bit too visible for my tastes.

I'm not sure what's on the main level, but the sign on the wall indicates the offices are upstairs, so that's where I go. The wall on one side of the second floor landing has floor to ceiling lockers, and the door is directly opposite. Expecting some kind of reception area, I push the door open and walk straight into what appears to be a large shared office space. The first person I see is Luna, her blue eyes startle when they shoot up.

"Most people knock."

Jesus, the woman is prickly, but for some reason it makes me grin, which seems to tick her off even more.

"Didn't realize you doubled as receptionist." I return what I know is a jab, intended to fire her up even more. With success.

"Kiss my ass, Strongbow." She's spitting now, rising out of her chair.

Deep chuckles draw my attention to the two others inhabiting the space. I lift my chin in their general direction. I like Jasper Greene, have had some interaction with him but the other guy—Barnes, I think—I don't really know.

"Thanks for coming," Gomez greets me, sticking his head around a doorway before he turns to the others. "Boardroom?"

"You nuts?" I bark out, when Gomez lays out his reasons for asking me here. "You're sending a woman undercover into an MC? Do you know how fuckin' risky that is?" I plant my hands on the table, ignoring the woman in question, who is turning purple in the face.

"Let me remind you again," Gomez says sharply. "Roosberg is a highly qualified agent."

"That may be so, but in my world; she eyes like a tasty piece of innocent candy. She'll get chewed up and spit out."

"Only if she'll let them." He leans over the table, mimicking my stance. "Besides, we'll plant her on the back of the bike of one of your most trusted guys. Someone who evokes a lot of respect, both inside and outside of your club, and gives her credibility. One of your officers."

"I was thinking Kaga? Maybe Yuma?" she contributes and I shoot her a hot glare.

"Kaga's old lady might take issue with that, and over my dead body you'll get on the back of Yuma's bike," I growl, the thought of that goddamn male slut anywhere near this sprite has me see blood. His claim to fame is banging a record amount of pussy at every fucking rally we attend, and he's none too picky either. Christ, it's a miracle his cock is still attached.

"Why?" she challenges me, and I get in her face.

"Because even just sittin' on the back of his fuckin' bike will leave you with a severe case of crotch rot." Her big blue eyes blink a few times before she shrugs.

"Oh."

"Yeah, oh. You ride on the back of anyone's bike, it'll be mine." I realize my mistake the moment it leaves my mouth, and I see the smug grin on Gomez's face. Should've left well enough alone, but I had to fucking hammer it home. Truth is, it probably is the best option. A few of my guys have witnessed the fireworks between her and me, and it probably wouldn't be hard to convince them something's going on.

Jesus. Even just thinking about that tight little

body snug behind me on my bike has my dick rise to the occasion.

"Perfect," the asshole says. "That's settled then."

"Wait—" she pipes up, but I ignore her protests.

"Thing is though, in order to sell it, we'll have to convince my guys first. We can fake it for the outside world, but all it takes is one of my guys getting drunk, getting loose-lipped, and your cover is blown. Can't do anything about most of them knowing she's an agent, but we can make it not matter."

"Excuse me—"

"So what are you suggesting?" Damian asks.

"I'm suggesting I'm picking my date up for a club barbecue tonight, taking her on the back of my bike, so there can be no mistaking in what capacity she's there."

"Over my dead body," Luna shouts.

"I'll be able to introduce her as mine to some of the guys from the visiting clubs. Will make her coming to the rally a lot more credible," I address Gomez, who turns to his fuming agent and slowly raises one eyebrow. I try hard not to smirk when I see the effort it takes for her to rein her shit back in.

"Fine," she bites off through clenched teeth.

"Excellent."

Special Agent in Charge Damian Gomez is fucking looking like the cat that got the cream, way too satisfied.

"Need your phone number and address."

She glares at me. "I don't share my address with

anyone."

"I'm not anyone," I shoot back. "I'm your new man. You want this believable, don't ya?" She doesn't take her angry eyes off me, and I can tell she's pissed I'm making sense.

"Luna…" her boss gives her a low warning. "Write it down for him."

Ripping a page from her notebook, with vicious scratches of her pen, she writes down her phone number and address. I'm pretty surprised to find she's not even five minutes from the clubhouse. Small fucking world.

"Be ready at seven," I warn her, tucking the paper in my pocket. "I'm doing the meat so I can't be late."

With a handshake for Gomez and a chin lift for the other guys, I head for the door, when I hear her voice behind me.

"But I don't have anything to wear."

LUNA

Fuck. Fuck. Fuck.

I don't know why I'm so nervous and it's pissing me off.

I should be pumped about the undercover assignment—those kinds of opportunities are rare for female agents—but instead of plotting moves, I'm contemplating fucking outfits. Nothing in my closet at home screams biker chick. In fact, all I have in there are suits for work, cargo pants and T-shirts—also for work—and an unhealthy amount of athletic wear. I own precisely one pair of jeans, and those are of the mommy variety and don't exactly scream biker babe.

With only an hour and a half left before I have to be home because he'll be knocking on my door— no time to go fucking shopping—I know there's only option open to me. One person who might be able to help on short notice, because she has a gasp worthy collection of fitted and flimsy.

"Bella, I need help," I come right out and admit when she answers her phone.

Bella is my teammate Jasper's better half, and a clothes horse. She's also short, like me, perhaps a bit more curvy, but she likes stuff super tight so it might fit me just right.

Thirty torturous minutes later, I'm pulling myself into a pair of stretchy designer jeans with holes. It's a concept I still don't understand, paying exorbitant amounts of money for jeans that look like they're ready for the trash can. I'm told it's fashionable. All right then. They look like they were painted on my legs, they fit so snug.

"Your ass looks outstanding in these!" Bella, of course, was all over my dilemma and has been using me like some overgrown animated Barbie doll to dress.

"I don't need an outstanding ass," I grumble. "I just have to look believable."

"Then you do need ass, and tits," she informs me, and I look down at my scant B cups. Not even a handful, maybe just a palm. I shake my head, knocking loose the image of Ouray's large calloused hands. "Don't worry, this tank has a built-in push-up shelf."

I have no fucking idea what a 'built-in push-up shelf' is, but I'll take her word for it. She hands me the teal-colored bit of material I don't think is going to do much to turn my tiny bumps into the required 'tits' she talks of, but I would be wrong. When she turns me to face the mirror, I suddenly have a fucking fruit basket under my chin.

My, "Holy shit, where'd those come from?" is immediately followed by, "I can't go out like this!"

Bella just chuckles behind me, fitting me into a soft, three-quarter sleeved, powder blue cardigan with sparkly glass buttons. "The jeans are rough and tumble, the tank is pure sex, but adding the sweater brings out the sweet. It makes for an irresistible contrast. You look delicious."

"Jesus, fuck, Bella, what have you done with Roosberg?" Jasper walks into the bedroom. I immediately blush red, feeling a little too exposed, and have a ridiculous urge to cover myself up with the bedspread.

"Doesn't she look amazing?" Bella coos.

"Squirt, we want her believable, not have every guy within fifty yards swallow his goddamn tongue."

The off-handed compliment feels good. Too good.

It's messing with my head. I don't like to stand out, but the prospect of turning heads is also secretly exhilarating. Turning one head anyway.

"Do I need high heels?" I ask Bella, feeling a little bolder and wanting a little extra height.

"Can you walk on them?"

"I can try," I offer, because I haven't really.

"Then no," Bella firmly shakes her head. "You'll totally ruin the sexy vibe if you stumble around. It might be cute with Keds or Chucks." At the blank look on my face, she throws up her hands and dives back into her bottomless closet, coming out with a pair of white tennis shoes.

"I have a pair of flip-flops at home," I suggest, but this time Jasper has an opinion.

"Not on the back of a bike. Also, those aren't great if you need to move fast."

He's got a point.

After a hug from Bella, wishing me good luck, and a brotherly word of caution from Jasper, I'm on my way home, checking out my enhanced boobage at every stop. Who knew?

By the time there's a knock at my door, I've been to the bathroom three times already and have had to resist pulling a plain T-shirt on for a little extra coverage. Too late now anyway.

I can't say I don't feel a pang of satisfaction when I pull the door open and the smug grin Ouray is sporting drops right off his face.

"Fuck me," he almost groans, looking me up and down before pulling me out the door. "I'm gonna regret this."

CHAPTER 5

OURAY

Jesus.

Who knew the woman could look like goddamn sex? Not that she's flaunting it, not in the way of some of the groupies, but just that hint of cleavage peeking out from the innocent sweater makes her look sexier than any other woman prancing around in lacy lingerie. Even her eyes, those big blue deceptively guileless orbs, hold a promise I know most men won't be able to resist. *Fuck.* The normally tightly wrapped and bristly agent looks like a sonofabitchin' wet dream.

Not what I expected at all when I pulled up her driveway to the small cabin, half-tucked in the trees, nestled high above the road below. From what I can tell, she has one neighbor, but behind her is nothing but space, and in front, a killer view. Nice. A surprise, actually. Just like the address she handed me earlier today, only minutes down the road.

"Put this on," I growl when we get to my bike, and I hand her the helmet I had to pick up this afternoon. I don't take women on the back of my bike, not ever, so there's never been need for a spare. I was tempted to pick her up in the truck instead, but I know damn well, nothing would make a statement like driving up to the clubhouse with her on the back of my bike. It would eliminate any question around why she was there and instantly identify her as someone important to me. "Been on a bike before?" I ask, brushing away her hands when she fumbles with the strap under her chin.

"Dirt bike. Once," she says with a self-deprecating grin, pointing at a scar in her hairline. "A singular experience I didn't care to repeat."

I can sense her nerves and throw her a grin back. "No worries. I won't crash us. Just hang on tight to me, and let your body lean in with mine."

Something I can't quite identify flashes in her eyes, gone as fast as it came. I swing my leg over and am about to instruct her how to get on, when I feel her swing up behind me, her body way too fucking snug against my back. When I glance back, I see her hands have a firm grip on her knees. "You gotta hold on, Luna." She moves them tentatively on my waist, trying to avoid as much contact as is possible, already wedged against me. "Yea, that ain't gonna work," I tell her, before I grab both her hands and pull them around my middle, biting down a curse when I feel her spectacularly wrangled tits press in my back. "Better get used to touching me, and having my hands all over you, if you want to pull this off. We're not shy at the clubhouse, it'll raise eyebrows if you act like I have the plague."

"So noted," she mumbles against my back.

The short ride up the mountain road is a good test she seems to pass with ease. Pulling up to the gate, manned by Rowtag and Wapi, one of our other cubs, we draw some raised eyebrows, but when Rowtag recognizes who's on the back of my bike, he scowls. I'm going to have to keep an eye on that one.

I have to help her again with her helmet and hang it off my handlebars while she fluffs out her hair. She's wearing it loose today, the thick blonde waves framing her face like a halo. She looks even fucking younger like this.

"How old are you?" I can fucking hear her hackles go up, so I add under my breath, "A pretty fucking important detail for your man to know, Sprite."

"Forty-one. Birthday in October. You?"

"Forty-eight and May." From the corner of my eye, I notice some eyes on us, so even as I'm answering her, I weave my fingers into her hair and cup the back of her head, my other landing on her ass. "Showtime," I whisper, just before covering her lips with mine.

Fuck. Her mouth is sweet, and despite the tension still coming off her, she plays her role really fucking well. Hands snaking around my neck, up on her toes, and her tits pressing against me. To someone watching she probably looks like she knows what she's doing, but her kiss betrays her. Her response is hesitant, apprehensive, when my tongue slips between her lips for a quick taste. A small groan escapes her, and I quickly pull away before I fucking bend her over my bike.

"Well, I'll be fuckin' damned."

I drag my eyes away from the high blush on her face to find Yuma watching us through squinted eyes a few feet away. Ignoring him, I hook my arm around her neck, and walk us right past him inside.

"Be prepared for the third degree from Momma," I warn her quietly before aiming her in the direction of the kitchen, ignoring the catcalls and whistles. Momma and Nosh will be the hardest sells. They know me best, they've met Luna in her professional capacity, and I feel like shit for lying to them, but it's important they buy into it. The rest of the club will automatically follow.

"I knew it," Momma says when she sees us coming in.

"That so?" I challenge. I don't have a clue what she thinks she knew, but I'm not about to argue. It works to our advantage.

"I could feel the sparks flying with you two in the same room," she claims smugly.

Nosh, who's sitting at the kitchen table—his favorite hangout—scrutinizes our faces closely to the point of uncomfortable, before he finally shrugs his shoulders.

It could work, he signs.

"Better get the grill fired up, boy. Them ribs gonna take a while to cook. Not too hot, or you'll burn them before they tender."

"And how often have I burned the ribs?" I raise an eyebrow at Momma, who knows damn well I don't burn meat. She dismissively waves her spatula and turns her back, but when I'm about to head for the grill out back, a quiet Luna still tucked under my arm, Momma stops us.

"Leave her here, I could use a hand." I swear the woman has eyes in the back of her head.

I don't really want to subject Luna to the Spanish Inquisition I know she's about to have put on her, but I don't really have a choice. Turning to her, I take her face in my hands and tilt it up. "You okay givin' Momma a hand?"

"Of course."

"I'll be out back. Come lookin' for me when you're done."

I wait for her acknowledging nod before I press a hard kiss on her lips and let her go. One last glance into the kitchen, I catch Momma's eyes in the reflection of the kitchen window—she hasn't missed a thing— before walking out to the back, where I know I'll be receiving a grilling of my own.

LUNA

"What would you like me to do, Mrs. Wells?"

The woman turns to face me with a scowl on her face.

"You can start by calling me Momma, just like everybody else," she snaps. "You mister and missus your way around this club, no one's gonna forget who you are."

"All right, Momma, what can I do?"

"Can ya cook?" I grin at the challenge in her voice. I don't get a chance to cook often but I'm pretty good, if I say so myself.

"Like a champ."

"That a fact?"

"Try me." I throw the challenge back with a grin and a wink for Nosh, who is eyeing us with interest.

The calculating glint in Momma's eyes should probably have been a warning, but I already threw my hat in the ring.

"Brussels sprouts. I make them for a handful of the guys, but the rest hate them, including Ouray. I want to see if you can change his mind."

"No problem."

I am so fucking bluffing and she knows it. I love my sprouts, but I'm not sure they'd be enough to get someone to like them.

For the next twenty minutes I'm cleaning vegetables, chopping fresh garlic, and mincing shallots. A few times I almost cut off a finger, my mind still preoccupied with the feel of Ouray's tongue stroking the inside of my mouth, his hand squeezing my ass. I'm mostly confused by my own response: I didn't want him to stop.

The club kitchen is large, but still Momma manages to crowd me when I toss the raw, halved sprouts in the wok with the rest of the ingredients.

"Ain't you gonna cook 'em first?"

"Nope. Stir fry so they keep a bit of bite. Do you have some hot sauce?" She hands me a jumbo-sized bottle from the fridge. I drizzle a little into the wok, stir it around, and pull the wok off the heat.

"I'll finish them up when the ribs are ready. Can't leave them sitting too long or they'll get mushy."

"Whatever you say," Momma says, rolling her eyes. "Why don't you go see if Ouray is ready for the meat?"

I have to say, it's a lot less comfortable walking out in a crowd of people I don't know, who all look at me with a healthy dose of suspicion, than it was earlier with Ouray's arm around my shoulder.

"Fresh pussy. Aren't you a sight for sore eyes?"

A man the size of a Mack truck, a nose that looks to have been on the wrong side of a fist one too many times, with massive amounts of hair everywhere steps in my path, his big shovel-sized hand rounding me to latch onto my ass. My move is instinctive as I twist around and aim my heel for his kneecap, wishing I'd chanced wearing high heels just for the added damage I could've done. Despite the flimsy tennis shoes on my feet, I manage to cause enough pain for the behemoth to stumble back a step. I'm in a half-crouch, my focus on him as I anticipate retaliation, when suddenly the guy is felled like a massive tree, going down on his knees in front of me.

Ouray. His nostrils flaring and his jaw twitching, he looms over the guy, bending down to get in his face.

"That's your one and only pardon, you son of a bitch. That ass you tried pawing belongs to me. You hear me?"

"I didn't know, Chief," is the guy's grudging response.

"Actually," I pipe up. "Last time I checked that ass belongs to *me*."

I realize quickly I probably would've been better off shutting my trap, when that nostril-flaring, jaw-twitching glare now is directed at me. Oops. An uncomfortable silence follows, during which way too many eyes flit back and forth between Ouray and me, waiting for things to escalate.

Unexpectedly, Ouray rolls his eyes heavenward. "Fine," he concedes, reaching out and pulling me to him, putting his own big paw on my rear. "The ass may belong to you, but I fuckin' claim exclusive rights." I don't get a chance to respond before I'm bent backward over his arm, my mouth bruised in a ravaging kiss that makes the earlier ones seem like chaste pecks in comparison. I swear the man is probing for my tonsils, his tongue is so far down my throat, and all I can do is go along for the ride. With my arms wrapped tight around his neck, I let myself be carried away, no longer aware of my surroundings. Overwhelmed with his taste in my mouth, his scent in my nose, and the feel of his strong arms holding me up, I lose all control of my body.

I don't become aware of the hooting and hollering until Ouray slowly lets me up, both of us breathing harder than is decent in public. When he pulls me flush against his front, I momentarily freeze at the hard press of his erection in my stomach, but I hold my ground.

"Jesus, Sprite," he whispers in my ear. "You're a quick study."

I'm still trying to figure out what that means exactly, when we sit down at a bunch of end to end picnic tables for dinner. While Ouray is arranging the ribs and burgers in large aluminum trays, I hurry inside to finish off the Brussels sprouts. A splash of soy sauce, a little ginger, and a quick stir through over high heat and they're done.

"What's this?" Ouray asks, when Momma shoves the serving dish under his nose.

"Done my sprouts a different way. Come hell or high water, I'll make you eat them yet."

"You've tried for the past thirty odd years, woman, what makes you think I—"

"Oh shut it and give it a go," she snaps impatiently. She instructed me not to mention anything so his response would be 'honest' so I'm keeping my mouth shut.

Ouray carefully scoops up three or four halves

and deposits them on his plate, a fair distance from the rest of his food. I almost laugh out loud at the look of disgust on his face.

"Don't laugh," he growls, spearing one on his fork and reluctantly bringing it up to his mouth.

"Please, Momma. Save us all from this torture, will you?" a man who was introduced to me earlier as Kaga, his second-in-command, pleads with the old woman, but from the stubborn look on her face, it's clear she's unmoved. "I don't get why we can't just stick to corn on the cob."

"Don't be going too far with that." Ouray points at the dish Momma's holding. "Goddamn, why didn't you ever make 'em like this before?"

Momma's eyes narrow on me as she holds out the bowl to him. "Gonna need that recipe," she mumbles, leaning in, but Ouray hears and raises an eyebrow at me.

"No shit?" He spears another sprout and pops it in his mouth, watching me. I just shrug.

At dinner I make note of names, clubs, roles, and any other tidbit of information that I can pick up. I'd almost forgotten the reason I'm here in the first place.

Most of the guys are Arrow's Edge, but there are a few from visiting clubs. There are quite some women too, but I can't get a grip on who's with who. The only ones I know are Momma and Lea, Kaga's wife, who I met earlier. Nobody bothered introducing me to the others and I plan to ask Ouray about that later.

The party gets rowdier the later it gets, alcohol

flowing and occasional tempers flaring. More than once I watch as Ouray steps between two guys and quietly seems to diffuse the tension. I notice he's only had a beer or two before dinner, but has been chugging back bottles of water since. I'm on my second beer myself, making it last. Not drinking would stand out, but as long as I have a half full bottle in my hand, I'm left alone.

I watch as one woman accompanies yet another biker into the clubhouse. I think it's her third. Not hard to imagine what goes on in there. "Who's she?" I ask Ouray softly, pretending to snuggle up to him. It's a little disturbing how easy it is pretending to be his date.

"Britney. Club groupie."

"She get paid or something?" I ask. "This is the third guy."

"*Fuck*. That's gonna be trouble," he mumbles, looking after them before he turns to me. "And no, she's not a hooker."

"She does it for fun?" I know I sound naïve, but it flies out before I can clamp down on it. The concept is alien to me, so I'm trying to understand.

"Britney? She mostly does it to stir up trouble. It's not new. Guess I'll have to have another talk with her before someone fucking starts shooting." He indicates one of the guys, who is staring at the clubhouse with barely suppressed anger. "That's Paco. Good man, bad judgement when it comes to that bitch."

I flinch at his use of that word, but when she walks

into the bathroom ten minutes later, it doesn't take me long to agree with him wholeheartedly.

"You got money?"

I'm washing my hands at the surprisingly clean sink when I hear the slightly nasal voice behind me. I look up to see her leaning against the wall, a smug little grin on her pouty lips.

"Money?"

"Yeah. Like are you rich or something?"

"Hardly." I grab a handful of paper towels and dry my hands.

"Hmm. Into kinky shit?"

I swing around, tossing the wad of paper in the trash can. "What can I do for you?"

She looks me up and down with distaste on her face.

"There's gotta be something that puts you on the back of his bike. The man likes his pussy hot and his tits ample. You ain't got none, and you look like a cold-ass choirboy instead of a hot-blooded woman."

Ah. A case of jealousy. I recognize it, even if I've never actually been the subject before. It's an interesting experience. Best way to deal with it is not to respond. She's clearly baiting me, and I won't bite. I try walking past her, but she moves faster, blocking the door. She doesn't know how big of a mistake she's making.

"You don't want to do that," I warn her in a calm, gentle voice.

"Do what? I asked you a question and you're bein'

a bitch, all rude, ignoring me."

"I'm gonna give you to the count of three, and I suggest you get out of my way, or I'll move you myself."

I can tell she's weighing the odds, until she finally steps aside.

"Go ahead. You're lucky I'm not in the mood to tussle with little girls tonight."

I already have the door open, hanging onto my temper by a thread, when she voices those last words. I'm about to give her a taste of my little girl fists when an arm snakes around me, pulling me against an already familiar body.

"You're not just a bitch, you're stupid too," Ouray says over my head. "Luna could take you apart limb by limb with one hand tied behind her back. I warned you, Britney, one more drama with your name on it, and it'll be the last time those gates open for ya."

"I can't remember much," the woman says with a calculating smirk. "On account of your cock being down my throat at the time."

CHAPTER 6
OURAY

Fucking Britney.

Even now, three days later, Luna is stiff as a board when she climbs behind me on the bike.

I don't get women. First off, I really don't see what she thought she had to gain by targeting Luna with some wild story. Sure, I had my dick in her mouth. I was in the middle of telling her off when she dropped to her knees, ripped my jeans open, and stuffed my limp cock between her lips. I'm damn lucky she didn't use her teeth to hang on when I shoved her off. Like that was going to help her get on the back of a bike. That's what she's after, we all know it. Poor Paco has a hard-on for the woman, but isn't ready to claim her as his old lady—thank fuck for that. As a result she's been spreading for whoever wants a piece, in hopes jealousy will get him to give in.

As for Luna, I don't get her at all. First she hates my guts, then she lights up like the fucking Fourth of July with my tongue in her mouth, before finally freezing me out altogether. This is all supposed to be fucking make-believe, and still I end up feeling like my dick is in a vise. This is why I don't do goddamn relationships.

Instead of driving off to meet my guys at the clubhouse before we ride out, I climb off the damn bike and swing around on Luna.

"Wanna tell me what bug crawled up your ass? This little setup of yours is not gonna fly if you're sitting behind me like a goddamn plank, giving off frigid ice maiden vibes to anyone watching." I notice a little too late that in my frustration I've said something that has her face go blank, and I mean totally impassive. No trace of any kind of emotion, not even anger. She's shut down on me, and that pisses me off even more. "I see I'm gonna have to kiss some blood flow back into your ass," I snap, grabbing the sides of her helmet and closing the distance between us.

"Don't you dare…" Her voice is low, almost a growl, as her eyes suddenly light up with fire. Good. Fucking better than that dead stare I got earlier. "…kiss me to prove a point."

I hold up just shy of her lips, my nose almost touching hers, as I take stock of all I see swirling in her eyes: challenge, anger, frustration, longing, hurt and…fucking hell. She tries to hide it, but there is definite fear there. I instantly let go of her head.

"Shit. I'm sorry." The words feel alien on my lips. Guess I don't use them a whole lot.

"No, don't. Let's..." Her eyes flit away before they come back to mine. "You're right. I'm...I'll be fine. Let's just go." I'm surprised to hear her stumble over her words, and I'm itching to dig in and find out what the fuck is going on in that head of hers, but she's right, we should make tracks. We've got guys waiting to get going on this three-day party.

With a simple nod, I slide back on my bike and wait for her arms to circle me.

It's near the noon hour when we pull onto the large parking lot of the Harley-Davidson store. This is where clubs congregate. There's stuff going on in other places, but we always start out here.

I help Luna with her helmet and with an arm slung around her shoulder, I walk her in the direction of the beer tent. Halfway there, I feel her arm snake around me and her small hand tuck into my back pocket. *Perfect.*

"Pint?" I ask her when we sidle up to the bar.

"A bottle of something if they have it."

"Ale okay? They should have some Brewer's Blond."

"Sure. Isn't that a local micro-brewery? I think I've had it before. Pretty good."

"It better be." I grin at her. "Belongs to the club."

"The brewery?" She seems surprised.

"The brewery and the restaurant." Of all our local investments, that one provides the best return.

I guess my pride shows because she smiles back at me. "A gym, a yoga studio, and a restaurant. That's pretty impressive."

"We also own an apartment building along the river, but Brewer's Pub is our main source of income. Every year since the club started sponsoring this event, as well as the annual blues festival, our market has almost doubled."

"Clever."

"I wouldn't believe a word out of this sonofabitch's mouth." The voice belongs to the president of the Amontinados MC who walks up behind me, throwing an arm over my shoulder, his eyes sharp on Luna. I'm tempted to ignore the bastard, but a slight lift of her eyebrow reminds me she's here for a reason.

"Luna, this asshole is Mico—"

"Manny," he interrupts.

"Right, Manuel Salinas."

"Manny to beautiful women," he says, leaning in to offer her a hand, but instead of shaking it, he pulls her closer, pressing a kiss on her fingers. I know what he's doing—it's nothing new—but for some reason now, with Luna, it makes my blood boil. I would've jumped in if Luna hadn't jerked back from his hold, immediately stepping close to my side.

"I'd say I was pleased to meet you, but I'd be lying," she says with a saccharine sweet smile for him. "Not a fan of strangers putting their lips on me. Asshole move, especially with my man standing right here."

"Oh, don't be like that, beautiful. Him and me don't mind sharing, do we, brother? Wouldn't be the first time."

"That's enough, you cocksucker." I shrug his arm from my shoulder. Every fucking chance he has the bastard brings that incident up. That was two decades ago and both of us were drunk out of our brains. I can't even remember the chick.

"I may be, but I don't remember you complaining." I don't miss Luna's sharp intake of breath, as Manny throws me a wink.

Just fucking great. The little bit of headway I made since picking her up is gone as I look into her stone-cold eyes. She quickly hides them with a little smile, and I'm relieved when a group of the Amontinados calls Manny over.

"Catch you later, *hermano,*" he says, punching my shoulder and wiggling his eyebrows at Luna. "Later, beautiful."

The moment his back is turned, Luna steps away from me, but before she can get too far away, I take her hand, walking with her in the opposite direction to where a bunch of vendors have stalls set up. Some sell clothes, some leather goods, memorabilia, and of course food. We kill some time checking the wares and I end up buying her a Harley T-shirt, ignoring her when she argues.

"You hungry? We should probably eat something since alcohol will be flowing all damn weekend."

"I could eat."

I lean in to whisper in her ear. "See those picnic tables over there? Those are the Shiprock guys. I'll introduce you and you can do your thing while I grab us a bite."

Wheels, the big burly president, observes us closely as we approach. "Have a seat," he rumbles in his deep voice after I shake his hand.

"I'm just gonna grab some food. Be right back," I tell him, but motion Luna to sit down. "Keep an eye on her for me."

"Not gonna be a hardship."

LUNA

This guy is as wide as he is tall, and probably in his sixties maybe even seventies.

I'm surprised to find he's still riding. The Shiprock MC President just finished telling me about the annual Rocky Mountain ride. He's a chatty guy once he gets going, which is probably why Ouray put me at his table. That, and the fact Wheels is apparently a family man. Devoted to his wife of more than forty years. His daughter married a stockbroker and lives in Denver, and his son is Road Captain for the club. He even has two grandsons who are part of the MC.

A real family affair.

"So is the plan for you to eventually retire and hand off to your son?"

He regards me from under his bushy eyebrows. "You always this nosy?"

I guess I hit a touchy subject. "I'm just curious. I don't really understand the life. I mean, I haven't known Ouray that long, and I'm still learning. Besides, from what I gather, most clubs are not like Arrow's Edge."

"That's for damn sure. Gotta hand it to the kid, he vowed to take the club clean, and fuck if he didn't do just that. Wasn't a popular move either." By *the kid* I assume he means Ouray, who seems to be taking an awful long time to get some food.

"How so?"

He leans back, folding his hands over his belly. "It wasn't just some of the members who didn't much like it. The move impacted more than just the Arrow's Edge. Fucked up some longstanding business arrangements made back in the seventies and eighties between clubs. Loyalties broken. Wasn't pretty then and some of that still festers, but Ouray, he stayed his course. I admire him for that."

"Alcohol makes you loose-lipped, old man." A gray-haired man, wearing a clear family resemblance, clamps a hand on Wheels's shoulder, who doesn't even turn around to acknowledge the newcomer. "Who's the fresh pussy?"

I try hard not to flinch at the crude descriptive as

father and son both seem to scrutinize me.

"She's on Ouray's bike, which means hands off, kid."

The younger one has a calculating glint in his eyes. "Ouray don't put bitches on the back of his bike. Not fucking ever." His voice is raised and he's drawing attention from a couple of other tables around us. I can feel the curious glances on me like tentacles.

"First time for everything," I offer with a shrug.

"You're not his type," he fires back.

"How do you figure?"

"I've got eyes," he says, pointing over my shoulder.

When I turn around to see what he's talking about, I see a familiar tall blonde draped all over Ouray against the side of a food trailer. I have a fraction of a second to decide what an appropriate reaction would be: storm off and jeopardize the assignment, or make a stand and maybe gain credibility.

I pick the latter, as I get up and stalk over to where Ouray seems to be in the process of untangling himself from the woman's hold. He sees me coming, and with a bemused twitch of his lips watches, as I grab onto one of the girl's arms and pull her back, sliding myself between the two of them.

"What the fuck?" It's the woman from the yoga studio.

"My man you have your hands on." I pull myself up to my full height, still inches short of being able to get in her face.

"Don't be ridiculous," she scoffs, looking me up and down, clearly finding me short of measure. It was mostly for show before, but my real temper is flaring as my hands curl into fists. "I know enough to know he belongs to no one."

"Down, Sprite," Ouray mumbles behind me, curling an arm around my waist, before addressing the other woman. "Like I said, Heidi, caved once, and as you fucking well know—I never showed my face for seconds—'cause it never shoulda happened in the first place. I've got me a good thing right here." He tightens his arm around me for emphasis, and for a moment I let myself imagine this is real.

"Your loss," she counters, tossing back her hair in dramatic fashion. "Wouldn't have wasted your time had I known you were into boys."

Good thing Ouray is keeping me tight against his front, or I might've gone after her. "Easy." His breath feathers against my ear and a responding shiver ripples over my skin. "We've got eyes on us," he says when I start to break away from his hold. "Better make this good."

He swings me around so my front is pressed against the side of the food truck, my hands braced on the warm metal. Fingers tangle in my hair, pulling my head back and to the side, so he can reach my lips. I instinctively open, every sense on sharp when his tongue sweeps in, claiming my mouth, as his hot hard body presses up behind me. Instead of panic at being confined, I relax into it and reach back to curl a hand around his neck. It's not until I feel his touch slipping low on my stomach, fingers dipping into the waistband of my jeans, I freeze and my muscles tense up. Immediately his hand stills and his lips leave mine. "Easy," he says again. "Got carried away."

We manage to stay away from any additional confrontation the rest of the afternoon, and I'm able to learn a little more about the various clubs as I tag along with Ouray while he mingles and mixes.

It's probably four when we roll out. The only other person joining us is Paco, with the rest of the club hanging behind. Ouray says he wants to get back to the clubhouse to check on the boy before tonight's festivities, so I just tag along.

"I can drop you home for a bit, if you want," he offers, twisting his head back when we're stopped at a light.

I glance over at Paco to see if he's watching, but he seems distracted, looking off in the distance. "I'm okay. Don't like to advertise my address."

"Gotcha. Momma will have something ready on the stove. Some of us older guys don't wanna go all day like we used to."

"I'm not real good in the party scene myself," I admit. "Swore it off many years ago."

"You wanna catch some of the music after? I usually drive out with the truck so Nosh can come out for a bit. He can't really hear the music, but he likes to stand by the speakers and feel the vibrations."

I don't get a chance to answer because the light

turns green, but it would've been yes. I should probably be concerned that the more I learn about the man, the more I warm up to him—despite his apparent sexual proclivities. I should be running for the hills instead.

CHAPTER 7

OURAY

How old are you?

The boy looks at me and then back at Luna, who asked him the question.

Twelve. Christ. *Did you ever shoot anyone?*

They've been at this for the past ten minutes, exchanging questions. It was Luna's idea when we found him sitting on the couch, staring at the wall. She ignored his blank stare and plopped down beside him, chatting up a storm with her hands. Initially he barely responded, but when she suggested he ask her anything he wanted, his interest was perked.

The kid seems to have a healthy fascination with Luna, which she doesn't seem to mind exploiting to get information from him. The rapid-fire questions have been revealing, even though she's been careful to mostly keep it light. She's been asking things like favorite food, favorite color, favorite action figure, with only an occasional personal question slipped in. He barely notices that she's doing a bang-up job of drawing out pertinent information. We know he's an only child, we know he doesn't know his father, and that he lived with his grandparents. And now we know he is twelve years old. It may not look like a whole lot, but it helps us narrow things down.

Yes. I didn't like it though. Do you go to school?

Not anymore. When will you teach me to fight?

Maybe we'll have some time tomorrow? Luna throws me a look and I shrug my shoulders. We'll make time. *How long have you been living on the streets?*

The boy throws me another look, and sensing my presence may be what's holding him back, I get to my feet. "I've got some shit to look over before dinner," I lie, and I can feel his eyes following me out of sight.

Fifteen minutes later, Luna sticks her head around the door of my office. "Momma says dinner's on in five."

"Good. We'll head back to town after, if you don't mind being squeezed between me and Nosh in the truck."

"Sure."

"Any more luck with the boy?"

She slips into the office, softly closing the door before she sits down across from my desk. "Only kid, twelve years old, was raised by grandparents after his mother overdosed. He took off almost a year ago, from what I can gather. I get the impression he's not *from* here, but he won't let on how he got here. He's a smart kid. He doesn't trust though—something happened to him. He says he likes it here, but I get the sense he's waiting for the other shoe to drop. It'll take time."

"It's more than we knew before," I admit.

"If I could make a suggestion?"

"Feel free."

"He doesn't like his name. Doesn't seem to like being reminded of who he was. We can push to find out more background, but I think you might accomplish more in the long run if you allow him to forget. For now. Give him a nickname like everyone else here has. Make him feel accepted without pressuring him. Give him a chance to trust he's safe here. I have a feeling he'll talk when he's ready."

"Not a problem. Maybe I should've bunked him in with the other kids instead of Momma's spare bedroom." Luna shakes her head sharply at that.

"No. I don't think that's a good idea. Not yet anyway."

I look at her surprised. "Why is that?"

She glances at her hands before eyes filled with sadness come up to meet mine. "Because I think he was abused. Momma says she can hear him slide a chair in front of his door every night."

I have a hard time swallowing down my dinner after that. Especially with that skinny boy across the table, his big brown eyes glancing at me over his plate.

"Where are we going?"

Luna pulls against the hold I have on her hand.

The clubhouse is loud with the party that inevitably follows the Friday night concert in town. This too is tradition, with the various clubs in attendance. Some of these guys will go right through until we ride out for the parade on Sunday.

I used to be one of them, but since taking up the gavel a decade ago, I've changed my ways. Someone has to keep their wits about them. With alcohol flowing freely, often already short tempers tend to flare, which is challenge enough when it's our own guys. Add members of different MCs together and you're sitting on a goddamn powder keg. I'm surprised we haven't had a blowup already.

It's almost two when I decide to call it a night. The heavy partying didn't start until after the young ones were hustled off to bed by Nosh and Momma, who left about an hour ago to their cabin behind the clubhouse. The moment they walked out, the lid came off the party. Out of respect for Momma, most guys keep things PG while she's around, but in the hour since the door closed behind them, all restraint has gone out the window.

Fucking Britney has been spread out on the pool table like a goddamn smorgasbord for every horny bastard to sample, while Paco watched from a distance. Finally he grabbed one of the girls who shows up at every damn club party, planted his ass on the couch beside me, pushed her down between his legs, and whipped his dick out.

That does it for me. Luna's tight little body has been playfully rubbing up against me all goddamn night, but at that display, she all but froze up on my lap. I'm guessing the lack of inhibitions is making her uncomfortable, which is why I'm calling it a night.

"My room." I'm already pushing open the door to my office. These are my private quarters: office, bedroom, and bathroom. Through the office is the only access, on purpose.

"I should go home." Luna stops just inside as the door falls shut behind her, and she looks like she's about to jump out of her skin.

"I can't leave," I explain. "I've gotta be here in case shit hits the fan."

"I can find my own way home," she says defiantly, folding her arms under her breasts.

"And blow your cover?"

"How so?"

"You're supposed to be my woman. No one would buy me letting you go off alone. They expect you in my bed. Especially this weekend."

"I can't sleep in your bed. Besides, I don't have any of my stuff here."

"Sure you can." I grab her hand again and lead her into my bedroom through the door on the other side of the office. It's nothing special: a king-sized bed, a dresser, and a recliner in the far corner. "You take the bed, I'll take the recliner, and I have extra shit in the bathroom. Momma always makes sure it's stocked." I let go of her hand and walk over to my dresser, pulling out a T-shirt I toss at her. "You can sleep in that. Tomorrow morning when everyone is still sleeping it off, I'll take you to your place and you can pick up some stuff for an overnight."

Her eyes get big. "You expect me to sleep here again tomorrow?"

"Christ, Sprite, you're giving a guy a complex. I don't usually stay here, but on weekends we have club functions, I do. We all do. So yes, I expect you in my bed again tomorrow."

I can almost hear her internal struggle, but finally she nods. "Toothbrush?"

"Second drawer of the vanity."

With a firm nod, she makes her way into the bathroom, clutching my shirt, and closes the door behind her. I let out a sigh, I'm not looking forward to spending the night on the recliner. I wouldn't even have offered if I didn't suspect the woman is hiding something under that badass FBI agent shield. Something that makes her jump at a touch, and tight as a bow at the sight of too much skin. It's probably for the best, since I've been fighting for control over my body around her. Fuck knows, I might crawl all over her while sleeping. I'd send her screaming from the room if she felt the size of my hard cock.

My condition doesn't improve when she walks

out of the bathroom a few minutes later, her clothes clutched in front of her and my T-shirt hanging down almost to her knees. The threadbare material does little to hide her modest curves underneath. For a tits and ass guy, I'm surprised at the surge of lust at the tease of her compact shape. I quickly grab a pair of old sweats from my dresser, since I doubt she'd appreciate me sleeping in the buff like I normally do, and dive into the bathroom.

The cold shower helps a little, but when I walk back into the bedroom, and see her small body curled up with her back to me in my bed, my dick immediately responds. Un-fucking-believable. For the last few years, the damn thing has needed more than a little encouragement to get hard, yet doesn't seem to have any problems jumping to attention around this woman.

I can tell she's awake from the way her shoulders are bunched high and full of tension. She visibly flinches when I grab one of the pillows off the bed and stretch out on the recliner. This is going to suck.

At some point I must've drifted off, despite the loud music filtering into the room, but loud banging on the door has me shoot upright. When I look over I see Luna sitting up in the bed, her knees drawn up to her chest.

"We've got a problem, Chief. It's Paco." I recognize Lusio's voice, and jump up, motioning Luna to stay in bed.

"Go back to sleep. I've got this," I tell her when

I see her flip down the covers. After a moment's hesitation, she nods and pulls them back up.

The clubhouse is unusually quiet, and I see why when I walk into the common room. A young guy wearing the Moab Reds colors is hanging on the bar, blood streaming down from a nasty cut on his cheek, a few of his brothers in a semicircle in front of him. Near the front door, Kaga and Honon are holding back Paco, who is clutching a broken beer bottle in his hand.

Fucking hell.

I'm in front of Paco in two strides. His eyes wild as he strains against the death grip his brothers have on his arms. From the corner of my eye, I see Britney sniffling on the couch, two other chicks with their arms around her. Brilliant.

I clasp a hand around Paco's neck and force him to focus on me. "Let go of the bottle, brother."

"He hurt her," he grinds out between clenched teeth, the stench of alcohol wafting over me. "The fucker hurt her."

My blood runs cold, but I hold on to my own temper. "I'll deal with that, but you've gotta let go of the bottle. Let the boys take care of you."

With Paco being led down the hall to his bedroom—I'm sure the guys will keep an eye on him—I turn to the bleeding kid, ignoring the other men surrounding him. "You touched her?" He looks up, almost confused.

"Ain't that was she's here for?"

"Don't work that way in this clubhouse."

"She was spreading for everyone."

I inch up on him until my nose is almost touching his. "That may be so, but no still fucking means no."

"You've grown into a bunch of fucking pussies." This comes from the Moab Red's VP and I swing on him, sensing my boys inching closer.

It takes me another five minutes to get these guys out of the clubhouse without further bloodshed, and shut down this party. By the time I get back to the bedroom, I fully expect Luna to be asleep, but she's still sitting up in bed, her arms protectively around her legs.

"Everything okay?"

"Go to sleep, Sprite." My voice sounds tired, even to my own ears, and instead of the recliner, I grab the pillow and climb into bed.

"What are you doing?"

"What does it look like?" Without another word I turn my back on her, punch my pillow, and close my eyes.

I finally hear her slide down in the bed, and minutes later her breath deepens. I drift off not long after.

LUNA

I can't breathe.

I wake up with my face pressed against warm skin and my limbs are pinned by a heavy body. Panic sets in as I struggle to get free.

"Relax." The gruff deep voice manages to filter through the edge of fear. *Ouray*. The instant he rolls away, I scoot up against the headboard, panting heavily from the sudden rush of adrenaline.

"What the hell do you think you're doing?" I spit out reflectively.

"Sweetheart," he drawls, propping his head up on his hand and regarding me with amusement. "You're the one who snuggled up to me in the middle of the night. I just followed suit."

"Bullshit." I try to ignore the flutter in my stomach when I look at his face slightly rumpled with sleep, and heavy-lidded eyes staring back at me.

"Whatever makes it easier on you."

He seems to ignore my glare, instead rolling the opposite way and out of bed. He's not wearing a shirt and his sweats hang low on his hips, exposing the swell of a firm ass. From his lower back, a tattoo of a single arrow runs all the way up to his neck. I'm not fast enough to hide my interest when he turns to face me, a knowing smirk on his lips. His wide chest, where my face was pressed just a few minutes ago, is covered with hair, narrowing over his stomach before disappearing under the edge of his waistband. Once my eyes hit that region it's impossible to miss the prominent tent in his pants. *Shit*. I immediately look away.

"Involuntary, Sprite. Although, I have to admit it's been a while." I'm unsettled with conflicting feelings of aversion and curiosity, my stomach twisting in knots as I try to regain some control. "Why don't you grab a shower while I go see if Momma has coffee ready? We can head over to yours after."

I watch from under my eyelids as he snatches a shirt from a drawer and walks out of the room, tugging it on as he goes.

Cody is sitting at the kitchen table with Ouray and Nosh when I walk in a bit later. I remember the promise I made him when he looks up at me with disappointment in his eyes.

He says you're leaving.

I quickly look over at Ouray, who gives a little shrug. *I have to get a few things at home,* I tell Cody, *but I won't be long. I'll bring back some of my gear.*

Like what?

I have a pair of extra boxing gloves you can use. I think our hands are of similar size. "Do you guys have a bag here somewhere? For him to practice on?" I ask Ouray.

There's a couple in the large garage. We use part of it as a gym.

Momma slides a cup of coffee and a plate of bacon and eggs in front of me. I turn to thank her. "You need some meat on those bones," she mutters. "There's nothin' to hold onto."

"Wouldn't say that, Momma. She fills my hands nicely," Ouray says with a wink, earning a smack to

the back of his head from the older woman.
 "Mind your mouth when there's kids around."

86

CHAPTER 8

LUNA

"Do I have time to grab a quick shower?"

I'm mopping my face with the bottom of my T-shirt, noticing too late the kind of interest my midsection seems to draw. Ouray's eyes are dark when I glance up, and he reaches out to yank my shirt back in place. My little workout with Cody seems to have drawn an audience.

The kid was outside waiting when Ouray and I got back from my place. He seemed almost surprised when I pulled the promised boxing gloves from my tote. I got the sense he's been let down a lot in his short life. After a quick change into my gym clothes, I went to look for him in the garage where he was already pounding the snot out of one of the suspended bags. I was going to show him a few basic defensive moves, but changed my mind when I saw him swing his fists.

Instead, I showed him the proper stance, straightened his gloves, taught him a few techniques and training routines, so he can practice on his own. What he lacks in size and strength, he more than makes up for in enthusiasm.

Thirty minutes later, I'm sweaty from exertion, looking around the garage to find half a dozen guys watching me. Normally that wouldn't faze me—I can probably take every one of them—but it's the way they look at me that makes me very uncomfortable. Ouray isn't too pleased with the attention either, he throws his arm over my shoulder and marches me to the clubhouse and through to his quarters.

"No more fucking tights and titty-shirts next time," he grumbles, almost shoving me into the bedroom, and immediately my hackles go up.

"It's perfectly normal athletic wear. There's nothing wrong with it," I protest.

"Maybe not in a goddamn yoga studio, but here you might as well parade around fucking naked."

"That's ridiculous," I sputter, but he grabs me by the shoulders, leaning down into my face.

"Not in my world it ain't. Now get yourself in the shower, we're riding out in twenty." He turns me around and shoves me in the direction of the bathroom, swatting my ass when I start walking. When I swing back to give him a piece of my mind, he's already leaving the bedroom.

Asshole.

"I can't accept this."

I shove the butter-soft leather jacket back at the vendor, who seems amused by our back-and-forth. Ouray—bulldozer that he is—simply hands over a wad of cash and grabs the jacket from the guy. With one of his large paws on the back of my neck, he marches me around the side of the building and pushes my back against the brick. From a distance it looks like we're having a quiet moment, but up close I can feel the tension come off him in waves.

"Want this to work? Then stop drawing attention by fucking arguing with me every step of the way. *Jesus*, you're exasperating. I'm getting you a fucking jacket because you need one on the back of my bike."

"But I can pay for—"

His flat hand slaps against the brick beside my head and he rolls his eyes heavenward. "Christ, give me patience," he mumbles, before he continues with threatening calm. "In *my* world, I pay. Away from my world you can do whatever the fuck you want, but when you're on the back of my bike, I get you what you need.

"That's just dumb."

"It's what's gonna keep your ass safe as my woman. Some of these guys even get wind you might be a plant, we both might be in a world of hurt."

It's then I clamp my mouth shut. He's right. I keep

forgetting we're acting out a part, it sometimes feels all too real.

"We've got eyes on us," he mumbles, his head dropping low so his lips are almost brushing mine. "Time to kiss and make up—try not to knee me in the gonads."

His lips are bruising as he leans his entire body into me, pressing me back against the wall. My arms snake around his neck as he slips a hand under my shirt, pulls up my knee with the other, and grinds his hips between my legs. I gasp into his mouth at the rush of heat pooling low in my belly, and I shiver when his fingers brush the skin under my breast.

"Get a fucking room!"

The taunt is like a cold shower and instantly my body seizes up.

"Goddammit, Sprite. You make me lose my head."

I'm still gasping like a fish out of water, and don't get a chance to react before he wraps his arm around me and starts walking.

The crowds are thick, especially around the Hot Bike Chopper Show where Ouray introduces me to a few more bikers who were part of their ride along HWY 550. It's tough to get a good bead on these guys. They all seem to wield that danger vibe, although I'm starting to suspect that's more show than substance for some. It's an aggressive bunch, even in the way they interact. Always with something of an edge. Ouray is the same way, although I find him to be a contradiction. I've seen him with Nosh and Momma—the way he is with Cody or me—and there is a gentle side to him that only seems reserved for some. He comes across as rough, hardened, when dealing with the rest of the world. I'm guessing it's that way for a lot of these men. They protect their soft spots with a thick layer of bristles, much like I try to do myself. I'm not that different.

Perhaps that's why I'm more suspicious of the few who stand out as more socially apt and charming. Who knows, they may use their charm to hide their dark side.

Regardless, I make mental notes for every individual I encounter, hoping to hell I can retain it all until I can write it down.

"I'll be damned."

I swing my head around at the familiar voice and smile wide when I spot Keith Blackfoot with a surprised look on his face. Keith is Durango PD, but more importantly, he's a good friend. I slip out from under Ouray's arm and give Keith a hug.

"What are you doing here?" I ask.

"I'm thinking I should be asking you that question," he fires back, looking over my shoulder with a dark expression on his face. I turn my head to find Ouray staring back with an equally menacing look.

Oops.

"She's here with me," Ouray almost growls, as he curls an arm around my stomach and pulls me back against him.

Keith's incredulous look shifts to me, and I shrug, smiling sheepishly. "I am. With him, I mean."

"Seriously, Luna? Of all people you pick a guy like him? Do you know how they treat their women?"

Ouray's hold tightens around me to the point of discomfort, and I put a soothing hand on his arm, while keeping my eyes on Keith. "Stop," I caution him, my voice low so it doesn't carry. "First of all, you're generalizing. He's good to me. Secondly, I understand you feel protective of me—and believe me, I appreciate it—but I know what I'm doing."

Without telling him straight out I'm working a case, I'm trying to convey it with my eyes. Not sure how successful I am, since he is still throwing daggers at the man behind me. Who knows, I may even be sending off mixed messages, since I seem to have a hard time remembering this is a job myself. It's hard to think like a professional when just the strength of his arm holding me to the heat of his body is enough to scramble my brain.

"We're drawing an audience," Ouray mutters over my shoulder.

Sure enough, a number of bikers are watching the exchange with intent curiosity, and I quickly turn to Keith, mumbling, "Call Damian. He'll explain."

Finally, a flash of understanding hits his eyes and breathing in deeply, he nods his head. "Will do, but I'm holding you responsible for her safety," he adds for Ouray's benefit.

"*Jesus,*" I hear him grumble behind me. Next

thing I know, I'm being marched to the beer tent with only "I need a fucking drink" as explanation.

OURAY

"Wanna explain to me why that cop feels the need to protect you?"

Goddamn. I've been stewing on that question all damn day for more than one reason, but mostly because in voicing it I admit—even to myself—I care a fuck of a lot about the answer.

My guard down after a good meal, a couple of beers, and a day of her scent in my nostrils, it slips out.

We're back at the clubhouse, sitting outside at one of the picnic tables, taking a break from the loud music inside. She glances at me, her eyebrows drawn, before turning her gaze down to where her fingers are picking at the label on the beer bottle she's holding. She keeps me waiting a long time before she finally answers.

"He's a good man," she starts, and I'm afraid I'm not gonna like what's coming. "We met at a party in college. He was a senior, me a sophomore. I… uhh…got into a situation, and he helped out. Just met him the one time, but I guess it left an impression. When I moved to Durango, I was surprised he still remembered me. Still sees me as that college kid, though. Still feels the need to throw himself in the role of protector."

"He have any claim on you?"

Fuck. I'm doing a shit job of holding back.

A little smile tugs at her lips. "I'm thinking you haven't met Autumn yet? She's a force to be reckoned with. I'm pretty sure he sees no one but her. Head over teakettle." I carefully let out the breath I've been holding. "Things could never have been like that between us."

There's something in the way she words it that has a new knot form in my gut. Something that's nagged at me from the first time she flinched at my touch. She doesn't seem to do that anymore, though. I sling an arm around her shoulders and let my fingers draw circles on her skin. Instead of pulling away, she seems to snuggle in even closer.

"I really want to kiss you right now," I mumble, my lips brushing the shell of her ear.

"Since when do you ask?" she whispers.

"Since we're alone out here. No one to convince. No one but you and me."

Her nostrils flare and she slowly lifts her face to mine, both interest and uncertainty in her eyes, but her lips form, "Okay."

The kiss starts sweet—a brush of lips, a tentative lick along the seam of her mouth—a soft introduction, as if it was our first. A slow and languid exploration of taste and texture, but when I feel the slight scrape of her blunt fingernails at the nape of my neck, my instincts take over. Sliding my hands under her arms, I haul her over to straddle my lap, her hot core burning the erection straining against my fly.

Soft sounds slip from her throat as I knead the firm globes of her ass in my hands, and I can barely sit still as she almost involuntarily rocks her hips on the hard ridge of my cock. I move a hand between us and up to palm a perfect handful of tit through fabric, plucking her hard little nipple between thumb and finger. Half prepared to feel her pull away, I'm surprised when she presses herself deeper into my hand. Encouraged, I pull down the neck of her shirt, the cup of her bra, exposing the pale flesh and pink tip to the outside air.

Her head drops back, eyes closed, and mouth slack, as I run my lips down her neck and chest, sucking her nipple into my mouth. She groans deep with every tug of my lips, and I can't hold my hips still, dry fucking up into her warm heat.

"Inside," I mumble, tugging her shirt up and sliding an arm under her ass. "Hold on."

She drops her head to my shoulder as I walk her inside, through the crowd to the back, her limbs wrapped around me, and her heart beating hard against my chest with every step.

I kick the bedroom door closed behind me and approach the bed, twisting as I let myself fall, so she ends up on top. Instantly her mouth latches back onto mine, and I can taste the fire on her little tongue. *Fuck yeah.* A hellcat. I have both hands free to explore bare skin, one sliding up her back, while the other slips into the back of her jeans feeling the smooth skin of her ass against my palm. I run my fingers along her crease until I encounter the hot silk of her arousal coating her pussy.

"On my face," I growl against her mouth, pulling my hand free and working her zipper, pushing jeans and underwear down, using my foot to pull them off all the way. All I can hear is her shallow breaths and when I glance up in her flushed face, she looks back at me, her eyes glinting under heavy lids. "Grab onto the headboard, Luna."

She does as I ask, as I settle her over me, the rich scent of her invading my senses. Primed and ready, her pussy is deep shade of pink, plump and glistening. I moan at the first taste of her and her body shudders in response.

"*Please...*"

I find her clit with my thumb, rolling it under the pad, as I tease her folds with my tongue. It's not until I wrap my lips around the little bundle of nerves and rim her entrance with a finger, that I feel her startle above me. I immediately move both hands to her ass, pull her down on my mouth and work her with deep tugs and firm flicks, not letting go until she cries out her release.

Her body is still shaking when she suddenly climbs off me, and I watch her tight little ass disappear into bathroom. For once I'm not sure what to do. If it wasn't clear before, it's fucking obvious now she has some issues.

The decision is made when I hear a crash coming from the bathroom and I swing out of bed. "Luna," I call her name, knocking on the damn door which she locked. "Open the fuckin' door." I'm about to kick it down when I hear the click of the latch and shove my way inside.

She's sitting on the edge of the tub, wrapped in a towel, with blood oozing from a couple of nasty cuts on the knuckles of her right hand. I take a step inside and feel crunching under my feet.

"What the fuck?" There are shards of glass from the mirror in the sink and on the floor. "Jesus, sweetheart—what did you do?" The eyes that look up at me are veiled. I can't get a bead on her state of mind, but it can't be good if she puts a fist through my fucking mirror. "Let me see." I take her hand and examine the cuts. "You may need some stitches. Let's get you dressed and I'll take you over to Mercy."

"No." As fragile as she looks, her voice is firm. "Superglue will do," she says, flexing her hand as she looks at it herself.

"Shit, Sprite. You're a fuckin' pain in my ass."

"Sorry," she mumbles.

"Don't freak, I'm gonna pick you up before you get glass in your feet too." She nods and I bend down to slip my arms under her, carrying her, towel and all, back to the bed. "Sit here, I'll be right back."

She's still in the same spot when I return with a first aid kit that luckily includes some superglue. She hisses when I quietly rinse out the cuts, dabbing the biggest ones dry before applying a bead of superglue and pressing the edges together. Her middle finger has a cut right across the knuckle so I wrap and splint that one, otherwise she'll just keep opening the wound. She doesn't say a peep while I tend to her, but when I try pulling the dirty towel from her grip, she struggles to hold on.

I lean down, dropping my forehead against hers. "Not gonna maul you, darlin'. I'm just gonna clean you up so we can get some sleep."

She stares in my eyes for a minute before nodding. "Just don't get any ideas," she quips, trying to cover her unease, I'm sure. "My hands are lethal weapons."

I snort in response. "They sure as fuck are."

Ten minutes later, the bathroom is cleaned up. I've taken another cold shower, and Luna is tucked in bed when I enter the room—but not sleeping. Her eyes follow me as I bypass the recliner and climb under the covers beside her.

When she pulls the sheet up to her chin, I have to laugh. "Fifteen minutes ago you were riding my face. A little late for you to get shy." I notice the deep blush on her cheeks, but I'm crass on purpose. She was on fire right before whatever is fucking with her mind had her pull back behind her defenses. "Come here." I roll on my side, hook an arm around her midsection, and pull her back against the curve of my body. "Any chance you want to discuss why you jump when I want to slide my finger in that hot pussy of yours?"

"Crass," she mumbles, her back stiff.

"Factual," I counter, tugging her a little closer and shoving my face in her hair, where I mumble, "Guess you're not ready to talk to me. I can wait."

I haven't even addressed why she decided to plant her fist in my mirror. Or her reflection.

CHAPTER 9

LUNA

"Glad you finally called in. I was about to send out a rescue team."

I hear the admonishment in Damian's voice, even though he wraps it up nice. This isn't like me, and he knows it. I'm usually on the ball and by the book—the ultimate professional—but there is nothing professional about the way I'm handling this assignment. I don't even recognize the person I'm becoming around Ouray. It freaks me out.

"I don't think this is working out."

The heavy silence on the other end of the line has me squirming on the edge of the bed.

I woke up with a throbbing hand and a heavy load of guilt. The bed was empty, Ouray already gone, and the quick shower I took did nothing to stop the churning in my head.

"Want to explain that to me?" he finally asks.

"I'm not sure I'm the right person for the job. Things are getting complicated."

"Ouray?" Sometimes Damian's acute insight scares me. Especially when he sees right through the cover I try to maintain. "Luna?" The prompt comes when I stay silent, not knowing how to answer. "There's a reason you're perfect for this job, you know?" he offers. "It's clear as day you hold the man's interest, and you haven't been as good as you think at hiding your own. The only way this will work is if you two are believable as a couple, and after the heated discussion I had with Blackfoot last night, I'd say you are successful. Even after explaining the assignment to him, he still doesn't buy that's all it is."

"You don't understand," I sputter. "I'm afraid I'm losing focus."

"Bullshit. You're the most focused person I know." I'm not sure he'd be saying that if he'd seen me last night. I feel the heat of a blush remembering the scene in this very bed. "The most successful lies are the ones that hold a grain of truth," he reminds me. "And let me ask you this—do you think I'm any less of an agent now than I was before I met Kerri? Or Jasper, for that matter, after he hooked up with my sister?"

"Of course not," I protest immediately. "But that's different."

"Not that different at all. Fuck knows I had my reservations starting something in the middle of an investigation, and I know Jasper did as well."

"I don't do relationships."

"Well, maybe it's about fucking time you did. Loosen up, Luna. The world won't fall apart if you let go a little."

I don't get a chance to respond because he's already hung up.

I'm still sitting on the edge of the bed when Ouray walks in with a mug of coffee for me. I don't even flinch when he bends down to press a kiss on my forehead.

"You done in the bathroom? I'm just gonna hop in the shower, we're riding out in fifteen. Momma's got waffles this morning, you may wanna go grab some before they're all gone."

He's right, by the time I get dressed and make my way to the kitchen, slipping by a scowling Rowtag to find the big platter on the table is empty. Damn.

"Saved you some," Momma says with a grin, as she pulls a plate from the oven.

I sit down across from Cody who is wolfing down the last of his waffles, with half an eye on mine. *Not a chance*, I sign before digging in, and I notice him looking at my hand with curiosity.

What happened?

I look at my bandaged hand and flex it a few times. *Got it caught on a nail.* That seems to appease him, although Momma—who's been paying attention— seems less convinced, throwing me a raised eyebrow.

Ignoring her scrutiny, I return to my plate, eating

my first waffle with relish.

Can you teach me again today? Cody asks when I look up.

Not sure if there will be time today. Tomorrow?

Cody just nods, getting up to deposit his plate and milk glass in the sink. I hate the look of disappointment on his face, so I grab his arm when he passes by my chair on his way out of the kitchen.

I promise. You practice that bag hard today, and I'll teach you some self-defense moves tomorrow after breakfast.

This time I get a lopsided smile—my first one—and it spreads an unfamiliar warmth through my chest. He has a dimple. I hadn't noticed that before.

"Gonna be a charmer, that one," Momma notes, staring after the kid. "Still skittish around my boys. I don't even wanna imagine what that baby's been through. It's a damn shame." The warm feeling disappears, replaced by a pang of nausea at her words.

No longer hungry, I manage two more bites before setting my fork down on my plate, just as Ouray saunters in.

"You done with that?" I nod, and he wastes no time shoveling the leftover waffle in his mouth, before dumping the plate in the sink. "Let's go."

We're fortunate with the weather. A little chilly this morning though, so he insisted I wear my new leather jacket.

It must've rained at some point during the night, because Ouray had to wipe down the seat of his bike, but the skies are clear when we ride out.

The sound of motorcycle engines is deafening as the parade snakes through Durango. Hundreds of them. Curious onlookers line the streets, and I can't help but wave back at some of the excited kids taking in the spectacle, and their smiles are contagious. By the time we get to the end, my cheeks are aching.

From there we head to the Sky Ute Casino where we park the bikes, and everyone goes their own way. Ouray and I grab a burger from one of the vendors before wandering over to have a look at the motorcycle stunt show.

"Your first rally?" Wheels, the president of the Shiprock MC, asks me when he joins us at the protective barrier, giving Ouray a barely there chin lift. I'd noticed him toting a large American flag, riding a three-wheeler in the parade. Wouldn't mind trying one of those myself.

"It is."

"You guys heading out on the poker run?"

"I don't know what that is, so I can't tell you," I admit, looking over my shoulder at Ouray.

"Like a road rally, or a treasure hunt," he explains before turning to Wheels. "A few of my guys like that stuff. I prefer the poker cards they have in here." He tilts his head toward the casino. "When are you guys rollin' out?"

"Depends on how drunk my guys get." He looks toward the beer tent at a group of bikers wearing the Shiprock colors and shakes his head. "Fuckin' looks like it'll be tomorrow morning," he grumbles before turning back to Ouray. "What day you gonna head out to Ruidoso?"

"Monday, I think. Seventeenth. We'll hit it in one day. Momma booked us in at Canyon Cabins. You stayin' there again this year?"

"That's the plan. We can ride together? Meet up in Bloomfield in the morning?"

"I'm good with that. Salinas will likely hook up as well."

"You tagging along, little one?" the old man asks me, and despite his cocky grin, the eyes are gentle in his scraggly face.

"Sure as fuck is," Ouray answers for me, throwing a possessive arm around my shoulders. "On the back of *my* bike, ya dirty old man."

Wheels bursts out laughing, a deep raspy sound, soon replaced by a nasty cough that sounds like he's trying to dislodge a lung. When I put a concerned hand on his arm, he brushes me off and walks away, still hacking.

"Is he okay?"

"Emphysema, but the motherfucker refuses to use his oxygen in public. Come on," he steers me toward the casino. "Got a poker table I'd like you to meet."

"I won!"

I grin at a very giddy Luna, flapping her ticket in my face.

She got annoyed losing at the poker table earlier, abandoned me, and for the past forty minutes has been trying out the slots. Apparently with success, judging by the neat four digit number on her ticket.

I'd left her in my bed this morning, purposely creating some distance after spending half the night with her limbs wrapped around me, trusting me more in sleep than she does awake. Don't get me wrong, I got a kick out of watching her come undone with my mouth on her pussy, but it was torture not burying myself balls deep inside, with her warm body plastered against mine. I took my breakfast into my office and spent the next hour staring at the goddamn wall, wondering what the fuck I was doing with a woman who clearly comes with a shitload of baggage.

Still, the moment I heard the water turn on in the bathroom, I couldn't think of anything but her hot as fuck naked body in my shower, and any reservations flew right out the damn window.

Seeing her now, she looks so different from the buttoned-up, straightlaced public servant I first met a few months ago. With a blush high on her cheeks, eyes shining with excitement, and that wide-mouthed grin, she looks almost carefree and full of life. I can't resist pressing a hard kiss on her lips.

"Congrats, Sprite."

"I've never won a single thing in my life," she whispers, her arms wrapping around my neck, smiling up in my face. Fuck, she's beautiful when she lets go.

"Happy for ya."

"Thirty-four hundred dollars. That's more than I take home at the end of the month. I don't even know what to do with it," she continues to babble as we make our way over to the cashier. "Wait! I know, I can buy you dinner."

"Not buying me dinner, Sprite."

"Why not?" A frown forms between her eyebrows as she looks at me. "This isn't gonna be much fun if you won't let me share."

I roll my eyes at her attempt at emotional blackmail, but apparently it's working because I find myself saying, "Fine." When she proposes the swankiest restaurant in town, I put my foot down, though. "Have a hankering for Chinese. Been a while. Let's do pick up and take it home."

"Should we bring enough for everyone else?" she asks, doing up her helmet on her own.

"Fuck no. Most of the guys will be out 'til all hours and you'd just insult Momma. Besides, I wasn't planning on heading to the club. Thinking more along the lines of your place or mine."

"You have a place? I thought—"

"Yeah, I've got a place. I may stay at the club when there's stuff going on, but most of the time I go home."

I can almost hear her thinking, but she doesn't say anything as she climbs on the back of my bike. Not until we walk out of May Palace on Main with enough food to last a week. She insisted ordering everything she liked off the menu.

"My place," she says with a determined look.

I open my mouth to object, thinking I'd like to get a taste of her in my house, but I end up closing it again. She'll feel more comfortable in her own digs, which means I may be able to pry a bit further into that pretty little head of hers.

Luna's cabin is basically one large rectangular room, housing a small kitchen, a table with four chairs, and a sitting area around the old stone fireplace. On the other side of the entrance is one bedroom and the bathroom. Very basic. Very Spartan. Very fitting the way Luna would like the outside world to see her, but not at all representative of the warm-blooded woman I've glimpsed underneath.

"Shit," she swears from the kitchen.

"What's up?"

"I only have two beers left."

"Plenty. I'm happy with water." She looks at me with a disbelieving smirk on her lips. "I am," I confirm, sitting down at the table. "Don't get me wrong, I drink, on occasion, but never more than two or three. Won't catch me rolling into bed hammered anymore."

"Anymore?"

"Did plenty of that when I was younger." This time I have to grin myself. Fuck, it's a miracle I can remember anything of my twenties and thirties. Most of those years were spent drunk, high, and buried into some willing chick. Not that I'm about to share this fact.

"Isn't that what they say? Wisdom comes with age?" She pulls out some plates and cutlery and sets them, along with the two beers, on the table.

I snort. "Yeah, that wasn't it. More like doctor's orders. At thirty-seven my liver was already good 'n pickled, and I like life too much to piss it away."

"Yikes." She starts sitting down, but immediately straightens up again. "You're gonna have to excuse me, there won't be room for food if I don't get these damn jeans off."

I'm scooping some food on our plates and when she returns, she's wearing an old pair of flannel pajama pants. I watch as she sits down across from me, folding one leg under her on the seat. Clearly much more at ease at home than sitting in the clubhouse kitchen. She doesn't seem as hyperaware of her surroundings either.

"Better?"

"Much," she mumbles, already attacking her dinner. The next few minutes we eat in silence when she suddenly says, "My therapist says I use alcohol as a numbing agent." The moment the words leave her lips, her shocked eyes shoot up and her hand clamps over her mouth. I try not to let my surprise show at her unexpected revelation, and shove another forkful of Hunan beef in my mouth. "I don't know why I said that." She plays with a piece of sesame chicken with her chopsticks before tossing them on her plate. "That's a lie—I know."

I follow suit and put my fork down, folding my hands under my chin as I catch her eyes. "Talk to me."

"Last night…" she starts, hesitantly. I wait her out. "I don't do that."

"What? Sitting on a guy's face?"

"Jesus, Ouray—do you have to be so blunt?" She rolls her eyes and I give myself an internal pat on the back for getting her riled up. Truths tend to fly when a little temper is involved. "Yes, *that*. Letting a guy touch me, period. I'm…"

"Come on, darlin', you came this far—don't chicken out now." If looks could kill, I'd be blowing out my last breath.

"Fuck you. I haven't had anyone touch me in years," she spits out.

"Years? Like two years? More?" She nods, so I push a little harder. "Five? Ten?"

"Since college, okay?" she finally snaps.

Well, fuck.

I don't get a chance to respond before she jumps up, snatches the plates off the table, and stalks over to the sink.

"Sprite—"

Almost relieved at the sudden peal of her phone, I snap my mouth closed. Not like I had any fucking clue what to say.

CHAPTER 10

LUNA

The small shopping plaza parking lot is jam-packed with emergency vehicles by the time I get there. Local PD, fire and rescue, and an ambulance. Damian mentioned one of the depository's employees was injured when he called, but the fact the rig is still here does not bode well.

I spot Dylan with one of the Durango detectives, Ramirez, standing in front of the store window.

"Give me the scoop." Both men look up when I approach.

"Two armed suspects forced their way into the store, just as the female employee was locking up," Ramirez reports. "From what she tells us, one held her at gunpoint while the other stuffed their backpacks with merchandise. Her manager, who'd been in the back office preparing the bank deposit, came out carrying a shotgun when one of the suspects turned and fired."

"Injuries?" I already know the answer when Ramirez solemnly shakes his head.

"Victim expired from a single gunshot wound to the chest by the time we got here. The girl's physically okay but distraught, so we put her in the back of the ambulance for now to get cleaned up."

"Did you talk to her, Barnes?"

Dylan shakes his head. "Was leaving that for you."

"Mind if I go talk to her?" I ask Ramirez.

"Have at it," he says, gesturing to the back of the ambulance. "Her name is Amber Jensen.

When I open the back of the rig, I find the young woman sitting on the stretcher, drinking from a bottle of water. Her hands still stained with what I assume is her manager's blood. The EMT with her is Bella, whose newly pregnant belly is starting to show under her uniform.

"I'm surprised Jas still lets you work the nightshift," I observe jokingly.

"Not his call to make," she bites off, apparently not finding my comment amusing.

"Good point," I mumble, climbing in and turning my attention to the girl. "Hi, Amber, my name is Luna Roosberg, I'm an agent for the FBI. I know you've already spoken with the detective, but if you don't mind, I have a few more questions to ask. Do you feel up to it?"

Her face is blotchy, and her eyes weary, when she

looks at me. Still, she nods in agreement.

"I'll be right outside," Bella assures the girl, giving her shoulder a squeeze.

There isn't a whole lot more Amber tells me, than what she'd already mentioned to Ramirez. Two armed suspects, their faces covered with bandanas and beanies pulled down low over their eyes. She only heard one of their voices and believes that guy to be the leader. The other one never spoke and was the one who kept a gun aimed at her. The leader was the one who shot her boss.

"What color were the bandanas?" I ask, having learned this past weekend that some MCs use a specific color. Some guys will tie them around their head, others will walk around with them tucked in their back pocket. When I commented on it, Ouray explained they likely had a heavy padlock tied to the other side. Makes for a handy weapon, you could make a serious dent in someone's skull swinging one of those around. With that bit of information, I spent a lot of time checking out backsides.

"Black, I think. Although it may have been navy."

Arrow's Edge uses navy bandanas, as does Shiprock. Mesa Riders have black, red for the Moab Reds, and the Amontinados don't seem to favor a specific color. I'm not sure if there is anything I should read into that, but it's interesting enough to make note of.

"Did you happen to see them leave?"

"I...Ed, he was bleeding. I was crawling over

to him. Tried to stop it, but there…there was just so much of it." She starts sobbing at the memories. I'm sure they will haunt her the rest of her life.

"You did all you humanly could," I reassure her, feeling awful to have to push, but it would go a long way if we could identify a vehicle. "So you didn't see anything, but maybe you can recall hearing a car or maybe motorcycles?"

"Not motorcycles. We've had enough come by this weekend to recognize the sound. Although I did hear an engine start up at some point. Like I said, I wasn't really paying attention, the only thing I can tell you is that it had a weird whining sound."

Again, not sure how helpful that information is by itself, but this is worth noting too.

"One last question, and then I'll leave you be— you mentioned the suspects we both armed—can you recall the skin color of their hands?"

She seems to think on that for a minute before turning to me. "They were wearing gloves."

So much for potential fingerprints.

I leave her in Bella's good care and walk inside the dispensary, making sure to stay away from the body still lying in a large pool of blood on the far side of the counter.

"Edward Linden. Thirty-four," Dylan recites from the driver's license on the inside of the wallet in his hand. He points to a snapshot of the victim with his arm around a pretty brunette, a toddler wedged between them. *Shit.*

It's close to two in the morning when I finally get home. After leaving the scene, Dylan and I went back to the office to type up a report with everything still fresh in our minds. The only one there was Jasper, who seems to prefer being there to staying home alone while his wife is on shift.

I can smell the Chinese we had earlier tonight the moment I open my door, and my thoughts immediately go to Ouray, who I all but kicked out when Damian called. At the time it was a welcome reprieve. I'd already said more than I wanted, and knowing Ouray, he wouldn't have left it alone. He's the kind of guy who will dig until he gets to the bottom, no matter how deep I keep that shit buried. Even Keith, who was there at the time, doesn't know the full story.

He kissed me hard on the lips when I tried to shove him out the door. "Call me when you get in, so I know you're safe."

"I'm a trained FBI agent," I'd snapped at him. "I can take care of myself."

"Humor me," had been his short reply.

I resist as long as it takes me to throw the leftover Chinese in the fridge, wash up the dirty dishes, and turn off the lights, before I sink down on the side of my bed, tapping out a quick text.

Me: **I'm home. Night.**

Two seconds later a message comes back.

Ouray: **Get some sleep, Sprite.**

I wonder if he was waiting up for me.

OURAY

I'm surprised as fuck when a tired-looking Luna walks into the kitchen the next morning.

"Figured you'd still be sleeping."

I made someone a promise, she signs, grinning at a slack-mouthed Cody, who starts pushing back from the table. *Finish your breakfast first.*

"You should eat somethin' too," Momma says, setting a cup of coffee by the empty spot at the table.

"Thanks, Momma, just coffee is good. I had something earlier."

The moment she sits down, I pull her chair closer to mine, tag her behind the neck, and plant a proper good morning on her. "That's better," I mumble against her lips, satisfied to see a slightly dazed look in her eyes.

"The boy," she whispers, her eyes flitting to Cody, who looks between us with open curiosity.

"Nothin' wrong with him seein' some lovin'," Momma declares with a dismissive wave of her hand. "Better that than fightin'."

"I guess." Luna shrugs, and the two launch into a conversation about violence on TV and in games and the impact on kids. All the time she keeps tabs on me from the corner of her eye.

After she rushed me out the door last night, I thought for sure she'd be running for the hills, which is why the last thing I expected was to see her this morning. Figured I'd have to chase her down at some point. Didn't get much sleep myself, our conversation playing through my mind while I was waiting to hear she got home okay.

Ready, Cody? she asks when the boy shovels down the last bite of his bacon.

Not Cody anymore. Ouray calls me A-h-i-g-a.

Luna glances at me with an eyebrow raised before asking the boy, *What does that mean?*

He who fights, he tells her with a grin.

It actually had been Nosh who suggested the name. Although, I'd been the first to use it last night when I found him beating the virtual crap out of a disgruntled Rowtag in some electronic game they were playing on a TV in the common room. Rowtag left in a huff. That boy's temper hasn't let up one bit since we brought him here. He'll turn twenty-one in a few months and will technically be eligible for a patch, but that's not going to happen unless he does a complete one-eighty before then. I'd hoped he would've shaken that boulder-sized chip on his shoulder by now, but I see another come-to-Jesus talk with the kid may be necessary.

I follow Luna and her charge to the garage at a distance, noting instead of her skintight athletic wear, she is wearing a pair of sweats and an oversized hoodie of some thin material. She's hiding that tight body I know is under there well.

The boy eagerly follows directions when she tells him to pull down four of the mats we have hanging on the far wall to form a soft surface. I almost laugh out loud at the eager grin on his face when she invites him to attack her. Five attempts later, he's not smiling anymore, frustrated when she once again lands him on his ass, this time when he comes at her from behind.

She has his full attention now though, and he's focused when she shows him how she managed to evade his attacks.

"Instead of standing there gawking, why don't you come give us a hand?" she calls out, looking at me.

I know what's coming; I'm being used as a guinea pig, and I'm pretty sure she won't be as gentle with me as she is with him. "Careful with the nuts," I whisper under my breath when I reach her. It earns me a sharp little elbow in my ribs, which Ahiga apparently thinks is hilarious, because for the first time I hear his laugh out loud.

"You'll recover," Luna mocks with a grin.

"I wouldn't be so sure, not at my age."

In the next five minutes, she puts me through my paces without once coming close to my package, for which I'm grateful. The boy looks on with eyes as big as saucers, taking in every single move. At some point, Nosh wandered in, cackling loudly each time my ass lands on the ground.

"I need you to come at me from behind this time."

Determined to get the upper hand at least once, I kick off my boots and drop them at the edge of the mat. "What's that for?" she asks, watching me.

"Only fair," I tell her with a shrug. "The boy can't hear someone coming up behind him either."

"Fine by me. If you want, you can blindfold me too, so I don't see your shadows."

I don't have to be told twice. I pull the do-rag from my back pocket, roll it up, cover her eyes, and tie it carefully behind her head. Then I bend my head down, my mouth next to her ear, and whisper, "We play this game again, we do it without an audience and close to a fucking bed."

I smile at the sharp intake of breath. Taking her by the shoulders, I twirl her around a few times, before backing up just a step. I wait her out—staying perfectly still as she tilts her head first this way and then that—but when she shifts on her feet, I move.

I've barely even wrapped my arm around her neck when she turns slightly, and before I can follow suit, she has her small hand firmly wrapped around my sac, exerting firm controlled pressure. Every time I move, she twists a little harder. I barely hear the loud baying coming from fucking Nosh over the roaring of blood in my veins. Fucking hell, ten minutes ago the thought of those small hands feeling me up was a fantasy, but those little fingers digging in feel more like a goddamn nightmare.

"Uncle," I call, lifting my hands in capitulation. She lets go, rips the bandana from her eyes, and grins wide, while I rub some blood flow back in my package.

But her smile disappears quickly when she sees Ahiga's face drained of blood, his eyes big on where my hand is still massaging my junk. Shit.

It's okay. I didn't really hurt him. "Tell him, Ouray."

"Don't think he's worried about that, Sprite," I tell her, removing my hand from my crotch.

From the corner of my eye, I see Nosh backing out of the garage, I'm guessing to give the kid some space.

Look at me. Luna, clueing in, places herself in his line of vision. *When you let something scare you, you give it power—but when you challenge your fears— you take control.*

The boy's eyes flit back and forth between us, before settling on me. *Aren't you mad?* His fingers shake as he forms the words.

No reason for me to be mad, boy. Luna wants you to know how to look after yourself. So do I. He nods, still looking unsure so I clarify. *When you're grabbed by someone bigger, you're not strong enough to fight them off, but you can be smart enough. Like aiming for the most vulnerable spots: eyes, knees, and crotch. A man is most vulnerable between his legs.*

Suddenly anger flashes in his eyes flash, while his hands fly with choppy motions.

Not true.

For the second time in as many days, bile crawls

up my throat, robbing me of the ability to speak.

"Maybe not before, but now it is," Luna says out loud, signing simultaneously, as she takes a step closer to the boy. "You're smarter now. You can take control, but that's not all—you have people who will protect you. I will..." She slaps a hand to her chest, before pointing it at me. "So will Ouray...Paco...Nosh, and can you imagine what Momma would do to anyone who wants to hurt you?"

The last comment has his lips twitching.

I think I've had enough for today. I can be back on Wednesday, but probably later in the afternoon or early evening. We'll practice some more, okay?

It takes a minute, but he eventually throws her a universal okay sign, and with just a sideways glance for me, walks out of the garage. When he's gone I lean down, with my hands on my knees, fighting hard to hang on to my breakfast. A hand lands on my shoulder and I take in a deep breath before straightening up.

"He'll be okay," she says, but her face is strained.

"I get my hands on who did that to the boy, I'll rip off his junk with my bare hands and shove his cock so far down his throat he'll choke on it."

"I'm already looking," she admits. "Trying to track down where he may have come from."

"You knew."

"I suspected."

"Because you recognize it?"

My statement is met with silence. I know I'm taking a big chance, but I wait it out.

"Probably." Her voice is soft, barely audible, but I don't miss a single syllable. I cup her face in my hands and lean my forehead against hers.

"I'll fucking do the same to him, unless you want to feed him his junk."

Luna's lips move without really making a sound.

"What was that?"

I'm not quite sure what she said, or maybe I don't want to know. She tells me anyway.

"*Them.*"

CHAPTER 11

LUNA

"Do you have a minute?"

Jasper looks up from his laptop. He's alone in the office when I walk in.

"Sure."

"I have a favor to ask. Ouray took in this boy, he's a street kid—troubled—I need to find out where he's from, but I have little to go on, so it may require some creative digging. I've tried and reached the end of my skill set."

"My specialty." He grins, stretching his fingers. "What can you tell me?"

"The only name he'll give us is Cody, and I'm pretty sure that's his real name. He's twelve, is deaf, has been on the street for a year, and says he went to school until about a year ago. He was picked up in Cortez but isn't from there, although I have a feeling he's not that far from home. Doesn't know his dad, and mom died of an overdose when he was eight, and he was living with his grandparents when he took off."

"I assume you've scoured missing persons reports?"

"Yes, I have. No luck."

"Do you have a picture of the kid?"

I pull up my phone and find the covert picture I took when he was engrossed in a PlayStation game, and send it to Jasper's email. It's not great, only three-quarters of his face is visible and he's looking off camera, so you don't really see his eyes, but it's better than nothing.

I snapped it on Monday, after his freak-out in the garage. I didn't stay long, telling Ouray I'd probably be bogged down at the office with the new developments in the case. He didn't argue too hard, just said he'd be in touch. I haven't heard a thing for the past two days, and I wonder if I've managed to scare him off. As much as my common sense tells me that's a good thing, it doesn't feel all that way.

Our pretend relationship didn't feel so fake from the inside. There was certainly nothing fake about the orgasm he gave me, or the physical response he seems to have to me. Too many lines are blurred—some crossed—and I should be glad for the break so I can reframe some boundaries, but instead I'm restless. So many things swirling through my mind I can barely keep track. Unsure what to do with my feelings, I shove them down, and focus instead on something concrete—like finding information on Cody so I can track down his abuser. Clearly with no success so far.

"What's the interest? If you don't mind me asking?" Jasper, who was looking at Cody's image on his screen, turns to me. I shake my head, unsure how much to tell him.

"Kid's had a rough go. He's given me reason to think something happened to him. Something bad."

Jasper's eyes narrow. "You don't say."

"Hmm. Bad enough he's leery of men."

Jasper growls deep in his chest. Bella told me a while ago Jasper grew up in the foster system himself. I hadn't known. It's surprising how we can trust each other with our lives in this office, but not enough to share. We all seem to be holding information back. I know I do.

"Leave it with me," he says under his voice when Damian walks in.

The rest of the morning we go over every piece of evidence we have from the latest robbery. The coroner retrieved the bullet, a .45 millimeter slug, from the victim's scapula where it had lodged. But that information is only helpful if we have a weapon to compare it to. We interviewed Amber again, but she had little to add.

Other than Arrow's Edge, the other MCs all seem to have left Durango in the past few days. Next stop for most of them will be the annual Golden Aspen rally in Ruidoso, New Mexico in a little over two weeks. And Damian wants me on the back of Ouray's bike again.

"You up for that?" he asks, challenging me. "You'll be out of state and pretty much on your own. It'll be even more important to look like you belong."

"I am, and I know."

"Yeah? So how come you've spent the past few days hanging around the office until all hours of the night, instead of securing your place with the club?" I squirm under his intense scrutiny. Something that doesn't go unnoticed and he gentles his tone. "Luna, if this is too much, I need you to tell me."

I'm tempted, just for a second, but then I think of Ed Linden's kids, of his wife, and I know I can't walk away. Cody, Jesus. I'm already too invested in that boy to turn my back now. I refuse to linger on any thoughts of Ouray. "It won't be a problem," I assure him.

"Good, then finish up any loose ends you have on your desk, hand the rest over to Dylan when he comes in, and focus all your attention on the assignment."

"I can't just not go to work, that wouldn't be credible either," I protest.

"Didn't say you couldn't check in, but within reason."

"So noted," I respond less than graciously as I walk out.

It's near three o'clock when a soft ping announces a message on my phone.

***Ouray:* The boy's asking about you.**

The text irks me. It's not like I would forget my

promise to the boy. Annoyed, I stuff my phone in my pocket, hand over the last of my files to Dylan, and with a curt, "I'm off," march out of the office. Ten minutes later, when I turn up Junction Creek Road, it occurs to me my irritation may be more about what Ouray doesn't say in his message.

"Hey." The man himself is having a smoke out front when I pull my car next to an old pickup on the other side of the collection of bikes.

"Hi." I know I sound snippy, but I can't seem to help myself. I try to slip by him but a strong arm blocks my path.

"Haven't seen you in two days, and that's all you have to say to me?"

"Could say the same thing about your damn text," I snap back, when I notice a very curious Lusio leaning against the gate, observing us closely. *Shit.*

A firm tug and I'm hauled against Ouray's firm body. I lift up my eyes to find his face just inches from mine.

"*Christ*, you can be a pain in the ass, Sprite. Would'a kept you here on Monday, but I thought you needed some space. A couple of hours, a night, but not two fucking days without a word."

"Oh."

"Yeah."

The semi-grunt is closely followed by a thorough kiss to hammer his point home. By the time I come up for air, I can't even remember what got me so worked up in the first place. I put a hand on his chest and look up at him.

"How's Cody doing?"

"Momma says he still shoves the chair in front of his door, this morning he voluntarily started talking to me. Progress in my books."

"It is," I confirm, disengaging myself from his hold. "I promised him some time in your gym, if you don't mind?"

He raises an eyebrow. "You've gotta ask? You gonna stick around after?"

There's a whole lot more to that question than just face value, but I answer in the same casual manner. "Planning to."

The faint tug at the corner of his mouth shows that pleases him, and my step is a bit lighter when I make my way inside to find my grasshopper.

OURAY

"You're the best, Momma."

She grumbles when I kiss her cheek, still not happy that I'm planning to feed Luna at my place, a job she'd like to lay claim to. She did pack a couple of servings of the massive apple crisp she made this afternoon.

"Tell that boy to wash before showin' up for dinner," she calls after me when I go in search of Luna.

I'm stuffing the dessert in my saddlebags when Lusio ambles up beside me.

"Feisty, that one," he says, looking over at the garage. "May wanna have a gander. Rowtag just wandered in there and I think she's going off on him."

Dammit, I can hear the raised voices now. Rushing over, I just catch the cub taunting her to take a swing at him. Stupid cocky fuck.

"Don't think you wanna take that on, boy," I say calmly approaching him from behind. He swings around at the sound of my voice. "She wiped the mat with me and I'm twice your size."

"The bitch owes me a rematch." He sounds almost petulant, and I wonder where we went wrong with this one.

Over the past years, a few of the kids we've taken in have stayed on to become part of the MC. Others have gone off to college, and some ended up enlisting with the armed forces. No matter their story, their age, or their path, they all came here as boys—and left as men.

I'm not sure why Rowtag is different, but I'm starting to doubt there's a man to be found in him. He's still very much the angry teenager he was when he first came here.

"You don't talk about my woman—or any woman for that matter—like that. I've never taken a hand to you, boy, but you're this fucking close to getting your ass handed to you. You better change your attitude right a-fucking-way, or you'll not only never get that patch you've been gagging for, but I'll personally strip you from that leather vest and toss your skinny behind on the other side of that fence."

I never take my eyes off him, and never raise my voice, calmly staring him down as I hear affirming grunts from a few brothers who have come in behind me. It's not until after he stalks out, pushing past me with a furious scowl on his face, that I turn my attention to Luna.

Wide-stanced, hands on her hips, and her chin high, she looks like a five foot tall warrior woman. Sexy as fuck. All the more so when I notice she's been shielding the boy behind her.

You okay?

The responding big grin on his face is a surprise and I have to chuckle when he signs, *She's badass.*

No shit. "Lusio?" I throw over my shoulder, noticing Yuma and Wapi, another of our cubs, looking on.

"Yeah, Chief?"

"Keep a close eye on the hothead. And I mean close, I don't want him to take a piss without you knowing about it."

"Got it," he confirms, following Rowtag out.

I turn to Yuma. "You plan to stay here tonight?" He nods. "Good. Anything comes up, I'll be home."

I wait until they've gone before I turn to Cody. *Gonna take my girl home. Tomorrow you and me are gonna talk about school...* He doesn't like that, I can tell, so I add, *But your assignment tonight is to kick*

Wapi's ass in Call Of Duty. *No one can beat him, but I bet you can.*

The grin back on his face, the kid runs to catch up with him.

"I could've handled him," Luna says, gathering her things and walking up to me.

"I know, but that wasn't my point. The way he handles himself is a reflection on this club—on me—I needed to make that clear."

"I get it."

I sigh, tossing an arm around her shoulder. "I don't think he does, though."

<hr>

"I don't know how you bringing me here is going to help my cover."

Luna is walking into my house behind me. She hadn't been happy when I told her to follow me to my place. Since I live almost across from the clubhouse on a rise overlooking Chapman Lake it took us two minutes to get there, and she's still grumbling after parking her car in front of my garage.

I stop in the small hallway and turn to face her. "More than staying at the clubhouse would," I explain. "My brothers know I don't bring women here."

"For real? Not ever?" The surprised look on her face is cute, and I snag a finger in the front of her shirt, pulling her close for a firm kiss on that slack mouth.

"Not big into relationships, Sprite. Never had the

urge to share more than my dick."

"Yikes," she grimaces, pulling back. "Crass. And more than I needed to know." She sidesteps me and walks into my living space.

I bought this place eight years ago, wanting a place of my own to withdraw to, but still close enough to the clubhouse. Other than the great location, one of the main attractions was the huge floor-to-ceiling glass panes all along the back of the house. My place sits higher than the surrounding area, and the land slopes down from the rise to the crisp mountain lake below. The view is fucking ace.

Apparently Luna agrees, because she's immediately drawn to the windows.

"My God, and I thought I had a good view—this is stunning."

I set the container with Momma's dessert in the fridge, grab a couple of beers, and join her by the window. I hand her a bottle over her shoulder, slip my free arm around her middle, and pull her back to my front, my chin resting on her head.

"Didn't mean to offend you." Fuck, that sounds stiff. Apologies don't come natural, and I almost choke on the dry words. "Only thing I was interested in before was getting off and getting out—is what I meant to say." I feel her stomach muscles contract and wonder if I made it even worse.

"Wow," she says, in a funny voice. "You sure know how to charm a girl."

Definitely fucked up again.

I see her face scrunch up in the window's reflection and turn her around, fully prepared to grovel. But the moment her eyes lift up, she throws her head back and bursts out laughing. She's got a great fucking deep, full belly laugh I can feel ripple over my skin.

"Smartass," I grumble, but I do it with a smile on my face.

Crisis averted, I get down to pulling shit together for dinner. Luna takes over prep for the salad, while I put together skewers. Steak, onion, bacon, chunks of fresh pineapple and Haloumi cheese. When there's nothing left to do but fire up the grill, I lead Luna out on the deck off the kitchen, and she tells me about her session with Cody. Apparently they talked a little about what happened a couple of days ago, but she doesn't elaborate much, and I don't push it. I probably trust her more than I trust myself handling that boy right.

It takes just a couple of minutes on each side for the skewers to be ready, and we end up eating out on the deck.

"This stuff is amazing," Luna says around a mouthful.

Damn, even her healthy appetite is sexy. I know this is supposed to be part of a job for her, but if I believed that's all it means to her, I would never have brought her here. Still, I wish she were here without an ulterior motive. As for me, my ass is already royally fucked. Case or no case, I like her in my house, I like where this is going. Complications and all.

"Glad you like."

"I'm actually surprised you didn't serve up something fried or even ordered. This is pretty healthy fare."

"Momma's a great cook, but with a small army of hungry guys to feed every day, she's more concerned about filling bellies than she is about nutritional value. She's all about the stick to your ribs kinda food—unfortunately in my case—it settles in my gut." I slap a hand on my belly.

"Hardly," she snorts, putting her own hands on her stomach as she leans back in the chair. "God, I'm stuffed."

I bite my lip to stop myself from letting the lewd thought that immediately springs to mind slip. Besides, I had another reason for whisking her off to my place, where we would have some privacy.

"Leave the plates," I tell Luna when she starts stacking stuff up. "I'll take care of them. Sit down, I got somethin' to say." I can see her defenses go up immediately, and I know she's probably been waiting for this, so I barge right in. "You said *them*." It's almost like I slapped her so I quickly grab for her hand. Better would be having her in my lap, but I'll take what I can get. "Pretty sure I know what that means, Sprite. Don't need a blow-by-blow, but I can listen and I can be patient." I'm actually not that sure about the latter, but I can sure as fuck try. "So I'm not gonna push, but one thing I need from you is names."

I've been stewing on this for a while. Since my

younger days, both on the streets and in the MC, I've lost my appetite for violence. That scene in the garage on Monday fired it right back up.

She shakes her head and stares out in the distance. "Can't give you those."

"Like hell you can't. I don't know—and I don't care—if these motherfuckers are behind bars or on the other side of the world. Even if they're already in a hole in the ground, I need their names, so I can piss on their graves." My voice has risen with anger and Luna yanks her hand back as she pushes out of her chair. Instead of running off, as I expected her to, she paces a few steps either way before she stops in front of me, her hands on her hips, and fire shooting from her eyes.

"I can't give you those, because I don't know who they are!"

CHAPTER 12

LUNA

I'm angry because to this day just talking about what happened all those years ago still makes me feel like puking.

I even went to see Gary Patterson, my therapist in Aztec, yesterday. He was surprised when I called to see him outside of my normal scheduled appointment once a month, but made room for me over lunch. It's all we talked about.

Gary is the only one who knows as much as I do. For years he's been trying to convince me that the more I talk about it, the more I acknowledge it happened to me, the less power it will have in my life. He calls it 'unresolved trauma.'

It took me long enough to seek help in the first place. When I was assigned to the La Plata County FBI field office, and first moved to Durango, the promise of a new start had me seek out counseling to deal with my past. Gary had me open up to him, which was a huge step for me, but I haven't been able to move much beyond that point.

Maybe what I needed was a good incentive.

He seemed encouraged when I told him I'd developed an interest in someone. In actual fact, he said, "About fucking time," before launching into a pep talk that had me convinced I could do this, right up to about five minutes ago.

I focus on Ouray, who looks back at me without blinking, challenging me without saying a word. I grab onto the railing behind me and take a deep breath.

"It was a Halloween party at a frat house," I finally manage, and once started, the words seem to fall from my lips unchecked. "My first one, and I was excited to dress up. It's funny because growing up in the Netherlands, I was worldwise to a lot of things, a lot of things my fellow students seemed more naïve about. Like drinking, which I'd been legally allowed to do since sixteen there, but a lot of the kids here were only just exposed to. Also about sexuality. I had experimented as a teenager—little was considered taboo in Holland. I had no concept that the silly cat costume I was wearing might be considered a sexual provocation."

"Shouldn't matter what you wear," Ouray says in a surprisingly soft voice.

"Maybe so, but still, it apparently gave the impression I was 'free game.' I was flattered when two guys—one wearing a Superman costume, and one dressed as Freddy Krueger—started dancing with me. Both had on masks. That's about as much as I remember. I wasn't drunk, so I figure they must've slipped me something in the beer they handed me." I snort, remembering how stupidly innocent I had been. "I recall being led up a set of stairs. I recall the masks—still sometimes see them hovering over me in my dreams. I remember them pulling the turtleneck sweater I was wearing to cover my face, and trying to fight when they ripped off my tights, but other than that, I don't remember much."

"*Jesus*." His voice is still gentle, in contrast with the clenched jaw and fisted hands on the armrests. "Tell me you know you hold no responsibility for what happened to you."

I shrug. It's one of the things I've struggled with most, what—if any—my part may have been in what happened. It's why I am the way I am. Not simply guarded around men, but not trusting my own judgement of them. I tried a few times since to connect with men on a physical level, but I panicked and backed out every time. It just seemed easier to avoid any involvement altogether.

"Rationally I do. Emotionally…that's a whole other kettle of fish."

My eyes drift off in the distance as the silence that follows my words stretches, and I can't help wonder what he is thinking. He may have made it clear he has more than a passing interest in me—even pushed me to tell him—but now that he knows how fucked up I really am, will he look at me the same?

I startle at a tentative touch of fingers reaching for my hand, and turn my eyes back to find him leaning forward, pressing his lips to my palm.

"I'm struggling," he says breathing hard, and my heart falls. I almost pull my hand back when he continues, "I should be telling you not all guys take what they want without permission, and yet what I really want to do is pull you down on my knees, hold you tight, and kiss the fucking starch out of those lips."

I search his face to find sincerity behind his words. I take a step closer and climb onto his lap, my eyes holding his as I press my mouth to his. Tentatively, his arms slide around me.

I hold no illusions I'm all better now, but being able to feel safe in a man's arms—this man's arms—is a sweet victory all on its own.

He lifts his mouth from mine, kisses the tip of my nose, and then we both turn our eyes to the beautiful view.

"What's Blackfoot's involvement?" he asks after a few minutes, and I realize even sitting together quietly, his mind never stopped churning.

"First time I met him was when he walked in, looking for an available bathroom, and found me lying on the bed." I remember that part clearly. I'd just come to, freaked at the sight of him, and scrambled up the bed. The first thing I noticed was the pain, and it took me a second to realize I was half-naked. "He wanted to call 911, but I wouldn't let him. I was still fairly new in the country, and convinced it must've been something I did wrong. Heck, I wasn't even clear on what just happened. I convinced him to take me to my dorm room, even though he wasn't happy about it. It was the first and the last time I saw him until moving to Durango. Seeing him was a shock."

"So nothing was ever reported? You never found out who?"

I bristle at his words and straighten up. Probably because they echo my self-recriminations. "I was young, thousands of miles away from home. My mom passed away the year before, and I used money I inherited from her on my eighteenth birthday to finance my ticket and my studies. My father had already moved on to another wife, was starting a new family," I reply defensively. "All I wanted to do was keep my head down. I switched my majors from English and history to psychology and criminology, and focused on my studies. And no—I never went looking."

"Easy, Sprite," he soothes me with his voice before pulling me back against his chest. "It was just a question." With his fingers lightly stroking my arm, I eventually relax again, despite the barely restrained tension I feel coming from him.

Each lost to our own thoughts, we sit like that until the sun is almost gone from the sky and the mosquitos come out in full force. Grabbing plates and bottles, we make our way inside, and take care of the dirty dishes without exchanging a word. The silence becomes oppressive and, drying my hands on the kitchen towel, I speak up.

"I should probably head home."

Rather than objecting, Ouray just nods, and the uncertainty I was feeling settles further in my bones like an ache.

"I'll follow you," he announces, as I dejectedly make my way to the door.

"No need. I know where I'm going."

An arm wraps around my chest from behind, and his breath stirs my hair. "I'll follow you," he repeats, firmer than before. Not in the mood to bicker, I simply open the door and lead the way outside.

I'm not a crier, but the tears burn hot in my eyes on the drive home. Annoyed with him, and with myself for the show of weakness, I pull the car up to my place, and without looking back or even acknowledging his presence, march up to the door, my keys ready in my hand.

"Oh no you don't," his voice rumbles behind me, and I'm swung around by a firm hand on my shoulder.

OURAY

I back her into the door and block her with my body.

"I'll be the first to admit I know fuck all about

what goes on in a woman's mind, but darlin', I sure as hell can tell when a woman is upset."

She keeps her eyes closed as I brush a fingertip over her cheek and bend down to cover her reluctant mouth with mine. A risk, because if she wanted, she could have me castrated in a split second. I taste the stray tears on her lips even as I feel her leaning into the kiss.

"Tonight was heavy," I mumble, tilting my head so I can look her in the eye. "Was hard for me to listen to. I can't even fuckin' imagine what it must've been like for you to talk about. For me it doesn't change a goddamn thing, I still want you the same, I'm just feeling a might murderous right now. Gonna need to blow off some steam, and now's not the time to do that in bed. I'll head over to the clubhouse, pound a bag for a bit, maybe have a drink, and hope I burn off enough I can sleep. You need some good rest too. Tomorrow we pick up where we left off. That's all."

I fucking hate seeing her eyes mist over, but she smiles when she nods her agreement. I take her keys and unlock the door for her, before I drop a quick kiss on her lips and walk back to my bike.

Instead of heading straight for the clubhouse, I return home. I wasn't lying, I need to blow off steam, but what I want first is to get some answers.

"Blackfoot," is the curt answer when I call. Didn't take me long to find his number. He's the only lead I have.

"She told me." I don't even bother introducing

myself, but he's not stupid.

"Nice try, she doesn't talk."

"You found her in a room in a frat house during a Halloween party, half-naked and terrified. She refused to report anything and you took her to her dorm room."

I hear the hiss of his breath over the line. "*Jesus.* She told you."

"Who were they?"

The brief silence is thick, and threatening. "Say what?"

"Not buying for a second you didn't know what was done to her the moment you saw her, Blackfoot. Don't fuck me around. The two guys, Superman and Freddy Krueger. Who were they?"

"Two of them?" He sounds wrecked. "I hustled her out of there, dropped her at her dorm as she asked. Then I went back to the party. I tagged the guy dressed as Superman right away, bragging about his fucking conquest to some dumb kid. The moment he walked outside for a smoke, I was on him. Dragged him into the garage and beat the crap out of him. Pretty sure he never recovered."

"Oh yeah? How's that."

"When he was out cold, I clamped his balls in a woodworking vise. Hard enough to leave him bleeding. I took off after that. It fucking never occurred to me there'd been two of them."

I didn't expect this and it takes the wind out of my sails. I'd been nursing my rage at Keith for not taking any action all night. Hearing he had taken action is deflating. It takes me a moment to recalibrate.

"Any suggestions how I might be able to track down Freddy Krueger?" I finally ask.

"Is this for Luna or for you?"

The guy is faster on his feet than I am, asking a question I should've been asking myself. "Both," is my honest response.

"Right. Luna is an FBI agent, she probably has more ways than you and I combined to find these guys. You may want to consider why it is she's never made an effort to find out for herself."

Fuck. Another good point. "What are you, a motherfuckin' feminist?" His snort is loud and immediate.

"Far from. I was recently introduced to the beauty of domestic bliss, and let me give you a friendly tip—learn to listen. Your wants don't measure up to their needs."

"Relationships sound like work," I grumble, which apparently is funny too, since he starts to chuckle.

"Fuck yeah, but trust me on this one: the payoff is huge."

I sure as shit hope so. I'm not a fan of handing over my balls, but ending up with Luna in my bed would be the ultimate reward.

"Anything you can tell me is welcome, Blackfoot. At least let me see if I can find them first. Give Luna the option then."

"You default on that—you harm that girl in any

way—I'll be up your ass so far, you won't know where you end and I begin." His doubt is evident. Heck, I'm not even sure myself if I can hold back if and when I find them, my rage runs so deep.

"She's not a girl, she's a woman, and so noted."

A deep sigh, and then he finally gives me something to work with. By the time I hang up, I have half a page of the notepad filled with my chicken scribble. I hope to fuck I can read it back.

It's two-thirty when I roll into bed, eyes burning from staring at my laptop for hours. But I now have a list of possible names for Freddy Krueger.

CHAPTER 13

LUNA

"Please spill. I'm desperate. All my shirts have boob stains and the closest thing to adult conversation this week was on cloth versus disposable diapers in the baby aisle at the grocery store. Let me live vicariously through you."

"Amen," Autumn echoes, a new mother herself.

I snicker at Kerry's impassioned plea.

Damian's wife and mother to their almost one-year old son, Dante, organized this girls' night out. Motherhood is apparently not without its drawbacks, and she needed a break.

This whole sisterhood business is still pretty new to me. I always kept to myself, not quite feeling at home in a gaggle of females, but in the past few years here, I haven't been able to escape it. I never had a choice. Kerry and Bella declared me a 'sister' and therefore I was, and newest addition, Autumn, isn't any fucking help either, she settled right into the group. She's married to Keith Blackfoot. The fifth woman, Marya, Kerry's assistant, and myself are the only two unattached ones.

I'm still the odd one out, though. All four other women are mothers or mothers-to-be. Autumn's new baby is barely two months old—I'd kill to get a glimpse of Keith playing daddy tonight—and Bella is three and a half months pregnant.

It's a little ironic Kerry picked The Irish for our night out, not only can't three of the five women drink, but the pub is also where most first responders and local law enforcement hang out. Not exactly the most girly bar in town for sure.

Yet here we are, and by the looks on all faces turned in my direction, I'm on the hot seat. It's Bella's fault. She asked me how my hot biker and I were getting along, which of course had them all turn on me.

"It's nothing serious. Just testing the waters." I try to brush it off, not really able to disclose my involvement with Ouray is for a case. Either way I'm lying and these women seem to know it. This is very serious—at least it is for me.

"Right," Kerry mocks. "Because you always wear skintight jeans, a kick-ass sexy leather jacket, and a shirt that makes your tits look like a freaking fruit basket."

I immediately glance down. Sure enough, my

barely there boobs look far more promising than I know they are. I check Bella, who is smirking behind her glass, she's the one who suggested this bra. She's been giving me fashion advice these past few weeks, and I've done more shopping—mostly online, thank God—than I think I ever have in my life. The result is a biker babe worthy closet. I keep telling myself it's all for the job, but secretly I kind of like the way I look.

"It's complicated," I try again.

I'm not lying, the past week—since opening up to Ouray—has been both interesting and oddly frustrating. He took me out Friday night to Brewer's Pub, another of the club's business interests, on a double date with Kaga and his wife, Lea. Another night he came over to my place for dinner and a movie, and I've spent some time at the clubhouse, hanging around with the boy who attempted to teach me to play *Fortnite* on the game system, and eating Momma's dinners. I'm learning more about the club life every day, but each night Ouray would leave me at my door, my lips still bruised from his kisses, but nothing more than that. Hence my frustration.

"It's always complicated." This from Autumn, who raises an eyebrow. "But is it worth it?"

"Come on, Luna. You've made me the only spinster at the table—you owe me," Marya pipes up. Her husband abandoned her with three kids, then under ten, three years ago. "All these women have good guys, sure they're hot, and they're all alpha as fuck, but you've snagged yourself a genuine 'bad boy.' Share, woman."

We're sitting in a booth near the bathrooms and given it's a Wednesday night, The Irish is not too crowded, most patrons are hanging around the bar. If I were to share, chance of being overheard would be minimal. I glance around the booth, all eyes still on me, and with a deep inhale, decide to take another leap.

"He's not as much of a bad boy as you guys might think he is. A little rough around the edges maybe, but his club isn't involved in anything criminal, hasn't been since Ouray took over the gavel. He can actually be quite gentle, especially with Cody or me."

"Who's Cody?" Bella asks.

That launches me into an explanation of the club's charitable work—taking in street kids—and more specifically about the boy who is quickly making his quiet way into my heart. Apparently my friends can read me like a book, because they all look at me with knowing smiles.

It doesn't mean I'm off the hook, as Autumn quickly makes clear. "Sweet, but get to the good stuff already."

"I'll second that," Kerry prompts, provoking the others to make encouraging sounds.

"Little to tell." At the dubious glances I hasten to add, "We haven't exactly…not that we haven't… done some things, but not…well, you know."

It's Autumn, who puts a comforting hand on my

arm when I start to stammer. "You don't have to go into details, darlin'," she says in her Texas drawl. Reminding me a little of the way Ouray calls me that, usually when he's trying to get a rise out of me.

"It's not that—exactly—it's that there aren't a lot details to go into. Although I do know he's got some skills."

"Shit, I knew it," Marya says, fanning herself with a beer coaster. "Damn, how I wish for a singular warm body with the same collective abilities as my toy collection. I don't think I'm asking for much, other than maybe regular shower habits. Bad BO is such a turnoff." The booth is quiet for a second following her words, before we all bust out laughing.

"I'm not sure of all his skills," I clarify when hilarity dies down. "I just know his mouth and tongue are lethal."

"No shit?" Bella leans forward on the table. "You haven't had a chance to check out the wares, so to speak?"

I squirm a little in my seat, feeling the scrutiny. "We're taking things slow, although I can report he seems to have impressive equipment."

"Always a bonus," Marya points out, causing another titter around the table.

"Truth is…" I start, second-guessing myself even as the words leave my mouth, "…going slow is for me. I had a bad experience many years ago. I told him about it, and since then he's backed off anything but kissing and it's getting on my nerves. I'm frustrated, because each time he walks away, I'm left…turned on and unsatisfied."

I don't notice the silence in the booth until I finish talking. Autumn is the first one to speak up, and she does so in her usual straightforward manner.

"The traumatic experience in college you told me about—the first time you met Keith—it was rape, wasn't it?"

I respond with a shrug, feeling both relieved and decidedly uncomfortable. It's terrifying to expose yourself when you've worked hard to keep a low profile for most of your adult life. I know the questions are coming, and I steel myself, determined to answer honestly.

I've had opportunity to see each of these women at their most vulnerable over the years, it's only fair I allow them the same.

I owe them that much.

OURAY

I'm a fucking saint.

Other than a short stint in junior high with a cute little redhead with freckles—whose name I can't even remember—I've never had to exercise this much restraint. It's more painful than I recall. Of course, at eleven, I didn't have joints that start protesting with vigorous exercise, and my hand and wrist have gotten their share in the past little while.

I didn't even see her last night—she was out with some friends—but apparently all it takes is her voice on the phone to have me hard as granite. She called to tell me she got home okay, as I'd made her promise, and I was struggling the entire time not to let on I was jacking off while listening to her talk.

"What's wrong with your hand?" Yuma asks, ambling into my office as I'm flexing my aching digits.

"None of your fucking business," I bark out, shoving said hand out of sight under my desk. "What's up?"

"It's about Rowtag. Overheard him with some of the other cubs, talking about putting the deaf kid in his place. Apparently Ahiga's been kicking all of their asses in *Call Of Duty*."

I shove back my chair and stand up, my fists clenched on the desk. "Where is he now?"

"Rowtag? I put him on guard duty. He's been bitching about you taking his gun away, so I gave him a baseball bat instead."

"*Jesus*." I run my hand through my hair. "And the boy?"

"Up at the shooting range with Nosh."

"Good. Thanks for keeping an eye out. I'll deal with the punk. He's starting to piss me off good."

I round the desk and head for the door when Yuma stops me. "Need me around tonight?"

"Nah. I'll be here. Why?" It should be obvious

from the shit-eating grin on his face, so I amend my question. "Who's the hapless victim this time?"

"New chick who moved into unit twelve at the River's Edge."

"Fucking hell, Yuma. Can't you find pussy that doesn't have some sort of connection to any of our businesses? Do I need to remind you what happened with that chick from Brewer's Pub last year? What was her name? Elise or something?" He blanches at the reference to the waitress he strung along for a month or two during the summer. When the girl found out they weren't as exclusive as she thought they were—she walked in on him with his hand down the panties of the new sous-chef in the kitchen—she went ballistic with a chef's knife. Yuma got off easy with just a nick on his palm when he tried to subdue her, but the other girl will have that scar on her chest the rest of her life. That whole scene played out during a busy weekend cocktail hour.

Alice, or whatever her name was, ended up pleading guilty to aggravated assault, and I fucking banned Yuma from Brewer's Pub for a year. Which, now that I think about it, is almost up.

"I don't do that anymore," he says, looking sheepishly.

"What? You want me to believe you're a serial monogamist now? Gimme a break, you and I both know, one of these days that pecker of yours is gonna get you into a whole lot more trouble than at the wrong end of a knife."

"So much for trusting a brother's word."

"Put my life down for you, *brother*," I emphasize, "but it will be a cold day in hell before I trust you to keep your dick in your goddamn jeans. Don't need more blowback on any of our businesses."

"Won't be any."

"Gonna hold you to that."

With a last glare, I stalk out of the office and go in search of another pain in my ass.

Some days, it's like watching over a herd of fucking preschoolers.

My talk with Rowtag is not improving my mood. The punk gets defensive, insisting he was just planning a friendly initiation to make Ahiga feel more at home. He's a shit liar and I warn him he's on really fucking thin ice, and that if anything happens to the boy, I'll have his cut. The idiot still has the balls to ask for his gun back.

"You can have it back when you grow the fuck up."

I turn my back on him when I see Luna's ride drive up to the gate. My mood instantly improves. I open the gate for her, and leave it to Rowtag to close.

The moment she gets out, I haul her in my arms and plant a heavy one on her.

"Whew…what was that for?"

There's a lightness about her, her smile open and her eyes bright. "You make me feel better," I admit, grumbling to cover the sappy words.

"Bad day?"

"Yuma is doing his best to fuck his way through the entire female population of La Plata County. Rowtag is firing up the cubs to give our boy a hard time." Her demeanor instantly changes and I can see the claws coming out. Fucking momma bear. "No worries, I've got that handled. But worst of all is I haven't had your taste on my lips in fucking forever." That makes her smile.

"Exaggerate much? I'm pretty sure you had your mouth on me two nights ago," she teases.

"Too fucking long," I emphasize, stealing another hard kiss before asking, "Not that I'm complainin', but what brings you here in the middle of the afternoon? I thought you had to work 'til five?"

The smile on her face turns even brighter. "I've got something to tell you, but not here."

"Is this bedroom news or office news?"

She shakes her head, lowering her eyes to the middle of my chest, but that fucking smile is still there. I'm afraid to hope what that coy little smirk might mean, but my cock is about to burst free and sing alleluia already.

"I'd say office," she says, busting my balloon, but then she adds, "first."

I not so patiently wait while she says her hellos to everyone, taking her sweet time, until I finally grab her hand and drag her into my office.

"Sit," she says, her face beaming. I lower myself down in my chair as she sits her ass on the desk just inches from me. "So—I know I may have overstepped a little, and I don't know how you guys usually handle this, but I want you to know other than Jas and me, no one knows."

I don't know what the fuck she's on about, but it can't be that bad if she's looking this happy. "Go on," I prompt her.

"I spent some time seeing what I could find out about Cody. He's still very leery of sharing anything about himself. Every time he lets a little piece slip, he shuts down right away. But…" she lets the word linger and I roll my eyes.

"Turning grayer here."

"I wasn't very successful, but I asked Jas to look into it. Don't worry," she says quickly when she sees me straighten up in my chair. "This is totally off the record. I trust him with my life. Anyway, all I had to give him were bits and pieces, and he only worked on it on his own time, but he thinks he found him. Cody, I mean."

It would be hypocritical to get pissed because she did some digging behind my back, when I've done exactly the same to her. I just hope to God she hasn't acted on what she's found out. Usually before the club does anything with that kind of information, it's run by the lawyer.

"Tell me."

"He's from Monticello: Cody Tyler Washburn, twelve years old, he'll be thirteen in December. There's no missing person's report. Jas ended up pulling information from the snippets of information the boy told us. He looked into known overdose cases. Filtered out the women who were listed as having a child or children of an age matching his at the time, and tracked him that way. He was five when she died, went to live with his grandparents in Monticello."

"Found his way to Cortez somehow," I point out.

"Hitchhiking, probably," Luna offers. "Risky for a kid. Anyway, he was with his grandparents for three years, when they took him on a church trip to Moab. A tractor trailer crossed into oncoming traffic and plowed into the school bus transporting the church group. The grandparents, along with five others, were sitting toward the front of the bus and died."

"Jesus," I hiss, wincing. The poor kid doesn't sound like he's had any breaks in his young life.

"Cody was sitting in the back with the other kids and got off with minor scrapes and bruises. Along with everyone else, he was checked out in the hospital in Monticello and Child Services was called in right away."

"Let me guess," I finish for her, the picture coming through clear. "He was placed in a home where something bad happened to him, he took off running, and whatever bastards were supposed to look after him, never reported it, because they'd lose their monthly check. Am I close?"

She leans in and kisses me hard on the mouth. "Bullseye."

"Poor kid," I mutter and Luna's expression turns sober.

"You know he needs help, right? This kind of tragedy and then abuse after that—not that hard to understand why he doesn't trust. I can only imagine the kind of problems he's bound to run into."

"We'll get him help," I promise her.

"Actually—remember I mentioned overstepping? Well, I contacted my awesome therapist in Aztec, who works together with a social worker who specializes in working with traumatized and abused children. And…" she adds with a smile. "She happens to know ASL."

"I see."

The smile drops at my response, which comes out much gruffer than I intended.

"Well…I may have made him an appointment."

I can barely contain my grin. "May have?"

"This Saturday at eleven. I know where it is, I'll take him," she rambles off.

"Come here." She eyes me suspiciously but eventually slides off my desk and onto my lap, and I waste no time in showing my appreciation.

"So you're not pissed?"

"Shit no. Every fuckin' day I find new reasons to like you."

CHAPTER 14

LUNA

To say I'm nervous would be an understatement.

I thought opening up would be the hardest, but I hate to admit Gary was right—confession does lighten the soul. I'm not sure what I was expecting in terms of a reaction but was surprised—in a good way—by how both Ouray and the girls responded.

It was Autumn who made a comment last night, when the conversation drifted into the bedroom, that really struck home. She said, "Sex is merely a physical expression of a state of mind. It's not the sex itself that's the goal, but the wish to feel connected— both in body and mind."

That's why I'm sitting on the back of Ouray's bike, my arms tight around his middle, driving to his place. He insisted, both that I get on his bike—which I finally conceded to—and getting away from the clubhouse. We weren't able to leave without letting Momma feed us first, although I wasn't able to eat much—my stomach already a little queasy.

"Relax," Ouray rumbles, reaching for my hand which is fisted around his belly, catching me as I glance over at his tense reflection in his rearview mirror for the third time in the short trip.

Easier said than done, as doubts about how the night would play out start creeping in. I'd been ready when I got to the clubhouse earlier. Feeling good about the information Jasper was able to dig up, and high on the pep talk I received from the girls last night, I thought I was ready for this. For sex. My body sure seems to be on board.

The heat in Ouray's eyes, knowing that's for me, is cranking up the anticipation. But it's also making me afraid I may not live up to expectations. What if I freak out and can't go through with it? I like Ouray. Okay, I really like him—he makes me feel worthwhile—but what if this is a disaster? I not only risk derailing the investigation, but losing him as well.

"You need to get out of your head," he says over his shoulder, as we pull up to his house. Shutting down the engine, he turns in his seat. "You're thinking too much. We're on a bike, I'm gonna be in control, but in bed? Sprite, you're in the driver's seat until you get comfortable there."

Straightening my shoulders and taking off my helmet, I give him a little nod. "All right."

"Want something to drink?" he asks when we

walk in. "I think I need some coffee."

"Just water is fine."

I follow him into the kitchen, where he fills me a glass of water, and I gulp half of it down. Then he turns away to make himself a coffee, giving me a moment to steel myself and come to a decision.

It's the rustle of my shirt, as I pull it over my head, that has him turn around. His eyes narrow and lips press together when I reach behind my back to unclasp my bra, dropping it to the floor as well. I notice his hands, grabbing onto the counter behind him, knuckles white, but he doesn't move. I kick off my Keds, undo my pants, and push them down my hips, taking my underwear along with them.

Panic hits me when he closes his eyes, but then he takes a deep breath, nostrils flaring, before opening them back up, his eyelids heavy. I can feel it on my skin as he takes in every inch of my body, from the tips of my toes to the top of my head.

"Killing me, Luna," he grunts. "Make the call."

"Bedroom," I whisper, my voice all but gone.

"Go on, upstairs, second on the right. I need a minute."

I start walking slowly, aware of his intense gaze following my every move, until I hit the first step, bolting upstairs and out of sight. My heart pounding almost painfully in my chest.

It's a big room with an equally big bed, unmade, and a shiver runs down my spine when I imagine Ouray tangled in the covers. There's a single dresser with a large flatscreen TV hanging on the wall above and two sturdy looking nightstands beside the bed, but little else in terms of furniture. Just the straight-back chair in the corner, a plastic laundry basket with haphazardly folded clothing on top.

I freeze when I hear his heavy footsteps come up the stairs, but instead of entering the bedroom, I hear them walk in what I assume is the bathroom next door. The sound of a shower confirms it. I'm not clear on why he's taking a shower now, but I'm pretty sure it's not because he didn't like what he saw. It was all in his eyes: even I recognize that kind of hunger.

The window overlooks the lake below and I take a step closer to take in the view. Not that I actually see anything, all my senses are focused on the man taking a shower in the next room.

It's probably just a minute or two—although it feels like a lot longer—until I hear the water turn off. I have my back to the room when moments later I hear the connecting door open.

"Beautiful," he mumbles, as I hear the rustling of sheets on the bed.

He's the one who's beautiful, lying back on his bed, one arm folded behind his head, his body unapologetically naked. I know my eyes are greedy, taking in my fill of him, until they focus on the heavily veined cock, resting hard and unyielding against his stomach.

"Ain't gonna bite you," he says when he notices me staring, his voice hoarse. "Doin' my best to keep my hands to myself until you tell me different, but fuck, baby…I might blow even with nothing but your eyes on me."

The idea I might hold that kind of power is what emboldens me, as I step closer to the bed—to him.

I climb on the mattress and touch my fingers to his skin, surprised to find it almost hot to the touch. His muscles ripple with every stroke of my hand.

"Luna…"

His voice is like a plea when I trail my fingers through his chest hair. Tracing his happy trail down, I lightly brush the tip of his angry-looking cock before sliding my palm down his length. Hot silk over hard steel.

The last dick I remember touching barely filled my palm. The Nebraska boy it belonged to looked promising enough with his wide shoulders and large hands, but it wasn't much.

My hand wraps around Ouray's girth—much more in measure with the man—and squeeze lightly, sliding it down to the root. He hisses sharply and my eyes shoot up to his face, immediately letting go.

"Did I hurt you?"

He barks out a strangled laugh. "Fuck no, but that doesn't mean I ain't in pain, darlin'. I need to touch you so bad." I scrutinize his face and see nothing that makes me anxious. "You want me to stop, I stop, I swear."

I feel surprisingly unselfconscious as I lay down beside him, my arms straight along my body. He rolls on his side, propping his head with his hand. With the other he brushes the hair from my face, before running an index finger along my nose, tracing my lips and down my neck.

"You good?"

"Mmm."

OURAY

The moment my mouth closes over her nipple, her back arcs off the mattress.

Jesus, she's responsive.

I got a taste of the real Luna, uninhibited, when I made her come sitting on my face, but I didn't fully appreciate the gift then. I fucking do now. She moans low in her throat when I suck her deep. She's primed, I can smell her arousal as her limbs move restlessly over the sheets.

"Touch yourself, honey," I mumble around her pert little tit. She doesn't hesitate, opening her legs and letting her knees fall open as she slips a hand between.

I lift my head and find the heat of her mouth with mine, while I run gentle fingers down her arm. I trace it down to where her hand is working between her legs. Instead of freezing, she moans down my throat as I entwine my fingers with hers, sliding into her silky heat. This time she lifts her hips when I find her opening and slip a digit inside. It doesn't take long for her to raise her butt off the mattress, chasing my touch.

"So close…" she moans when I lift my mouth, so I can see her when I add a second finger. Almost instantly her mouth falls open, her head tilts back, neck stretched, and I feel her muscles tighten around me as she comes on a deep guttural groan.

Rolling on my back, I pull her still shaking body on top of mine, stroking a firm hand over her back while she recovers. It doesn't take long before she lifts her head, looks at me with a smile on her face, and pushes up into a sitting position, a leg on each side of my hips.

"I want to feel you inside me."

Her words undo whatever little gain I've made getting both my heart rate and my cock back under control. "Maybe we should—" I barely get a word out before she presses her fingers to my mouth, leaning forward a little so her curls brush my face.

"Please."

"You take the lead—it's all yours—but Sprite, I can't guarantee I'll last without taking the reins." I reach over and grab the condom I tossed there, covering myself quickly.

"Help me."

She lifts her hips slightly so I can fist my dick and brush the tip along her flushed folds until I'm braced at her entrance. Raising my eyes to hers, I hang on to that connection as she slowly lowers herself. The moment her ass hits my thighs, I blow out the breath I've been holding. "You okay?"

"Mmm, full."

"I fucking hope so," I mumble, and I can feel her resulting laugh ripple over every inch of my body. Grabbing her hips, I still her movement. "Baby, I'm barely hanging on here."

Clearly enjoying her power, but still with a hint of wonder in her eyes, she starts riding me. I swear I'm breaking a few molars grinding my teeth, but when she throws her head back, her hand reaching down to feel our connection, I'm done.

Planting a foot in the mattress, I flip us, brace myself on both arms so I don't crush her, and take over.

Blood is roaring in my ears as I drive inside her, never removing my eyes from her face as she digs her nails into my ass. Not even when she uses her other hand to rub at her clit and comes loudly, her muscles milking my cock. Or too short a time later when I can't hold back, and clench my ass as I power balls deep and see stars with the force of my release.

"I can't breathe."

Her voice is mumbled underneath me when my arms finally give out and I collapse on top, trying to catch my breath. I'm getting to be an old guy, my heart is hammering so hard in my chest, I wonder if I should be worried this woman is gonna give me a coronary.

She sure as fuck is doing something to my heart.

"Stay."

She looks over her shoulder at me and smiles.

Never one to linger for the night after getting my rocks off, I'm starting to see the benefits. It felt great to wake up with Luna wrapped around me and—in the soft, early-morning light—picking up right where we left off the night before.

"I need to get ready, check in at the office, see if there's anything more that's come to light so I'm up-to-date when we ride out on Monday."

"A few of the Mesa Riders are coming in this afternoon. Their pres is a good friend of Yuma's. Momma's got a couple'a rooms done up so they can stay at the compound. I'd like you there."

"I can be there after work, but I was gonna ask Bella to take me shopping on the weekend. I'm going to need some more appropriate clothes, I can hardly wear the same two outfits the entire week."

"Here's a suggestion: check in at work, grab your shit together, and come back here, and I'll take you to get whatever you need this weekend." Because I'm not above a little extortion to get my way, I add, "Be a good opportunity for you to check out the Mesa boys up close."

She's not stupid, she knows exactly what I'm doing, but that doesn't mean I don't make a valid point. "Fine," she snaps, squinting her eyes at me when I grin.

I don't mind she's pissed at me—she's cute when she gets mad—all I care about is more nights like last night and mornings like this one.

"Fine," I echo as I swing my legs over the side of the bed. "Then I'll get dressed and drive you over to get your car."

Twenty minutes later, we stand beside her Jeep and I take her in my arms, kissing her hungrily.

"You're pissing Momma off, leaving without eating her breakfast."

"I know. I'll make it up to her." Luna grins up at me. "But I really want to get going, it's already nine." She untangles herself from my arms and climbs behind the wheel. "I should be back, five at the latest."

"Shoot me a text before you leave, so I can make sure those guys have left room for you to park."

"Will do."

I open the gate myself and watch her disappear down the drive, before I walk back up to the clubhouse.

"Fuck, he's a goner."

I look over at Kaga's voice to find him and Yuma— their asses leaning against their bikes, smoking a cigarette—grinning as they watch me approach.

"Fuck off. That ain't gonna happen." The guys immediately bust out laughing.

"Cuz it's already done, Chief," Yuma heckles.

The satisfied grin I wear walking into the clubhouse proves them right.

LUNA

"Careful out there," Damian calls after me when I walk out of the office and I show him a thumbs-up.

I should be fine, especially with the backup of the local FBI agents in my contacts list. They'll be working undercover, as apparently they often do at random rallies, and I probably wouldn't recognize them to see them. The burner phone numbers they provided me will at least allow me to get in touch when I need to.

Rain is coming down in buckets when I get outside. I run to my Jeep, soaked by the time I get behind the wheel. Water's already sluicing down the steep road heading up to our office building, and visibility is shit. With my wipers doing double time, I cautiously drive down the mountain, hitting my brakes when I see the traffic light red at the bottom. For a moment I think the car is hydroplaning. I lift my foot from the pedal and reapply, but there's nothing at all, my foot goes right down to the floorboards without resistance.

Fuck.

I try steering into the curb as I shift down, but I have too much speed. My wheels easily hop the sidewalk, and with my engine loudly protesting the high RPMs, I burst into the middle of the intersection, watching the large grill of a Mack truck rushing toward me.

CHAPTER 15

OURAY

Fucking Luna.

She was supposed to let me know when she left the office. It's five thirty, I haven't heard a peep, and she's not answering her goddamn phone.

The three Mesa Riders guys rolled in about an hour ago and are already half in the bag at the bar. They were already loud when I was having dinner with Ahiga and Nosh in Momma's kitchen. I foresee a rowdy night ahead and am glad when Momma suggests they take the boy over to their cabin to watch a movie. He may not be able to hear, but I don't want him walking in on some of the shit that can go on when these guys get together.

I follow them outside and smoke a cigarette, my eyes on the gate, waiting for Luna's Jeep to appear.

I spent most of the day in my office, catching up on

some paperwork and making a few calls. I managed to get a hold of Lawrence Brimley, our lawyer, and gave him the information Luna dug up about the boy. He's going to use that to do a bit of digging of his own, or at least his investigators will. Two things I hope to get out of this: the cooperation of whoever the hell the kid's placement worker is supposed to be, and the name of the motherfucker who put his hands on the boy. The reason I have Brimley take care of that, instead of doing it myself, is simple: he's as slick and refined as his name implies, and I'm a rough-looking, no-bullshit biker. I don't particularly get along with public servants of any kind.

Luna apparently being the exception to that rule.

Five forty-five, and still no sign of her, dammit. I try her cell again.

"Hello?" a man's voice answers, and immediately the hair on my neck stands up.

"Who the fuck is this, and what are you doing with my woman's phone!"

"It's Damian. She's getting checked out by EMTs right now."

"The fuck, Gomez. What happened?" I'm already fishing my keys from my pocket and jog to the truck. Don't want to risk taking my bike on the wet roads.

"Got into a crash just at the bottom of Rock Point drive. She just left the office and got broadsided by a tractor trailer—"

I don't even let him finish, end the call, and shove the phone in my pocket as I yank the door of the truck open.

"Rowtag!" I holler at the little asswipe. "Open the goddamn gate, right the fuck now!"

I think I broke every traffic law ever written getting there. My heart, beating like a fucking piston the whole way here, suddenly skips a few when I drive up to the scene. The first thing I see are the mangled remains of her Jeep getting pulled off the grill of a big-ass Mack truck.

I manage to circumvent the State Patrol unit blocking the road by pulling into the small strip mall. Slamming my truck in park, I hop out, my eyes focused on the ambulance parked on the side of the road, and find myself suddenly blocked by a large state trooper.

"Where do you think you're going?"

I ignore him and try to step around him, but he pushes in my chest with his extended fingers. Only then do I turn my eyes on him.

"If you're partial to those fingers, I'd remove them right the fuck now."

The trooper takes a step closer, and I just fucking know he's gonna feel the need to throw his goddamn weight around.

"He's good! Let him through." I look over the officer's shoulder to see Damian jogging our way, already holding out his badge. "He's one of us."

The trooper gives me a long stare before finally removing his hand. Good thing too because I'm this close to snapping them like twigs.

"Where is she? And why is that fucking ambulance still here?" I stalk over in that direction, Damian keeping up beside me.

"Because the woman is a giant pain in the ass. She won't go to the hospital." He sounds exasperated. "She's in the ambulance. They're patching her up. Maybe you can talk some sense into her."

The doors on the back of the rig are open, and I can see her sitting on the stretcher inside.

"Ahh fuck," is the first thing from her mouth as I climb into the rig. She holds up a defensive hand. "Don't you start with me, Ouray. Every goddamn man you see here has already felt the need to flex their testosterone-filled muscles in an attempt to save me from myself. If I had a dick, no one would question my judgement, but apparently when a woman says she's fine—agent or not—you guys just can't take her word for it."

Whatever it was I intended to say to her flies right out the window. She looks like shit, with a nasty gash on the left side of her head just in her hairline, which must have bled good, judging from the state of her hair and shirt. And I suspect she may at least have a few other dents and dings, looking at the way she holds her body, but that sharp fire in her eyes goes a long way to silencing my inner caveman.

"All right, Sprite," I concede, grabbing her hand and pressing a kiss in her palm. I can't get at her lips, the EMT is in the way, or I would've taken those.

Her mouth falls open as I sit down on the stretcher

beside her, still holding onto her hand. "You don't have anything to say?"

"Scared the piss out of me, I'm good and riled you didn't text me like you were supposed to, and I'm gonna wanna know what the fuck happened here, but other than that—no."

The EMT sits back to admire his stitch job on her head, before turning to me. "A hit to the head like this, she could have a concussion. I recommend she lets us take her into Mercy to get checked out."

"Amen," Damian says, leaning into the back of the ambulance looking at me.

"Why is everyone looking at him?" Luna stands up from the stretcher, looking like someone who's just come through battle. "I'm right here." She swings on Damian, stabbing a pointy finger at him. "If this happened to Jasper, or even Dylan, would you doubt their word even for a second?"

"I would—" he starts.

"You know what? Don't even bother answering that. We both know you wouldn't." Gomez looks guilty. "I've had it up to here with the pats on the head and the there-there attitudes. Especially from people who should know better than to treat me like some fragile flower."

Fuck, I'm glad I decided to keep my trap shut. She doesn't just swing a mean right hook, she can castrate a guy with a few words too.

Taking her lead, I get up and climb down from the rig, holding onto her hand as she gets out after me.

"Jesus, Luna. What happened?" I look up to find Keith Blackfoot stalking up. "The trooper says you ran a red light? What the hell were you thinking?"

I feel her bristle beside me at the same time my shoulders straighten at the accusation in his voice.

"Back off, Blackfoot," I warn him, but it's too late, Luna drops my hand and goes toe to toe with the much larger man.

"Like I told whoever the hell that state trooper was: I had no brakes coming down Rock Point Drive— no resistance at all. Now I gave all my information, got myself checked out, and now I'm going home. You all can go fuck yourselves." With that, she starts marching down the sidewalk and I have to hustle to catch up.

"My truck is right over there," I casually point out, slipping my palm against hers. It feels good when her fingers slip between mine and she holds on.

I'm not a particularly sensitive guy, but I don't doubt for a second she'd cut me off at the ankles if I gave her any reason to think I'm managing her. I thought about driving her home and staying there with her, blowing off the Mesa Riders back at my clubhouse, but I'll not be the one to suggest that.

Luna has her head turned, looking out the side window, as I drive off the parking lot, but I don't miss the furtive brush of a hand over her cheek.

LUNA

Goddammit.

Last thing I want is to be seen crying right after my tough guy routine back there, but I'm so flipping angry right now, I can't seem to stop the flow.

How ironic that the guy most likely to go all protective on me is the only one willing to trust my judgement. Or at least respects me enough to pretend, because I have no doubt he's fighting his instincts to take over, even now. Instead, he gives me space to get myself together, something I'm well aware is an anomaly for Ouray, but I'm grateful for it in this moment.

Christ, I thought that was it for me. If the truck hadn't already been applying the brakes, I don't think I would've walked away. It's a small miracle I got off the way I did, going by the state of my poor Jeep. Fuck, I'm going to have to get a new car.

"If we could stop at my place? I need a quick shower and to grab my things. I won't be more than ten minutes, tops."

His hand lands on my knee, giving it a light squeeze. "You sure you're up to it?"

"Yup. I'm good."

"Okay, your call. There's no real rush, so take your time."

His comment echoes his words from last night, and that easily, my mind is back there. The delicious memories all but drowning out the fear and anger I've been nursing.

"I'd love to know where your head was right

there," he rumbles beside me, and the blush I've been cursed with since childhood heats my face.

It's clear I don't need to answer, since his deep chuckle tells me he already knows.

"Mind if I make some coffee?" he asks when we walk into my house.

"Go ahead, make yourself at home. I wouldn't mind a cup myself."

He catches me just as I'm about to head into my bedroom and pulls me flush against his chest. His arms circling me tight. "Need a second," he whispers in my hair, and to be honest, the hug helps center me too.

I'm not sure how long we stand like that, but eventually he tilts my head back with his hand, presses a soft kiss on my lips and gives me a firm smack on my ass with the other.

"Go get your shit done."

I first pack whatever I think I need for a week in a large duffel. Then I strip out of my clothes in the bathroom, toss them in the hamper to deal with later, and make the mistake of looking in the mirror, only to groan at my reflection.

My naturally curly blonde hair is plastered against the left side of my head, caked with blood from the cut. I probe the shaved patch above my ear where the stitches hold my scalp together. The effect is less than charming, especially coupled with the bruises I can already see forming along the left side of my face. My shoulder on that side also shows signs of the impact.

Lovely.

Just as I step out of the shower, I hear Ouray's voice coming from the kitchen. He must be on the phone, I would've heard someone coming in. Opening the bathroom door a crack to let some of the steam out, I can actually catch the words as I quickly dry off.

"I'm telling you, you'll wanna check that car. Luna says she had no brakes—she had no goddamn brakes. Had fuck-all to do with hydroplaning." A brief silence follows, and then he speaks up again. *"Not in my job description, Gomez. That'd be yours. — Don't matter if that piece of junk is twice as old, you willing to leave it to chance? Check the goddamn brake lines."*

Brake lines?

My hands still just as I'm pulling on the one and only suitable clean pair of jeans. My assumption had been the same as Damian's obviously is: it's an old car, shit breaks down. Add to that the fact I'm not that great at maintaining it, it's been at least two years since it's seen a mechanic. It's not unreasonable to think wear and tear could've been the cause.

Check the brake lines. Holy shit.

I've been shot at before, been in fights, but oddly enough those incidents have little to do with me. This, though—this would be a personal attack. A whole fucking different kettle of fish.

I finish dressing and sling my duffel over my shoulder. In the kitchen, Ouray is leaning his ass against the counter, a mug in his hand, eyeing me closely when I walk in.

"I heard you on the phone," I announce, dropping the bag by the front door before walking into the kitchen.

Ouray hands me a second mug and shrugs. "Wasn't trying to hide it. I just made sure it was looked into. If it was wear and tear, I'm thinking you'd've noticed something before."

"Oh." I take a sip and groan out loud at the hit of caffeine. I'm going to need something to kill the throbbing in my head. I look around for the ibuprofen I keep on my windowsill, when Ouray produces the bottle, shakes a couple in his hand, and holds them out to me. "Get out of my head," I mumble, taking the pills and tossing them back with a swig of hot coffee.

"Fat chance. I'm just starting to find my way around in there."

"Shut up." I'm grinning as I toss back the rest of my coffee and set my cup in the sink. When I turn back, Ouray is fishing something out of the inside pocket of his vest. "What's that?"

"An old habit I haven't been able to ditch yet," he says, undoing a knot in a bandana that has a padlock attached to it.

"You told me about those. Works like a sap, right?"

"Yup." He finally pulls the bandana free, tosses the lock on my windowsill and faces me. "Turn around, Sprite."

I turn my back and feel him twist a braid in my

hair.

"You know how to braid?"

"Darlin', I used to have hair longer'n yours."

"Really? Wish I'd have seen that."

"Elastic?"

"Probably," I answer, digging through my junk drawer and coming up with one.

"Got some old pictures at the clubhouse. I'll show ya. Stand still," he orders when I want to turn around. "I ain't done yet."

With gentle hands, he covers my hair with the bandana, tying the three points behind my head.

"Now you can turn." I do as he asks as he tugs a little at the fabric, taking great care to make sure my stitches are covered. "There. Now you look like old lady material."

I never thought such an archaic and misogynistic term would fill me with warmth, but apparently from this man's mouth it does. "Thanks."

"Got no problem with you looking after you, but every so often you're gonna have to let me do the looking after."

CHAPTER 16

OURAY

"Holy shit, how many cars do you have?"

"Just two and a couple of bikes."

Luna walks into the garage, running her hand over the black on black Traverse I bought just last year. My old truck started looking pretty ratty, although the engine's still fine. But there are times when showing up on my bike, or in an old pickup, doesn't quite cut it when I don't want people to be distracted by what they think I represent. People are still narrow-minded as shit, and I had a good business deal go sour early last year, when I rode up on my bike.

It used to be I'd flip my finger at people like that, but with age I've learned that some people will never change. These days I'll drive the Traverse when I think my bike might hamper what I want to get done. I've been accused of going soft on the lifestyle, but when it comes to the welfare of my club, or the kids, I don't give a single shit about creed or convictions.

"Hop up," I offer, opening the door. "Damn thing even has ass warmers in the seats."

"Won't need that today," she says, a prim look on her face. "I'm pretty sure my ass is still wearing your fingerprints." I chuckle at her reference to our early morning gymnastics.

Last night had been a bust at the clubhouse. By the time we got there, a few of the guys were already passed out on the furniture. Red, the Mesa's president, and his old lady were going at it in my fucking bedroom. Apparently they weren't alone, as I discovered when I went looking for Yuma to give him a piece of my fucking mind, since he's the only one with access. I caught the bastard coming out of my bedroom, buck-fucking-naked, to pilfer the stash of good scotch I keep in my desk.

My bed, my office, and my fucking scotch are off limits, and the only reason that asswipe has a key is because the gun locker is in there. After tearing a strip off him, I collected Luna and took her home.

This morning I have to live up to my promise to take her shopping. Not exactly a fun exercise, but a necessary evil since I've got a few things I was going to get her for our trip anyway. Necessities in my books, although I'm sure she'll put up a stink before we're done.

"Got a preference where you want to go?" I ask her when I get behind the wheel and back out of the garage.

"Bella gave me the names of a couple of places downtown. It might be easier to park and walk?"

"Sounds good." Sounds a fuckofalot better than hanging around some mall. "I got one stop I wanna get over with first."

"I'm not in a rush."

She's clueless until we walk into the Harley-Davidson store and I make a beeline for women's apparel. "Really, Ouray?" She holds up a skimpy tank saying 'Best Tits In Town.'

"Perfect for ya," I tease, grabbing a pair of leathers off another rack. "But first try these on."

"Why do I need those?"

"For protection. We're gonna spend a lot of time on the road, Sprite." There's a stubborn set to her chin, so before she can launch into the protests I know are coming, I add, "Need to know you're as safe as I can make ya." This clearly was the right thing to say, because instantly her face softens.

I haven't exactly been successful at hiding my reaction to the bruises on her. The big black marks all along the left side of her body and face she woke up with this morning almost had me rush her to Mercy Hospital, but she promised me she was fine.

"Sure," she concedes, with a little smile.

"Boots too," I add quickly, since she's in a compliant mood. That earns me an eye roll.

"Whatever."

Her comment is dismissive but still she willingly

grabs the chaps and disappears into a dressing room. I head in the opposite direction, quickly grab a few things and toss them on the sales counter. "Start packing these up," I tell the woman behind the cash register before following Luna to the back. "They fit?"

"Gimme a minute," she mutters from behind the curtain. "I can't figure out if I have them on the right way. Something's missing."

"Show me." Before she can protest, I slip inside the small cubicle with her. "Damn, woman," falls from my mouth when I catch a glimpse of an ass cheek in the mirror and I automatically reach out to grab me a handful. "Not complainin', don't get me wrong, but those are supposed to go on over jeans."

"I know that, but the jeans are Bella's and don't want to accidentally damage them with all these damn buckles." She twists out of the handhold I have on her butt and starts undoing them.

"Come here," I tell her, pulling her in my arms. My eyes are focused over her head on the full-length mirror behind her, displaying a perfect glimpse of her creamy firm globes peeking out of her next to nothing panties. Framed by black leather, it makes for a mouthwatering view. "They look like a good fit."

Her head snaps up and she tosses a glance over her shoulder. "Perv," she hisses, shoving hard at my chest.

"I'm gettin' hard standing in the middle of the goddamn Harley store looking atcha, baby." I grin when her eyes do a quick scan of my crotch. "We're gettin' those chaps, and I'm giving you fair warning…" I lean in close to her ear before whispering, "…I'll have you bent over, wearing nothing but those leathers, watching my cock sliding in and out of you." A little hitch in her breath tells me she's liking that idea. I have to adjust myself and get the hell out of the dressing room before I live out my fantasy right here, right now.

The boots are next and quickly decided on. Thank fuck, Luna doesn't waste time when she's shopping, and she doesn't even argue much when I pull out my wallet. Maybe twenty minutes from the time we walked in, we're back outside. I toss the large bag with our purchases in the back of the Traverse and climb behind the wheel.

"Those boots are kick-ass," she grins from the passenger seat. "I'm getting a few inches lift out of those, and I bet I could do some serious damage in a pinch."

"I'm sure you could. Now that we've got your inner badass taken care of, want to hit up those girly boutiques?"

"Not particularly," she says, wincing. "But we probably should. Let's get this over with."

We end up hitting three stores. Luna buys a fuckload of clothes, mostly tees and jeans, but on my urging tries on a little dress that looks more like a silky nightie. She balks when I want to buy it for her, but when I point out how *badass* she would look wearing that dress with her leather jacket and brand new biker boots, she caves.

We hit the Wendy's drive-thru on our way out of town, and head back to my house where I haul in her purchases.

"Let's eat first," I suggest when she starts digging through the bags I dropped on the couch. Other than a piece of toast and some coffee before we took off this morning, neither of us have had much.

"What's this?" she asks when she sits down at the counter and spots the spare keys and garage door opener I put beside her burger.

"Keys are for the house and the SUV. Like I said," I explain when I see the look on her face. "I rarely ever use it, and you need some wheels until you get sorted. The house key is just in case something happens."

"Doesn't someone in the club have a key for emergencies?"

"Momma does, but I don't want you to have to go ask if you need it. Use it, don't use it, it don't matter, I just want you to have it."

She doesn't answer, but she does take a massive bite out of her crispy chicken sandwich, so I consider the matter closed. I count myself lucky she hasn't yet taken a strip off me.

But that changes when—lunch eaten—she goes and rummages through her bags of purchases.

"What the fuck?" She pulls out the two shirts I had them pack. One is a Harley one, but that's not what she's upset at. "You actually expect me to wear this?"

she asks, holding up the offensive scrap of fabric and I don't bother hiding my grin.

"Nothin' but the truth, darlin'. Those babies are definitely the *best tits in town*."

LUNA

I look over at Cody, who is sitting stiffly beside me in the passenger seat of the Traverse.

This is a damn sweet ride, but I'm not enjoying it half as much as I should, seeing how nervous the boy is.

He knows we're on our way to Aztec, and why, but he doesn't trust it. Explaining to him, without going into detail, I'd been hurt too when I was young, and was seeing a therapist myself, helped a little. He does keep glancing sideways at my face.

Stopped at a traffic light, I turn to him. *I was in an accident yesterday. And I got banged up, but I was lucky.*

He doesn't respond, just turns to look back out the window, and I need my hands to drive, so for most of the trip, we're each lost in our thoughts. It's not until I park in front of the clinic, that he taps my arm and signs.

Was he there?

Jesus. Had I known where his head would go seeing my face, I'd have made an effort to cover it up with makeup.

Who? Ouray? No, Cody—this was a car accident. My Jeep is totaled. Ouray wasn't even around, I quickly explain.

Ahiga. My name is Ahiga.

Apparently Nosh is grilling tonight, and he's doing it big.

I can smell the meat smoking from the road and by the time Ouray backs the bike into his spot, my mouth is watering even though I got the kid and me some donuts for the drive back.

He had been mostly quiet, although he did mention liking his therapist, and conceded to going back in two weeks. I wasn't going to push it, because I know only too well how emotionally taxing these sessions can be. I doubt she dug very deep, his first time there, but her thumbs-up at me when we left was encouraging.

"You look hot," Ouray says appreciatively, looking me up and down—again—when I get off the bike.

I almost killed him when I found him outside in his driveway, rubbing gravel on my new boots. "Makin' them look authentic," was his explanation. Apparently this is something he does with his own stuff. He doesn't like new, not even his bikes, the one exception being his Traverse. He also had my chaps out there, but those I snagged before he could mess those up.

I'm wearing the boots, one of my new pairs of jeans—those were already artificially ripped and roughed up, not Ouray's doing—and I have on one of the shirts he got me. The Harley one, I had to draw the line at the tits shirt. My hair is in two braids, and he tied that do-rag back around my head. I'm looking the part and I have to admit, I like this.

The only annoying thing is the bruising on my face that I didn't quite manage to hide with concealer.

"Quit rubbing your face, you look great," he tells me when I take off my helmet.

"People are gonna ask."

Apparently that's funny, because he snorts loudly. "Fat chance. Even if they were visible—which they're not," he emphasizes with a sharp look. "Not like they've never seen a woman with bruises before. You may have noticed we try not to get into anyone else's business."

I'm not quite sure I like the implication of that, but now's not the time to argue. Cody—guess I really should start calling him Ahiga—is running up, already moving his hands at warp speed.

Nosh is cooking lots of meat, but it won't be ready for another two hours. Can we go practice?

I throw a quick glance at Ouray who shrugs. "Got your stuff here?"

"I think I left my gym bag here last time. Should be in your room."

To the boy he says, *Give us fifteen minutes. Gonna say hello and Luna has to change. You can go on ahead.*

Ahiga gives him a thumbs-up and runs in the direction of the garage.

"I know it's too soon, but it's almost like he's a little easier around you," I observe, looking after him.

"Had a talk with him yesterday morning. Damn kid, at first he wouldn't come into my office, just stood in the door. It took me almost half an hour to coax him inside, and only then with the promise the door would stay open. I had to ask him if he wanted to stay, if I could make that happen. Goddammit, Sprite, you shoulda seen his face. I don't wanna disappoint him."

If I wasn't already falling for this man, that glimpse of vulnerability would surely tip me over the edge.

I slip my hand in his and follow him inside.

It's difficult trying to instruct Ahiga with my gloves strapped to my hands, but luckily he can read lips.

"Lift your hands, keep your face covered, even after you land a punch. You're dropping them."

He was eager to go a round in the ring, so I fit him with my sparring headgear. He was grinning from ear to ear as he started throwing punches. Landing one in my ribs, where I already had a nice sized bruise, the grin only got bigger, but it evaporated when I tapped him easily on the side of his helmet.

"Why don't you go clean up," I suddenly hear Ouray's voice behind me. "I'll take him through a few steps with the blocking pad until it's time for dinner." I hadn't heard him come in.

I strip off my gloves and turn to the boy. *You okay with that? Ouray taking over for a bit? I'm a little sore. You've got a mean jab.*

He does his best to hide the smug grin at the compliment, but fails, nodding his agreement. I do a little internal fist pump at his easy capitulation. It's a pretty big show of trust.

"I'll help," one of the cubs, Wapi, who must've wandered in behind Ouray, offers up. "I can hold the pad, so you can use your hands," he suggests to his chief.

I slip between the ropes and drop down from the platform, planning to sneak out, but Ouray catches me for a knee-buckling kiss.

"Make sure you lock both the bathroom and office doors before you have a shower," he mumbles, his lips still on mine.

"Why your office?"

"Don't wanna run the chance of anyone barging in on you, and I don't want you to walk out on anything. Gonna need to fucking fumigate that room before I'll ever sleep in there again."

My confusion shows on my face. "Not sure what you mean."

"Let's just say, Red and his woman like to go at it all the motherfucking time, and seem to enjoy extra players on the field."

It takes me a minute, but when I clue in a heated blush spreads over my cheeks.

"Oh."

"Yeah."

It's not until much later—after another noisy clubhouse party, complete with fisticuffs between one of the Mesa guys and Paco that had to be broken off—that I have a chance to satisfy my curiosity.

I'm straddling Ouray's lap, who's leaning with his back against the headboard. My breath is shallow and my skin is sticky from the explosive orgasm he just gave me. He held me up with his big hands on my ass, and with his heels planted in the mattress, powered up inside me. That was after he'd made me come the first time with his mouth.

I could shoot myself. So many years I've let myself be robbed of this fast addicting feeling of utter bliss. Although I'm pretty sure it's all about Ouray being the one to introduce me to all these wonderful carnal pleasures.

"So, Red and his wife, they're into threesomes?"

"Christ, now you come with that? I'm still inside you."

"I'm just curious."

"Apparently," he says with a shudder. "Can't unsee Yuma come out of that room naked as the day he was born, his fucking dick still half-mast. Gonna need to bleach my brain."

"Really?"

He pushes me back with his hands on my shoulder and dips his head to look in my eyes. "You'd be into something like that?"

"Me? Two guys? Jesus, Ouray, I—"

"Fuck. Sorry, Sprite, wasn't thinking."

"Are you?"

"Hell to the no. Don't want any guy even near my junk."

"What if it was another woman?" I push. I know he's had way more experience than I'll probably ever have in my lifetime, but I ask anyway.

He lifts his hands and cups my face. "Lord knows I'm not a choirboy. Yeah, I've done some crazy shit in my younger years, experimented plenty when I was mostly too drunk to care. I can barely remember any of it, but I can promise you, I'll never forget the first taste of your lips."

His words warm me, but still I shiver lightly as my damp skin cools down. Without moving us, he pulls the covers up to my shoulders.

"Still cold?"

"No. This is nice. Unless you want me to get off? Am I getting too heavy?" I can feel the vibration of laughter against my ear.

"Hardly. I may be gettin' up on fifty, but I'm pretty sure I could strap you to my back and carry you around for a day."

"Mmm. Mind if I pass?"

I listen to his heartbeat slowing down in his wide chest, as his hand strokes down my spine. I shift a little, hoping to hold onto his softening cock a little longer.

"Let me take care of the condom." He lifts me off him, which I'm not particularly happy about, and swings his legs out of bed. "Which is something we need to get fixed soon. I called a clinic in Farmington yesterday. Got us the first appointment Monday mornin'. It's a twenty minute ride from the diner in Bloomfield where were supposed to meet up. We'll head out an hour before the others, get me a test, and you a shot at the clinic, and be in time for breakfast."

"Do I get any say in this?" I sputter, trying to hold onto my temper and not slap at his hand when he palms the back of my head, pressing his forehead to mine.

"I shoulda checked. Just assumed you'd want to feel me inside you as much as I can't wait to feel your wet heat against my skin."

Well. Doesn't that just deflate the head of steam I was working up?

CHAPTER 17

OURAY

"Elk."

I turn my head in the direction Luna is pointing and sure enough, a small herd is grazing off the side of the road.

Early morning rides in these mountains are the best. There's no traffic outside of town, the air still smells fresh, and if you're lucky, you see some wildlife. With overnight temperatures dropping as summer moves into fall, your chances are better, as they slowly come out of the cool shade of the trees to find food in preparation for winter.

I used to prefer taking off by myself, but having Luna's warm body plastered against my back as the wind hits my face, is fast becoming my preferred way of riding.

Earlier, we dropped off our bags at the clubhouse.

Momma was already up and cooking, insisting we at least have a bite before hitting the road. Luna had driven over our stuff in the pickup, so Momma or Nosh could use that since the club truck would be coming to Ruidoso with us.

I gave instructions to the guys, leaving Kaga in charge, but I'm not sure how much of what I said registered—both because of the early-for-them hour, plus Luna seemed to provide a bit of a distraction.

I have to admit, she looks hot as fuck in her leathers. Hard to believe that only a month ago, she was dressed to minimize her appeal, and yet all decked out in black leather, she looks badass and more beautiful than ever.

The drive to Farmington is just over an hour, and we get there a little before nine. The wait isn't long before we're called in.

"The shot is effective immediately," the nurse says, after injecting Luna with the contraceptive. "But your test reports will take two or three days. I can mail them to you if you leave me your address?"

"Do you give results over the phone?" I ask, eager to get my all-clear. My question makes Luna shuffle uncomfortably beside me.

The nurse smiles a knowing smile, looking from one to the other. "You can call Wednesday afternoon to see if they're in yet."

I snatch up a card and shove it in my pocket.

"Obvious much?" Luna hisses under her breath as we walk out of the clinic.

"Sprite, it's fucking Planned Parenthood. It was obvious the second we walked in the damn door."

The effects of the muffin Momma fed us this morning are long gone, and I'm starving as we head over to Sonya's Diner in Bloomfield. We're about a third of the way there on Highway 64, when a couple of police cruisers with lights and sirens, speeding toward us, suddenly cut across traffic and into the parking lot of a small industrial building. Just as we turn south on the 550, another cruiser and a fire truck fly by. Clearly something's going on.

The parking lot of the diner is nearly full—mostly bikes. I'm guessing the Shiprock crew's rolled in as well. We walk in to loud greetings and shoulder claps in the crowded diner. The only available spots are a couple of stools at the counter.

"Wanna sit there or should I kick a few guys out of the booth?" I ask Luna, who looks a little overwhelmed by the sea of facial hair and leather. Much like the poor waitresses, who already look frazzled with the demand.

"There is fine."

Luna takes the stool next to Lea, Kaga's old lady, and the two immediately start up a conversation, leaving me free to look around the diner. Wheels catches my eye and motions me over. I hold up a finger for him to hang on, and quickly place my and Luna's breakfast orders, before making my way over.

"What's with all the bacon out there? I can still hear the sirens," Wheels asks quietly, leaning over the table.

"Not sure. Saw two pulling into a strip mall along the 64 when we were coming from Farmington."

"That on the south side? Not the Ace Hardware was it?"

"The one before that."

"Shit. That's old Eddie Burchfield's Gun Emporium. Fire?"

"Didn't look like one. I didn't stick around to see."

Wheels chuckles. "Prob'ly smart. Wouldn't mind knowing what's goin' on, though."

"Small town, I wanna bet we'll know before we roll out."

The old man holds up his mug at a passing waitress.

"Coffee?" she asks me after giving him a refill.

"I've got one getting cold over there." I push off the table and turn to Wheels. "Don't wanna leave her alone too long. Too many goddamn vultures here."

I can hear him cackle behind me as I make my way back to where fucking Manny is leaning over Luna.

"Back off, Salinas."

Ignoring me, he bends to whisper something in Luna's ear and a red mist bleeds into my view.

"Easy, Chief," I hear Paco behind me. Before I can take action, however, Manny suddenly bends over, mutters a few choice curse words under his breath, and backs into me. I shove him to the side, and note that he's using both hands to cup his package. When I look up at Luna, she shoots me a jaunty wink.

Right. I'm the one with the woman who's clearly capable of protecting herself.

"You oughta teach your bitch some respect, *hermano*," Manny hisses, and I swing back on him, getting into his space.

"Only to those who deserve it. Didn't take long for your true face to show, now did it?" I feel Paco at my back and sense a crowd forming around us. "And don't call me your brother—you turned your back on being a brother years ago."

With that I step past him and take my seat beside Luna, ignoring the scuffle behind me.

"Jesus," Luna whispers under her breath. "He was going for his gun."

"I know. There's a real hothead under all that charm. The guys'll calm him down. What'd you do to him?" I ask her, an eyebrow raised.

Her mouth twitches before she answers, "A sac squeeze 'n twist. Very effective for up close encounters."

"I can see that." I shake my head and grin into my cold coffee.

LUNA

That got tense in a hurry.

A diner full of bikers takes some time to look

after, so when Ouray got the bill settled, I follow him outside. Don't want to be at the center of another session of chest pounding.

He leans his butt on his bike and lights a smoke. "Sorry about that."

"Not your monkey," I tell him with a shrug. "Besides, it's always kind of fun to watch the shock on their faces when they realize I'm not copping a feel."

He snorts. "Jesus, Sprite, you're something else."

"What's with the guy anyway? I mean, I get he's a player, but I have the sense that scene back there had less to do with me and more with pissing you off."

"Yeah. There's some history."

He's not exactly volunteering information so I push. "I remember you called him Mico back in Durango?"

"His road name before he left the Arrow's Edge. Wasn't the friendliest parting of ways, but we've managed to stay civil. For the most part."

"Was his beef with you or the club?" I probe, keeping an eye on the police cruiser slowing down and pulling into the parking lot.

"Same thing. Let's just say he wasn't happy with the club's new direction."

"You mean going legit?" My eyes slide back to the cop who's still behind the wheel of his car.

"If you're looking at Manny for the robberies, you should also look at Red—Yuma and he have been friends for a long time, and Red made no bones he was not happy when I took the gavel instead of his buddy. Even Wheels, he may look harmless, but he's one of the most ruthless and feared MC leaders in the Four Corners area." I have a hard time seeing the old man in that role, but I guess if I've learned one thing in my association with Ouray and his club, it's appearances can deceive.

The sound of a car door closing has Ouray turn around and me look up. The officer is stalking straight for us.

"Morning, folks. Can I ask what y'all are doing here?" The tone is none too friendly.

"Breakfast," Ouray snaps, his hackles up right away. I put a calming hand on his arm and turn to the cop.

"Morning yourself. As my boyfriend just mentioned, we stopped for breakfast, met up with some friends, and we're off shortly to Ruidoso for the bike rally there." My shy smile and slight ramble are as fake as a three-dollar bill, but will hopefully function as a lightning rod for the already charged atmosphere.

"I see. You wouldn't happen to mind if I checked your saddlebags, would you?" He aims at Ouray again who bristles beside me. At this rate I'll be pulling my badge soon, even though I'd prefer not to wave that piece of information around.

"Do you mind if I ask why?" I jump in before Ouray blows a gasket and the cop's eyes come to me. "Not that I mean to be difficult, I'm just curious."

It's clear the man finds me a nuisance, which is just fine by me. I just don't want Ouray to antagonize him further.

"Investigating an aggravated robbery and assault. I'd like to know where you were between eight thirty and nine thirty this morning."

"None of your goddamn—"

"Actually, officer," I quickly interrupt Ouray, who gets up to his full height in an attempt to cower the shorter man. But I know the type, deriving power from his badge, and antagonizing him will only turn this situation, that is easily resolved, into one that has no chance of ending well. "At eight thirty we were at the Planned Parenthood clinic in Farmington for an appointment. I'm sure you can easily confirm that. We left at about ten after nine, and got here at nine thirty, which I'm sure the diner staff can attest to."

The man looks disgruntled when he asks, "Can I see some identification?" Without argument I pull my purse from the saddlebags and hand over my driver's license while Ouray just stands there glowering.

"Honey, give the officer your driver's license," I nudge him. Reluctantly he fishes his billfold from his back pocket and produces it.

"What seems to be the trouble here?" Of all people, Manny walks out with a few of his guys by his side.

"Not your concern, Salinas," the officer replies, locked in a battle of glares with Ouray.

"Come on, Berkland, don't you have somethin'

better to do than throw your weight around at a friendly gatherin'?" This draws the officer's ire, and he swings on Manny, who doesn't seem affected as the man gets in his face.

"Not when a man was left with a dent in his skull the size of my fist on the floor of his gun shop, not half a mile from here, as the result of an aggravated robbery. I'm gonna wanna check all of your buddies. Best call 'em out," he orders, poking a finger at a docile looking Manny, before getting on his radio to call for more units. Fabulous.

In minutes, three more cruisers arrive, and with a parking lot now full of aggravated bikers and half a dozen stern-faced police officers, the situation is tense to say the least.

It takes two hours for the cops to check everyone's ID for active warrants, while Wheels seems to be the one designated to keep the crowd under control. Amazingly out of the almost thirty bikers, only two guys end up cuffed and put in the back of the cruiser. One of Ouray's guys, Honon, has a bench warrant for a traffic ticket he ignored on an earlier pass through New Mexico this year, and the other is one of the Amontinados with a probation violation.

When we finally ride out a few hours late, and a couple of riders short, the mood is dark and the tempers short. And not just among the group, the officers weren't looking too happy themselves, having to let the rest go without recourse.

Ouray doesn't say much until we stop to gas

up, about three hours later, just the other side of Albuquerque.

"I need a word," he says, grabbing my arm and marching me to the far side of the small building, where he gets in my face. "What the fuck was that back there?"

"Sorry?"

"The little stunt you pulled with that cop, talking out of turn, making me look like a goddamn lapdog."

"Excuse me? You mean when I tried to stop you from getting yourself in a whole lot of trouble with that attitude?"

"I get what you were trying to do, but goddammit, woman, the only way I've stayed in the saddle, since taking the club legit, is the respect of my brothers and these other MCs. Without it, we'd have been overrun a long fucking time ago. Respect is my power, and you just publicly undermined that."

"Fine, then next time I see you dig a grave for yourself, I'm gonna go right ahead and let you bury yourself."

Already cranky, and now butthurt by his words, I slip from his hold, turn on a heel, and dive inside the gas station, looking for a restroom. Five minutes later, cooled down with some cold water on my face, and munching on a Snickers bar I needed, I march back outside without looking at Ouray, who is waiting by the bike. I grab my helmet from the handlebars, slap it on my head, and get on the bitch seat, pointedly looking at the road and ignoring him.

I can feel him staring at me, before he finally gives up with a deep sigh and gets on his bike. A few minutes later we're back on the road, the warm wind drying the odd tear rolling down my cheek almost as fast as it appears.

CHAPTER 18

Luna

My ass is sore.

I guess riding on the back of a motorcycle for five and a half hours will do that to you. The comfort of the bitch seat apparently only lasts so long.

My head is sore too. It would've helped if I had time to call into the office and hash over this morning's events with one of the guys, but since that was not an option, I spent the entire ride mulling over every detail, doing my own head in. I'm not in a position to get the particulars about the robbery this morning, so I can't confirm if there is any connection to the dispensary hits, or to any of the MCs. I had to make a judgement call, and decided not to use my badge and instead continue to fly under the radar.

Still, the whole scene left me feeling uneasy. From what I could overhear a couple of the officers say, there was minimal information they were able to get from the severely injured shopkeeper, but it was enough to have the hair on my neck stand on end. My ears perked up with the mention of two suspects, all in black, and although the poor man hadn't seen them leave, he recalled hearing the whining sound of an engine.

"I'll grab the bags," Ouray says, taking the helmet from my hands. It's the first time he's spoken to me since our brief stop the other side of Albuquerque. I can't bring myself to speak yet, so I just nod, and walk off to stretch my legs and explore the rustic setting of Canyon Cabins, where we're staying.

The basic cabins are spread out under a canopy of tall pine trees, with picnic tables outside each, and the clumps of motorcycles parked in front of most of them seem out of place. From what I can tell, the guys are sharing, three or four per cabin. Ours looks to be one of the smaller ones, sporting only one bedroom, so I guess it'll just be Ouray and me. I'm sure I would've been grateful for that before, but now the prospect of being alone with him is not something I look forward to.

Just as I round the corner of one of the larger units, I spot Rowtag leaning against the back of a van, sharing what looks to be a massive joint with another guy. I think I may have seen him ride with one of the other MCs. I distinctly remember seeing him sitting with Rowtag in a booth at the diner when we walked in this morning. Instead of walking into another confrontation with the kid—which will only hurt whatever reputation he has—I slip between two cabins and start heading back.

When I spot Ginger, Red's old lady—on the porch of a cabin two over from ours—I walk over to say hello.

"How's your ass?" she asks, grinning, when she sees me coming. I must be bowlegged, at least it feels that way.

"Tender," I admit. "Guess I'll get used to it."

"Fuck no. Unless you ride out with your man every time he hits the road, you'll feel it every time you go on a longer run. Extra padding doesn't really help either," she says, slapping her own rounded ass. "Best thing to do is grab a drink and take a nice long soak in the tub."

"Maybe I'll do that."

Wheels steps out of the cabin right next to ours when I pass by, and I smile at his chin lift. I feel his eyes follow me all the way up the steps of our little porch.

"Was wondering if you'd return." Ouray is sitting on a plastic white chair, holding a beer and with his feet propped up on the railing.

"I was just looking around."

"Want a beer?" he asks, getting up from his seat.

"No thanks," I stop him. "I've got to make a quick call and thought maybe I'd soak in the tub for a bit."

"Sore?" His face is marked with concern and it has me swallow down hard. Not so much because we got into it, but more because the argument illustrated how impossibly ill-suited we are. It makes me sad. The first time since…well, ever, I've felt this kind of connection to a man, and yet we are worlds apart.

"A bit." I manage a smile and head inside the small cabin.

OURAY

I was able to hear her on the phone inside. Sounded like she was reporting back to the office, but it's quiet now.

Doesn't surprise me to hear her suspicions were raised by that robbery this morning. Mine were too. I'm pretty sure we were the last ones to get to the diner, but I'm trying to recall if anyone else looked like they'd just arrived. The only person I really paid any notice to was Wheels, and he was down to the dregs of his coffee, so I figure he'd been there a while. I didn't really notice Manny until he tried to mess with Luna. It wasn't until the cop started asking about the bandanas, and the significance of the colors, that I clued in there might be some connection. Otherwise I might've paid closer attention when we first got there.

That was one fucked-up situation. Not a good start to our week. Of course it didn't help that I lost my shit on Luna, who's been quiet the rest of the ride, but I can't have her jump in like she did. I was pissed she shared about our visit to the clinic—that's no one's fucking business but our own—even if she did it to clear my name right off the bat. It was the first time I saw the potential pitfalls of this relationship.

Because that's exactly what this is: a relationship. She may want to crawl back behind her mask and pretend this is all about the damn case, but I saw the hurt in her face and it ate at me the whole ride here. Even with what I know will be some serious adjustments on both our parts to make this work, it's fucking well worth it for me. I'm too damn old to play around.

Determined, I head inside, dropping my empty in the kitchen sink. I can hear her in the tub and don't waste time—stripping down in the bedroom—before opening the adjoining door.

"What the hell, Ouray?" she snaps, trying to cover herself.

"We gotta talk."

Her eyes fly up to my face. "Not much to talk about."

"Bullshit." I climb in behind her, dropping a condom on the edge of the tub while I force her forward.

"Well, do we need to be naked for that?" She tries to scoot away, but I lock my arm around her waist and haul her back against me. She's stiffer than a board.

"Abso-fucking-lutely. All bared, Sprite. Nothing to hide behind." No response except for a soft snort. "First off, I might've handled that better."

"I have no idea what you're talking about," she snaps right away, betraying she knows damn well.

"No bullshit, Luna. I climbed down your throat, and even though my point's still solid, I could've made it another way."

She twists her head around and looks at me with disbelief. "Is that supposed to be an apology? Because if it is, it sucks." I grin at her fire. I'd rather have that than the straight face and blank tone.

"This won't be the only time we argue, baby—I foresee a future filled with those—but we can't throw in the towel at every fucking bump we hit on the way."

She's quiet for a bit, until I feel her body relaxing against me. "You foresee a future?"

"Not playing games."

"It's hard. Trying to find that line between personal and professional," she confesses, turning in the tub so she's facing me.

"I'm thinking until this shit is cleared up, it'll keep being hard," I agree. "I know I've gotta give you room to do what you've gotta do, but I ask you try and keep a mind about the way you do it. I wasn't kidding when I said I can't have you putting my position in question. Especially when it already looks like someone's trying hard to trip me up. I'm all for equality and shit, but not everyone in this world understands that, so if we could go easy—in public— I'd be much obliged."

"So noted." Her words are short, but the little smile she rewards me with says all I need to know.

Tagging her behind the neck, I stretch my legs and pull her on top of me, her warm skin slick against mine. "Now that we have that settled, what did the boss have to say?"

"Damian?" She props her chin on a hand resting on my chest. "They were already aware of what happened in Bloomfield. The MO looks to be similar to the dispensary robberies, as are the suspect descriptions. The only bit new to me was that the owner says he was hit over the head with a sap of some kind." I raise my eyebrows at that piece of information. "Yeah, I was thinking that too," she says without needing my words. "After you mentioned the padlock thing. I mentioned to Damian it might be another indication someone is looking to frame you." I know I had nothing to do with this, and I know Luna knows I had nothing to do with it, because she's been with me the whole day, but still it feels good to hear her say that. I scoot her up a little higher with my hands on her ass, and give her a hard kiss on the lips. "Which reminds me, he just got word earlier today there was a small cut in my brake line."

"Figured there might be."

"Right. So now the question is, when did it get there? And, more importantly, where did I get it? Damian is having a forensic mechanic from the Colorado Bureau of Investigation look at it. See if he can determine the first, so we can figure out the second."

"Good."

That's what I say, but my thoughts immediately go to the fact that damn Jeep was parked behind gates in the parking lot of my clubhouse. Even the thought it could have been one of my own brothers makes me sick to my stomach. I just don't know why any of them would, it doesn't make any sense.

Luna's soft fingers stroke over the frown on my forehead. "You're thinking too hard."

"That's not the only thing hard." I slightly tilt my hips so she can feel exactly what I'm talking about, before making quick work of rolling on the condom. "Convenient," she mumbles, smiling as she immediately opens her legs to straddle my hips. Even submersed in the warm water, I can feel the heat of her core. Her hand reaches up, trailing her fingers through the scruff on my chin. "We done talkin', Sprite?"

"Yeah," she whispers, her eyes on my mouth before they slide up, settling on mine.

I don't hesitate taking her lips, her soft skin sliding easily against mine, as her arms slip around my neck, holding on tight. Almost effortlessly, my cock finds her heat.

With our movement restricted in the slippery tub, all I manage is slow, shallow strokes, which all too soon prove not enough.

"Out of the tub, babe," I mumble against her skin, my hands on her hips lifting her off me. She grumbles softly in protest. "You'll get it back."

I get out after her, wrapping her in one of the threadbare towels, but before have a chance to lead her to the bed, she lifts herself on the bathroom counter. She lets the towel fall open, spreads her legs, and pulls one heel up on the cracked Formica.

Fuck, she's gorgeous. Innocence and temptation rolled into one. Her lips still swollen from my kiss, her pale skin flushed, and her plump pussy an invitation, she brings me to my knees. Literally.

She curves a hand around the back of my head the moment my mouth closes on her and her moans fill the small bathroom. When her thighs start trembling against my face, I surge to my feet, and with one smooth stroke, I bury myself to the hilt.

Having this tightly restrained woman come apart in my arms makes me feel like a fucking king.

LUNA

The distant slam of a screen door wakes me up.

I'm pinned to the bed, Ouray's much larger body wrapped around me, much the same way we fell asleep last night. He'd carried me to bed after making me come the first time, only to slip inside me again from behind. A large hand is still cupping my tender sex.

He grumbles in his sleep when I untangle myself and pad into the bathroom to relieve myself.

My phone is in my purse in the living room, but I'm guessing it's around eight. Still early, but there are some sounds of life coming from outside. I head back into the bedroom to grab some clothes to put on before I get coffee going, but stop in the doorway taking in the view. Ouray—now on his back—one strong arm folded behind his head, the sheet tangled around his hips displaying his broad chest, and one knee pulled wide. This large, powerful man, lying there so openly relaxed, is burrowing deep under my skin. In my life. In my heart.

I quietly get dressed and leave him sleeping in the bedroom to go in search of coffee. We probably should've gone to grab some groceries yesterday, because the cupboards are bare. There's a coffee maker and filters, but there isn't a coffee bean in sight. I grab my purse, scribble a note for Ouray in case he wakes up, and head out the door. We're not that far from town and I could use a walk to loosen up my stiff muscles.

The cabins are mostly quiet and I don't encounter anyone when I set out. About a mile down the road, I find a small grocery store that carries everything I need to get a decent breakfast together. I grab whatever I can carry—making note that at some point today we'll need to get more supplies—and head back to Canyon Cabins.

There are quite a few cabin rental places along this road and I notice a shitload of bikes. Looks like ours isn't the only group arriving early for the rally that doesn't start until Thursday.

About a block from the resort, I look up a side

street and spot a familiar figure standing beside an idling white pickup, talking animatedly to whomever is behind the wheel. I try to memorize the license plate, looking away quickly when the man turns his head in my direction.

Tempted to look over my shoulder, I instead focus on keeping my eyes ahead, my ears sharp for any movement behind me. No footsteps following, but I do hear the distinct whine of an engine moments later.

Not wanting to risk being overheard, I stop just inside the entrance to the cabins and sit down on a rock. I quickly dial the office, knowing one of the guys will be in.

"La Plata County FBI."

"Dylan, can you run this? White older model pickup truck, extended cab and covered bed. License 748 OAW."

"Gotcha," he answers easily. "Anything else?"

"Yeah. See who it's registered to and how they are connected to the Amontinados MC. Manny Salinas in particular."

"Will do."

"And Dylan? The truck's engine has a whine."

"You don't say?"

CHAPTER 19

Luna

I don't get a chance to tell Ouray what I saw. He and Wheels are sitting on the small porch, sipping hot coffee when I walk up to the cabin.

Ouray is grinning wide. "Could've saved you the trip, Sprite. Momma always loads that van up with supplies before we leave." He gets up and grabs the heavy bags from my sore hands. "Coffee in the pot." Leaning down, he plants a wet kiss on my pouting lips.

So much for my plan to surprise my guy with a hearty breakfast. I grumble a greeting at Wheels, and follow Ouray into the cabin where bacon, eggs, and a loaf of bread are mocking me from the counter.

"I was going to cook for you."

He drops the bags and turns around, taking me in his arms. "Appreciate it, but let me cook for you this morning, so you can grab a shower. Tomorrow you can have a turn. I have this fantasy of waking up to find you naked and barefoot in my kitchen."

I stick a finger between his ribs and he jumps back, barking out a laugh. "You can keep right on dreaming," I toss out, darting around him on my way to the bathroom.

When I walk out fifteen minutes later, I find Wheels still here, sitting at the small kitchen table wolfing down eggs, while Ouray is popping bread in the toaster.

"Coffee's on the table. You good with scrambled?"

"That's fine, thanks." I slide into the seat next to Wheels and take a sip of my coffee. Ouray shows up a minute later with two plates piled high. "I can't eat all that," I comment when I notice the amount of food.

"Anything you got left, I'll take off your hands," the older man offers with a grin.

"Just so you know," Ouray explains, popping a piece of toast in his mouth. "Wheels will try to hit anyone up for a meal."

"I ain't cookin'."

"Find someone else to beg food off tomorrow morning, old man. Me and my old lady got plans."

I glare at Ouray, who pretends not to notice, but Wheels throws me a wink. Sneaky old bastard.

I listen to the two men talking about their itinerary for the day. Something about going for a ride into the mountains. I get the impression this is something the guys do on their own, and since my ass is still protesting from the long trip yesterday and could probably use a break, I pass when Ouray tries to include me.

Twenty minutes later, I watch from the porch as the guys roll out, but before I have a chance to head back inside, Lea walks over.

"Morning," I greet her as she climbs up the steps. "Looking for coffee?"

"I'll take some if you have any left."

"I do. Come in."

"I actually came to see if you'd be interested in hitting the slots? There's a casino on the other side of town, and we usually slip out there when the guys are off doing their thing. They won't be back until dinnertime."

"Who's we?"

"Me, Ginger, a few of the other girls. It's kinda become tradition."

The invitation fits in quite nicely with my plans to see if I can get a bit more insight from the women. From what I can tell, Salinas is single, but he's a handsome guy and I'm hoping his movements are noticed. Anything to help me find out more, even spending the day behind a slot machine.

"How are we going to get there?"

"Jill, Hanshaw's old lady?" I recognize the name, he's one of Wheels' guys. "She's six months pregnant and her man wouldn't let her come on the back of the bike, so she drove down." Lea grins wide, taking a sip of her coffee. "Can't say he appreciated the surprise—

he was madder than a puffed toad she drove all that way herself. Not that it lasted long. Sounded like she found a way to tame the bear, from the sounds coming from their cabin last night."

Immediately my eyes shoot to our bedroom, where I'm sure we made some noise ourselves. *Fuck.* Lea must've noticed, since she starts laughing. "Walls are paper-thin, Sugar."

"So noted," I mumble a bit embarrassed. Wheels's cabin is on that side of ours and I'm pretty sure the window was open.

"You'll get used to it," she says, patting my hand with hers. "Most'a these guys don't give a rat's ass who hears or even sees them going at it. Although, once they stake their claim, they're not so hot on sharing ya. Unless of course, they're into that kinda thing." That reminds me of what Ouray told me about Red, sharing his woman with Yuma. "Not me," she hastens to tell me. "But I know some."

"So I understand."

"Ginger?" she probes and I just shrug. "Yeah, she can be a wild one. Not shy about it either."

"What about Manny?" I ask, figuring this might be a good segue into getting some more info on the guy.

"Now there's a juicy one," Lea comments with a wink. "From what I've seen, he's at least as adventurous—if not more so—as Yuma. I'm pretty sure Yuma draws a line when it comes to guys, but Manny doesn't seem to have any such boundaries."

Remembering the comment I heard the man make to Ouray, I almost wince at the mental picture it paints and quickly redirect the conversation.

"He doesn't have an old lady, does he?"

"Manny? Hell no. He draws enough attention. Believe it or not, there are plenty of women who seem to fall for the kind of game he put on you back at Sonya's. Though there's never been one able to keep *his* attention long enough. He's too far up his own ass to see beyond his ego. Manny is not one to mess with. Best to leave handling him to your man. He's always liked living on the edge, even predating his break with the club."

I offer more coffee but Lea waves it off. "Yeah, I heard something about that," I casually prompt and Lea readily fills in.

"Didn't wanna let go of the adrenaline rush. While most everyone else was on board with Ouray's vision for the future of the club, Manny took the offer to opt out without repercussions. The rest is history."

Sensing I'd be pushing my luck if I probed any further, I let the subject rest.

I like Lea, she's pretty straightforward and seems open in the way she describes her life with Kaga. In the half hour we spend chatting—before she announces it's time for us to meet the others—I learn she and Kaga have seven-year-old twins at home her mother is looking after, and she works part-time as a bank teller.

I'm sitting in the back seat of the large Yukon,

flanked by Lea and Ginger, while Jill and Britney—of all people—take the front. Apparently those two are good friends and when Jill decided to follow her husband to Ruidoso, Britney was quick to jump on that plan. So when Jill asks me how I managed to get on the back of Ouray's bike, I'm not completely surprised. Before I have a chance to respond, Lea—who probably knows which way is up—jumps in.

"That's not hard—she kicks ass and takes names. She actually took down Manny when he got too handsy, before Chief even had a chance to step in. She's his perfect match."

"True," Ginger offers, but Britney huffs from the front seat and Jill gives me a good once-over before returning her gaze to the road.

Ginger catches my eye. "It was an impressive move, but you best watch out with Salinas. Underneath that slick exterior, he's a snake. There are other guys with reason not to be happy with Ouray, but Manny is outright pissed, even though he hides it behind those smiles of his. I wouldn't put it past him to hurt you to get at your man."

"Over my dead body," I blurt out, earning appreciative glances from everyone but Ginger. She just looks pensive before muttering under her breath.

"Wouldn't put that past him either."

"Word," Jill adds.

It's not until we're at the casino—and I'm sitting next to Ginger at neighboring slot machines—that I have a chance to ask her about a remark she made earlier.

"What did you mean when you said other guys aren't happy with Ouray?"

I look at her sideways but she keeps her eyes peeled on her machine. At first I think perhaps she didn't hear me, but then she sighs deeply.

"I probably shouldn't have said anything," she finally says, shaking her head. "Red sometimes tells me stuff, and I know better than talk about it. He's gonna have my hide as it is."

"Look," I plead, my hand on her arm. "I'm not asking for details. This is all new to me, and I just want to make sure I don't inadvertently make things worse."

"It all should be water under the bridge anyway, but these guys don't forget easily."

"Which guys?"

She turns and glares at me. "I've already said too much."

OURAY

It's a perfect day for the ride into the mountains. Would've been better with Luna's warm body behind me, though. I didn't particularly care to leave her behind, but Kaga—who's been riding beside me— mentioned Lea would keep an eye on her. I didn't bother telling him Luna is probably the last person who needs looking after.

As usual, we stop at the No Scum Allowed Saloon in White Oaks, where they're expecting us. Normally only open Friday through Sunday these days, they still accommodate us every year. A small, almost dingy, roadside bar where they're not afraid of a couple dozen bikers dropping in to grab a quick bite and to drink a few. Most of us hang out back on the patio, which is twice the size of the actual building. They even have a stage for live acts on the weekends.

I'm listening to Wheels recounting tales of the good ol' days, when loud voices draw my attention. Off to the side, near the empty stage, I just catch Yuma poking an angry finger in Manny's chest. I'm up out of my chair the next second, but Wheels grabs my arm to hold me back.

"Hold up, boy. Red's right there, he'll set them straight."

I yank my arm back and turn on the old man. "My man, my business—and I'm far from your *boy*."

Wheels shrugs his shoulder. "Be my guest, but you stick your nose in, sparks are really gonna fly. Tension's high enough after your run-in at the diner."

I hate that he's right. I've done my best to avoid getting anywhere near Manny, especially since yesterday. He's succeeding in getting under my skin after that stunt with Luna, and he fucking knows it too: it's exactly what he wants. At best, we've tolerated each other these past years, but recently he's been purposely provoking. Normally I can handle that kind of crap, but when he takes on my woman, or one of my brothers, I draw the line.

I see Red sling an arm around an angry Yuma's shoulder and walk him in the opposite direction.

"Told ya," Wheels pipes up.

"Yeah, yeah. Ya did. I'm still gonna have a talk with him 'cause we're gonna have serious problems if he doesn't stop this shit."

It's not until later that afternoon, when we pull back into Canyon Cabins, that I have a chance to quietly pull Yuma aside. He follows me almost reluctantly to my cabin. There's no sign of Luna, so I assume she's off with Lea somewhere.

"Beer?"

"Sure." He takes the bottle I offer him and drinks down half of it in one go, wiping his mouth with the back of his hand.

"Wanna talk me what that was about?"

"Not particularly." He barely looks at me, but instead focuses his eyes on the window.

"I fucking insist." That earns me a quick glance, before his head drops down between his shoulders.

"Motherfucker is just yanking my chain. I lost my cool. That's all."

"Not like you to lose it, brother. It's one of the reasons why I trust you at my back. I'm the one with a temper, not you."

He lightly shakes his head before finally looking up. "Guess he caught me on a bad day. He's stoking a fire and I shoulda just walked away."

"What fire?"

"Jesus, you're a persistent son of a bitch. Fine. He's stirring the pot with some of our guys, trying to recruit them, flashing money, making promises. I called him on it and the fucker laughed in my face, called me a bigger pussy than my boss."

I can feel my blood pressure rise. "Why the fuck didn't you tell me about it?"

"Because it's my job and I knew you'd blow a gasket. Especially since he's been suggesting you've handed off your balls to your new pussy."

"I'm gonna have a talk with—"

"Hey guys," Luna says, walking in carrying a few grocery bags and wearing a smile that promptly disappears when she gets a load of our mood. "I'm interrupting something. Sorry, I can—"

"No need. I'm heading out anyway," Yuma says, moving to the door before he turns my way. "Leave this with me."

"What was that all about?" Luna asks when I pull her into my arms.

"Club business." I know that won't fly the moment I see her lips press together and feel her body stiffen. After that comment about my balls, it was a knee-jerk response. "I'll tell you, but I need a kiss first."

The way my focus narrows on just her when her mouth opens under mine, I wonder if there's not a grain of truth to it. This woman holds all the power over me.

I slide my hand in the back of her jeans, squeezing

her ass and slipping between her legs.

"Wait up," she mumbles against my lips. "Hold that thought. I brought home some stuff for dinner. I'm starving. You can fill me in while I cook. I have a few things I found out myself."

Reluctantly I let her go and take a seat at the table, filling her in while she putters around in the kitchen. She listens without interruption, making appropriate sounds until I mention having a talk with Salinas.

"Don't think that's a good idea," she says sharply, swinging around.

"Why the fuck not?"

"Because I don't trust him. He's up to something, and you don't want to get drawn into his game. Not until we know what he's up to. I never had a chance to tell you this morning, but I saw him."

"Manny?"

She nods. "When I came back from the grocery store. Saw him talking to someone in a white pickup truck. The engine had a distinct whine to it."

It takes me a second to put two and two together but when I do, I sit up straight. "No shit?"

"Nope. I called Dylan, had him run the license plate." She turns back to the stove and stirs whatever she's got cooking. It smells amazing. "Also," she continues, "I spent an interesting afternoon with Lea and her friends. Did you know your Britney is friends with Jill? Hanshaw's old lady?"

"Britney isn't anything to me," I correct her sharply. "But that news doesn't surprise me. She's been around long enough."

"Yeah, well, apparently she drove down here with Jill. She sure doesn't like me much, so I avoided her, and hung around with the others. I like Lea, and Ginger is okay too. She actually warned me to stay away from Manny Salinas. Gave me a little insight on the man. Told me he still holds a grudge, but apparently he's not the only one." She pulls two plates down from the cupboards.

"That's not a surprise either," I volunteer. "Arrow's Edge was part of a steady pipeline for guns through the Rockies along Hwy 550. When we shut down our link in the chain, none of the others were impressed."

She walks over to the table with two plates and sets one down in front of me.

"What's this?" I point at the plate with a bunch of green leaves topped with a pile of what looks to be chicken.

"Lettuce tacos. Don't judge, just try," she suggests with a half smile. I watch her fold one of the leaves and take a big bite, juices dripping down her chin. "It's messy."

"Messy looks good on you." Sexy as fuck, especially with those little sounds she makes as she eats. "It's good," I mumble after taking a bite myself. The shredded chicken is spiced up nicely for a bit of heat. In minutes I've emptied my plate.

"Want more?" She starts pushing out of her seat.

"You eat. I can get it," I insist, getting up myself. "By the way, did you hear anything back yet on that license plate?"

"Right, forgot to mention. Dylan shot me a message while I was at the casino with the girls. I was a little disappointed. The truck is registered to one Nathan Phillips."

The name is like a punch in the gut and I drop the spoon I'm holding, bracing myself on the counter.

"Are you okay?" I hear her concerned voice, but it's not until I feel her hand in the middle of my back I can take my next breath. "Ouray?"

"It's Paco."

CHAPTER 20

LUNA

"I'm so sick of motorcycles right now."

I turn to Lea, who is sipping on her drink.

"Every year I look forward to these trips. Time away from my rambunctious boys, but always when I get to this point I just want to be home, drive around in my comfy SUV, where I don't have to worry about bugs in my teeth or saddle sores."

"Amen." Ginger raises her glass.

We're sitting around a picnic table, watching, as the guys wander around yet another bike show. The third day in a row. Lea is right, it's getting utterly boring. If I didn't have these women to hang around with I'd be going out of my mind.

It's been a tense couple of days. Ouray was ready to track down Paco and tear a strip off him, but I managed to dissuade him for now. He wasn't having it at first. It took some fast talking on my part. With at least two suspects, it would stand to reason that if we confronted Paco, whoever the second one was would go to ground and we might never get this solved. I have to tell you, he would've been one of the last ones I might've suspected.

At this point I suspect just about everyone else. There's no way I can possibly monitor all, so I decided to call Dylan in for backup. Ouray was less than impressed when I told him, but he had to agree that having Dylan pose as my brother would be the easiest way to lend him some credibility. Not to mention add some to mine.

The handful of club members who saw him in official capacity won't clue in when they see him arrive in full disguise. Dylan is good at transforming his clean-cut exterior. I've seen him pose as a homeless guy and even I walked right by him.

That's why, when a big, bearded, burly-looking biker comes straight for our table, a grin on his face, I don't clue in who it is. Not until he calls out, "Sis," in a big booming voice.

"Dylan!" I jump up and walk into his widespread arms, leaving the other women staring curiously.

"Fuck, Lulu, don't call me that. It's Bullseye."

I almost choke holding back my laugh at the nickname he's given himself. When he was first assigned to the La Plata office, the guy couldn't hit the broadside of a fucking barn. Then James pulled him to Denver on a case, and apparently our junior agent spent a lot of time at the shooting range, because our first time out, he pumped an entire clip into a three-inch diameter circle. The target still hangs over his desk at the office as a trophy.

"Who's this?" Ginger asks from behind me, and I turn to the girls, my arm still around his waist.

"This is my little brother…" I throw a sideways glance at him, biting my cheek not to laugh. "…Bullseye."

"Well, hello there, handsome," she coos, eliciting a wink from Dylan.

"This is Ginger, and my friend, Lea. Both have men, so if you want to hang on to your testicles, I'd tread carefully," I warn him with an elbow to the ribs. "What are you doing here anyway? I thought you said you weren't coming?"

"Changed my mind. Figure it's time I check out this new guy of yours."

"Looks like you won't have to wait long. Incoming," Lea points out with a nod in the direction of a very pissed-off looking Ouray stalking this way. Shit. He probably doesn't recognize Dylan either.

"Hey, babe, come meet my brother," I call out, placing myself squarely between them in case he doesn't hear me, but his pace slows and his shoulders aren't up around his ears anymore when he gets near. Still, the first thing he does is pull me close and with a hard kiss on my lips, anchors me with an arm against his side. Only then does he look up at Dylan and offers him his free hand.

I provide introductions—again—and this time Dylan's road name already slides a little easier from my lips. It doesn't take long for Dylan to be absorbed into the group of men over by the beer tent, and I'm pleasantly surprised to see him make connections so easily. I have to admit, I haven't had much of an opportunity to see him work outside of the office—where there's a certain hierarchy—but he's impressing me so far.

"You never mentioned a brother," Britney, who'd come sauntering to inquire about the 'new meat,' says in an accusatory tone.

"Didn't know I was required to share every detail of my life," I fire back. Since building friendship with her is clearly not an option, I figure perhaps if I antagonize her, she'll let something slip.

"I figure since he's a biker and all."

"Not club related. He's a loner, generally goes where the weather is nice." Her interest is clear, which is why I immediately nip any hopes she has of ingratiating herself.

"Then how does he make a living? Is he like, independently wealthy or something?"

God how I dislike the woman, but this time I make no effort to hide it. "You don't give up, do you? He works when he needs money. Whatever he can get his hands on. Trust me, he's not your speed."

"No need to be snippy about it," she blusters, tossing her hair over her shoulder and marching off to where Jill is sitting on her man's lap. Both have been watching the interaction rather intently.

Christ, I'm starting to look at everything and everyone with suspicion. Britney appears to be trying her luck with Manny, who barely acknowledges her. He's deep in conversation with Red. Over in the beer tent, Dylan looks to be the center of attention in a group that includes Wheels, and most of Ouray's brothers. The only ones I can't locate are my guy and Paco.

Worried, I get up for a better vantage point, when an arm slips around my waist from behind.

"Looking for me?"

I let go of the lungful of air I've been holding at the sound of Ouray's voice in my ear. I turn and slip my arms around his neck. "I was," I admit, opening willingly when his lips cover mine.

"You okay grabbing something to eat from a vendor here?" he mumbles with his face in my neck. "I think everyone's gonna hang around for the band. They start at six."

"Fine by me."

"Good. We won't make it too late. It'll be an early day tomorrow for the parade and the party after often goes all night. You'll wanna be sharp: lots of booze which means lots of loose lips."

"Sounds like a plan."

One more heady kiss and he wanders back to the beer tent.

The phone in my pocket buzzes with a new message.

Dylan: That PDA for show? Dayum, Sis, who'da thunk?

I look over and catch him fanning himself, wearing a big grin.

OURAY

"Let's dance."

I raise an eyebrow at Luna's question. It's on my tongue to tell her hell no, I don't dance—ever—but her head is bobbing to the music, and I can't resist the big smile on her face. So when the band starts playing Eric Clapton's "Wonderful Tonight," I grab her hand, pull her through the crowd to the makeshift dance floor in front of the stage, and take her in my arms.

I shake my head at the whistles and catcalls from most of the guys. I'm the only sap dancing—the rest are all fucking women. I'd rather have a root canal than be the only fool out here, but the look on Luna's face when she looks up at me is worth every bit of torture. Pretty soon I don't even notice the heckles from the crowd, I'm lost in her blue eyes.

"Let's get a beer, darlin'," I finally whisper in her ear after the third slow song in a row, and grin when she easily slips her hand in mine.

"You owe me, you son of a bitch," Red grumbles over Ginger's shoulder when we pass him on the dance floor. By now there are quite a few guys with thunder on their faces, leading their ladies around.

"Fuckin' treason to the brotherhood, asshole." Kaga glares at me as Lea is pulling him closer to the band.

"Serves you right for makin' fun of your chief, brother," I fire back.

"I'm thinking I may have started a new trend," Luna says, a satisfied smirk on her face.

Grinning, I curl an arm around her neck and rub my knuckles on her head. "You're a shit disturber, you know that?"

Despite several attempts, I manage to avoid letting Luna drag me back out there. She finally gave up and is dancing with a group of girls.

Scanning the crowd, I'm looking for Paco again. I kept an eye on him earlier tonight, but he's been missing in action for a few hours now. It cuts, the thought one of my most trusted men is betraying me. It's enough to make me look at everyone through different eyes. My brothers, guys I'd consider friends, if I can't trust them, then what the hell is the purpose?

I pull my phone out of my pocket when I feel the buzz of a message notification, and swipe my finger over the screen when I see Paco's number come up.

Paco: **Need to talk. Alone. Behind porta-potty. I'm in trouble, brother.**

I take a quick look over where Luna has her arms up in the air and is bumping hips with Ginger, before heading to the john at the edge of the parking lot.

It's fucking dark back here. With floodlights

illuminating the lot, stepping into the shade of the trees behind the blue portable toilets almost renders me blind. I flick on the flashlight on my phone, and step deeper into the trees.

"The fuck are ya, Paco?"

I hear a light rustle behind me and start to turn, but before I can register anything, my world suddenly goes dark.

LUNA

"Have you seen Ouray?"

Kaga looks surprised at my question. "Not in a while, why?"

"I haven't seen him since I left the dance floor."

"Tried calling?"

"And sent texts. Nothing."

"Not like Chief. He's usually on the ball."

Dylan, who's been doing his own thing most of the night, walks over. "Something wrong?"

"Looking for Ouray," Kaga answers, scanning the crowd.

"Saw him heading for the can maybe half an hour ago." Dylan starts moving toward the portables and I follow right behind.

"I'll check the beer tent and see if his bike is still here." Ouray's second-in-command starts jogging in the opposite direction.

Two of the three stalls look to be occupied and we each pick a door to bang on. An embarrassed girl comes out of the one Dylan's standing in front of and he mumbles an apology. Finally the door I'm blocking opens to reveal a very pissed-off, gruff looking biker with a dirty gray beard almost covering his big gut. My eyes water when I get a whiff.

"Can't even take a fuckin' dump in peace," he grumbles, shoving past me.

I quickly take a few steps to the side, where the air is a little more tolerable.

"Jesus, pretty sure something died in there," Dylan comments, coming to stand beside me. "Did you try calling him?"

"Yes, several times. I'll try again." I hit redial on my cell, with the same result as before. "Nothing."

"Well shit. I hate to ask, 'cause from what I can tell you guys are quite cozy, but any chance he's off enjoying some extracurricular activity?"

"What?"

"Schtupping a piece on the side?"

"Christ, Barnes—can you be more crass?"

"Just staying in character," he says with an apologetic smile.

"Whatever. And to answer your question—no—he's not that guy." I'm surprisingly sure of that. Call it naïveté, but I'm generally good at reading people, and Ouray has been nothing but straightforward with me.

"Fine. So what would make him take off without a word?"

"An emergency," I suggest, although I'm not really buying that explanation. He would've let someone know.

"Don't think so," Kaga volunteers, as he walks up to us. "His bike's still there. He's gotta be around."

"Then let's find him. This is the last place he was seen."

I don't wait for the others and head around the back of the porta-potties. I hear footsteps following. It's dark, but a faint glow is visible from the brush about fifteen feet in. Turning on my phone's light, I aim it where I noticed the diffuse light, and move closer.

"What've you got?" Dylan asks behind me.

"Not sure. I swear I saw a faint light coming from somewhere around here."

A second stream of light hits the same area when Kaga uses his phone as well.

"I see it," Dylan announces. He steps forward, reaches down, and comes up with an iPhone, its light on. I immediately hit redial and watch the phone vibrate in his hand.

Kaga curses under his breath. "That's not good."

"No, it's not," I agree.

Just then we hear a bunch sirens in the distance and a cold fist closes around my heart.

CHAPTER 21

Ouray

Jesus, my head.

I smell fuel and try to open my eyes, but bright light is like a hot poker straight into my brain. I'm disoriented, it feels as if I'm falling forward as I'm slowly registering loud noises—yelling—and then the sound of metal grinding. The next thing I know, I'm pulled by my arm and tumble down, the fall jarring my skull.

"Stay still," a disembodied voice yells at me when I try to grab my head.

Hands pat me down, rifling through my pockets.

"Let EMTs at him. Looks like we have another head injury. He's bleeding."

I'm confused. I'm trying to make sense of what I'm hearing. Bleeding? I try to bring my hand to my head. *"Hold still or I'm gonna slap handcuffs on you."* Handcuffs?

Next I feel hands on me. "What…" I carefully squint against the flashing lights, seeing someone lean over me.

"You've been in an accident." A woman's voice this time. "Looks like you hit your head, you have a nasty cut."

"My bike?" I mumble.

"Your pickup, I'm afraid it's a write-off," she says as she places a collar around my neck. "Just a precaution until they can check you out in the hospital. Your friend is already on his way there."

I close my eyes as my mind is trying to process information as I'm being strapped to a backboard. There's something very wrong here.

"Call Luna."

"The police will take care of that," she says.

I hiss when I'm lifted, jarring my head. "My phone."

During the ride to the hospital, I start remembering. Dancing with Luna. A text message. Paco in trouble.

"I really need my phone." I turn to the cop who climbed into the back of the ambulance and is riding along. That's never a good sign.

"You didn't have one. You'll get your one call eventually."

Yeah, I'm in deep shit. If only I knew what I stepped into.

"You're not fucking listening to me. Find my goddamn phone and you can see the text for yourself."

The two cops seem unimpressed. I've tried to explain the events as I recall them a few times now, but I'm not getting anywhere.

Apparently I ended up behind the wheel of a pickup with Paco beside me, and a cache of stolen guns hidden under a tarp in the back. Some from a heist on a local gun shop earlier tonight, and a few they've traced back to the fucking Bloomfield robbery.

Looks like whoever has been trying to set me up is succeeding. At least with these yokels.

I'd really like a word with Paco.

LUNA

"This is bullshit."

The officer shrugs. "Following instructions. Both suspects are off limits until we've finished interviewing them."

"You're interfering with an ongoing FBI investigation," I hiss, trying to keep my voice low but the man doesn't seem to care.

"Call Damian," I tell Dylan, who's stayed beside me. Kaga is calming down the other brothers in the waiting room we were all hustled into. Emotions are high, and a mob of angry bikers isn't going to do Ouray any favors.

"Already did. He's on it. You've gotta cool it, Luna, or you'll blow this investigation and all the work you put in it will be lost."

I can't help snort. Who the fuck cares about work? Right now I'm more concerned getting in to see Ouray. Making sure he's okay. Getting these goddamn local cops off his ass.

"Are you related to Mr. Strongbow?" A young guy reminding me of Doogie Howser, with his pristine white coat and stethoscope around his neck, walks up.

"I'm his old lady."

With a hint of distaste he looks me up down. "Right. Well, your…Mr. Strongbow sustained a hard blow to the right side of his head in the accident. There was a small laceration we were able to close up with just a few stitches, and his scan was clear, but because he lost consciousness, we're keeping him for observation. He was lucky. From what I understand, the truck he was driving wasn't outfitted with airbags, so the damage could have been much worse. There's not even a mark on his chest where he must've hit the steering wheel."

"Wait," I call out when he starts walking away, my head spinning. "You said he was behind the wheel?"

"That's what I understand. The impact must've caused his head to hit the side window."

"But how would that be possible? Unless this is England and the steering wheel is on the other side, his injury should be on the left, not the right side of his head."

Dylan throws his arm over my shoulder, giving me a squeeze. "Good catch, Sis."

It's already early Saturday morning when the cavalry rolls in.

Kaga was finally able to convince the club members to head back to the cabins to grab some sleep, with my promise I'd call right away—once I get to see him—which hasn't happened yet.

Dylan also left, hoping to catch what—if any—chatter he might be able to pick up at the resort.

I'm outside getting a bit of fresh air to go with my disgusting vending machine coffee—both intended to keep me awake—when a black Explorer pulls into the parking lot. The man getting out of the SUV is top to toe G-man. Ill-fitting black suit, scuffed shoes, and mirrored shades despite the watery light of dawn.

He stops in his tracks when I approach him. I can only imagine the picture I make, with my ass-kicker boots, ripped jeans, and leather jacket—not to mention the messy mop of curls and haggard face.

"Special Agent Luna Roosberg," I introduce myself, holding out a hand he looks at as if I'm trying to pass on a communicable disease. Hardly promising.

"Special Agent Brent Nylander," he finally says, shaking my hand.

"Did my SAC explain the situation?"

"For the most part, why don't we go in and you

can fill in the blanks."

"I'd prefer not to be seen talking to you. Only a few know I'm FBI, and no one knows I'm working a case. Other than my colleague, Agent Barnes, and of course Ouray."

"Is that the gang's president?" he asks, and I bristle at the faulty presumption.

"Arrow's Edge is completely legit. A club, not a gang." I can't keep the edge out of my voice.

The man looks duly chastised, but I still worry about the impact his preconceived ideas might have. "Apologies. Club it is."

After that dubious start, I quickly update him with the latest information, including the inconsistencies of Ouray's injuries with the claim he was driving.

"What about the other suspect? Nathan Phillips?"

"Paco. Yes, he's in an adjoining room—both are guarded by local police—but I haven't been able to find out much about his involvement. All I've heard is that he was in the passenger seat. By the way," I add as an afterthought. "I believe the truck they were found in might well be the same one that was used in the chain of dispensary robberies in Colorado."

"Where can I find you?"

"There's a waiting room off the main lobby. I'll head back there."

It hasn't quite been an hour when Agent Nylander

steps into the waiting room and closes the door behind him.

"And?" I can't resist asking, having sat on pins and needles.

"Looks like Mr. Phillips will remain a guest of the Ruidoso PD a little longer, mostly because he seems unwilling to cooperate."

"Did you talk to him?"

"I tried. He won't talk to me either, but perhaps you'll have better luck."

"What about Ouray? Mark Strongbow?"

A little grin tugs at the otherwise rigid looking agent. "He talked to me all right. Mr. Strongbow was quite forceful in his opinions. None of which were particularly complimentary to local law enforcement. I believe the term is *spitting nails*." Brent Nyland is grinning now. "He also demanded to see you. Loudly."

I'm on my feet with my hand on the doorknob in a flash. "Will they let me?"

"Absolutely. The local chief of police was quite forthcoming once I explained our joint federal investigation trumps his local one."

All I want is to run to Ouray's bedside, but Agent Nyland leads me down the hall to see Paco first.

"How is he?" Paco asks me when I'm barely through the door, and I don't need clarification as to who he's referring to.

"From what I understand he's spitting-nails mad," I tell him with a glance over my shoulder at my fellow FBI agent in the doorway.

Paco follows my eyes and scowls. "What the fuck is he in here for?"

"Making sure I don't take off with the prisoners, I guess," I attempt to joke.

Paco's gaze return to me. "You forget I know you're a fed as well."

Right.

"I'm also Ouray's—you know that too—and I'm pretty protective of my man. Which prompts the question: why on earth would you turn on him like that?"

"I didn't. I know what it looks like, but I never—"

"Paco, your truck was packed with guns. That pickup is implicated in a string of robberies. Not only that, I have Ouray's phone, which shows the last message he received was from you, claiming to be in trouble."

"I lent the truck out to a friend, almost two months ago now."

I roll my eyes at that. "Really? Let me guess, you forgot your friend's name?"

He has a pained look on his face. "I rode down on my bike. You know I did. I couldn't believe it when I saw my truck peel out of the parking lot at the concert last night. I followed it to a dingy motel, just a few blocks up from where we're staying. I snuck around back and tried to catch a peek through the bathroom window, but that's all I remember until I woke up in the ambulance."

"Already someone has died, and another injured."

I know I'm taking a risk pushing him, but that name will finally give us something concrete to work with. "Who's the friend, Paco? The only way we can corroborate any of your story is if we know his name."

"Her." I have to strain to hear him, but it's enough to answer a few questions, and create some new ones as well.

"Britney," I suggest and he nods, looking defeated. "You lent your pickup to Britney. When was that?"

"A few days before the club took off on our ride north for the rally just outside Denver. She mentioned her car had died and she needed a way to get to her new job. My old pickup was mostly just sitting there. I bought a new truck last year, and never bothered getting rid of this one. I only use it for the odd dirty job. I let her borrow it."

"Britney," I repeat. "Oh, Paco."

I leave him staring out the window and close his door behind me.

"I don't need you to come in here."

Nyland stops with his hand on Ouray's door and regards me quietly before getting out of my way. I step inside, leaning my back against the door. The big bulk of a man lying in the hospital bed is turned away, and I wonder if he's sleeping. I must've made a noise, because suddenly his head turns in my direction, his blue eyes piercing the distance.

"Get your ass over here." His voice is hoarse and he looks like he's aged years since I saw him last night.

"You scared me."

"I know. Come here."

Closing in on the bed, I notice the bandage on the side of his head. "Are you hurting?" He doesn't bother answering, but grabs hold of my hand and pulls me down on top of him, folding me in his big arms.

"Not anymore."

—

"Has he found her?" Ouray asks when I end my call and sit down in the chair next to his bed.

The relief had been evident on his face when I mentioned what Paco had told me, but just as quickly had been replaced with anger. At Britney.

He'd been ready to call on his brothers, until I reminded him that they were likely setting up for the parade. Something Kaga suggested Ouray would want. He was right. It still took some convincing for him to let me call Dylan instead.

Britney may be involved, but as I pointed out patiently, she's not the only one. I know for a fact she drove down with Jill, and therefore could not have brought the pickup, which means someone else had. I'd seen Manny talking to someone behind the wheel, which we now know hadn't been Paco, but we still have no clue who it was.

It feels like the more information we get, the more lost we are.

"No. Apparently Jill's been looking too. She

hasn't seen her since before the concert last night. All her stuff is still at their cabin, though."

"Shit."

My sentiments exactly. Having Britney disappear doesn't exactly bode well for her. She may well have been a pawn in whatever game this is. It's clear whoever is pulling strings wants Ouray out of commission. If it wasn't for his inconsistent injuries, they may well have succeeded.

My biggest worry now is to keep Ouray safe, which is why I want to suggest keeping his release from police custody quiet for now.

"Right. It's concerning. Since the person or persons orchestrating this clearly stepped up their game with this last attempt to implicate you—plus Britney's disappearance—I think it's safe to assume they'll stop at nothing to get what they want."

"We don't even know what the fuck that is," he agitates, running an irritated hand through his hair that does nothing for his serious bed head.

"It's clear enough they want you out of commission, one way or another, and I'm not about to let that happen."

That earns me a glare. "Since when is it your job to look out for me? Fucking hell, woman, I've been looking out for myself all of my life."

"Since I'm the FBI agent in charge of this case. Since I don't want any harm to come to the man I care about. And since maybe, it's about damn time you had someone in your life looking out for you."

CHAPTER 22

Ouray

"I can't believe I let you talk me into running."

I feel like I've fucking handed my balls over on a platter.

"It's not running, it's strategizing," Luna fires back from behind the wheel.

Fucking doctor tells me no driving until I see a doctor back home to give me the all-clear on Wednesday. Load of bullshit. Of course Luna held on and ran with it. It took her all of ten minutes, and a couple of phone calls, to put together this plan to get me out of Ruidoso.

The guys are just finishing the parade tour, and we're already almost in Albuquerque.

"If my bike gets trashed by that snot-nosed—"

"Relax, Dylan is thirty-two—hardly a snot-nose—and he's not gonna trash your bike."

What had me cave to her plan was her mention of Nosh, Momma, Ahiga, and the other younger kids who stayed behind in Durango, virtually unprotected. The way this shit has been escalating, I can't discount the possibility they'll use anything in their power to get to me. Including the people I care about.

She also made a good point when she suggested we'd be more in control on our own turf. It's easier for her to handle law enforcement in her own jurisdiction, and I'll be able to get a better handle on things at home.

In the end I gave in, got in the back of the cruiser, and let myself be taken to the police station. This to throw off anyone who happened to be watching. There Luna was waiting with a black rental SUV we were going home in.

Since Dylan drove down with the bike in his truck bed, he'll take my bike home strapped down beside his, although I'm not sure when that'll be. He has the perfect cover to stay behind and make sure Paco is released from police custody, and kept safe as well.

I did call Kaga to fill him in on the plan. He'll have to pack up our shit and take the lead tomorrow, getting the guys home. As far as anyone else is concerned, I've been arrested and will be held in Ruidoso.

It's a fucking tough pill to swallow when you're not even sure you can trust your brothers anymore.

"Are you hungry? Want to pick something up?"

I blink awake, I guess I must've slept like the dead because it looks like we're just approaching Aztec.

"Jesus, you either have a serious lead foot, or those drugs they gave me knocked me right back out."

"Drugs and a head injury will do that," she says, her eyes on the road and a small grin on her lips. "And it's possible I may have leaned a little heavy on the gas at times." She throws me a quick glance. "Your color is a little better, though. The three-hour nap at least did you some good."

"Hmm. I guess I could eat," I answer her question. "Although I'm sure Momma has something cooking at the clubhouse."

"You think so? It's not like she's expecting anyone back until late tomorrow."

"True. Sonic drive-thru?"

"Fine by me."

Conversation stills until we take the exit to get to us to the fast food joint, when Luna breaks the silence.

"How do you want to tackle this?"

"Tackle what?"

"With Nosh and Momma, are you going to fill them in?"

I look over and catch her glancing back. She's being cautious with me. I can't blame her, I haven't exactly been a ray of sunshine. The events of the past days, my head is pounding so hard it blurs my vision at times—something I specifically avoided mentioning to the doc—and the fact I seem to have lost the careful hold I keep on my life, I guess I've been something of a bear.

Putting my hand on her knee, I twist in my seat to

face her. "I haven't thanked you for having my back—'preciate it. It matters. As for Nosh and Momma, I'll tell Nosh—he may have some valuable insights—but maybe we can leave it up to him to include Momma. Not that I don't trust her, but she loves all her boys, and the possibility one of them may be involved in this would hurt her. I don't want that on my head."

"She'll want to know what happened to you though. And so will the boy."

Automatically my hand comes up to the bandage covering the cut on my head. "I mention I had a spill. Wouldn't be the first time. Plus, it gives Momma a chance to vent her frustrations. If it were up to her, she'd make wearing a helmet mandatory."

"She worries."

"Every time we ride out."

Luna seems to think on that when she pulls into the drive-thru. Before placing our order, she turns to me. "So why don't you?"

"Some guys do, but it all boils down to individual choice. The last show of rebellion. If I take that away too, after taking the club straight, we'd be no more than a geriatric putt-putt club."

She's still snickering when a server comes to bring us our order.

Nosh comes ambling out of the clubhouse when we pull the rental up to the gate. With my keys back in Ruidoso with Dylan, I have no way to let us in.

The fuck happened to your head? Nosh starts signing the moment he gets a load of me through the windshield.

Fucking open the gate first, old man.

"Be nice," Luna mumbles beside me.

Where's Momma and the boy? I ask right away when I get out of the car, surprised the kid hasn't come tearing outside yet.

Groceries. Damn kid's a garbage disposal. Now what's with this? He stabs a finger at my head.

Long story.

Got nothing but time, boy, he returns, clearly not in the mood to wait any longer.

"Jesus." I throw my head back and let out a big breath. *Fine, I could use a drink anyway.*

"No alcohol until you get the all-clear," Luna feels compelled to remind me.

"Oh, for fuck's sake!"

Turning my back on both of them, I march straight into the clubhouse.

LUNA

Fucking knew it, Nosh says, none too friendly after we finish laying out the entire story, including my professional involvement. *Had my doubts in the beginning, but you two fucking pulled the wool over my eyes. Gonna break Momma's heart. Woman was over the moon you found your match.*

We're in Ouray's office—both men are sitting on

opposite sides of the desk—and I'm leaning against the wall. I blush at Nosh's words. It doesn't feel good to have kept this from them, but to be honest, it hadn't felt like much of a deception to me for a while already. Our so-called relationship may have been arranged, but it sure feels real to me.

I glance over at Ouray when he sits forward and reaches out for me. The moment I put my hand in his, he yanks me to him, pulling me down on his lap.

I have. Nosh lifts a dubious eyebrow as he sits back and crosses one leg over the other, his sharp eyes taking us in. *Found her, and gonna keep her,* Ouray signs, his arms around my middle.

That a fact? This time the old man focuses on me and clearly expects an answer, so I give him a tentative nod. The pause that follows gets uncomfortably long before he finally adds, *In that case, you tell Momma yourself. I'll keep the pup busy.*

As it turns out, I'm the one keeping Ahiga busy while Ouray talks to Momma.

We were just coming out of the office when they walked into the clubhouse, heavily loaded with bags and boxes of groceries. The moment the boy spots me, he drops the box he's carrying and runs over, his spindly arms closing around my waist.

Touched, and more than a little confused, I look up to find Momma's beaming smile.

"Boy got in a scuffle with one of the older kids and managed to deck him. Guess he's feeling a tad grateful."

I look down on his smiling face and ruffle his messy hair. *Nailed him, did you?*

He nods enthusiastically. *I think I made him cry.*

I bite my lip not to laugh. *You're gonna have to show me how you did that.*

He immediately latches onto my hand and drags me with him, out of the clubhouse, and over to the garage. Half an hour later, both of us sweating buckets, I remember I don't have a single piece of clean clothing with me.

"I stink," I warn Ouray, who pulls me close the moment I walk in the kitchen.

"Impossible," he mutters, his nose stuck in my damp hair.

Gross, Ahiga signs on his way to the fridge.

"Exactly. Which is why I'm going to have to run home. I don't have any clean clothes."

"Come with me." The order is curt, and Momma doesn't even look at me when she grabs an equally smelly Ahiga by the arm and heads past me, out of the kitchen.

"You best listen. She's on a tear," Ouray whispers in my ear, giving me a shove after her.

Great.

Like a lamb led to slaughter, I meekly follow the somewhat intimidating woman out of the clubhouse.

The moment we walk into the cottage behind the

clubhouse, Momma lets go of Ahiga. *You hop into the shower, son.* He doesn't protest, but obediently heads down the small hall and disappears through a door. I can see how Momma coerces the kind of respect she receives from all these grown men. She starts them young.

"Now you." I swing around at her stern tone. "I keep some stuff here for unexpected guests." She opens a closet door in the hallway and pulls out a pair of black yoga pants, an old Deep Purple shirt and a fresh package of Hanes panties, shoving the lot in my hands. "You didn't think I was gonna let ya run off without gettin' my say in, did you?"

"No, ma'am."

"Good. 'Cause that would not've gone over well. Why don't you grab a shower in the en suite in the master at the end of the hall? Clean towels and a fresh bar of soap on the rack behind the door. I'll meet you in the kitchen."

I guess it could be worse, I'm sure I'll get a tongue-lashing, but at least she didn't take me out back to shoot me.

The shower feels great, I realize I haven't had one since yesterday morning, and the hot stream helps to relieve some of the tension in my body. Unfortunately I can't stay in here forever, and eventually will have to show my face. I'd rather go straight to bed, but I guess that's not happening.

There's a teapot sitting in the middle of the small kitchen table, two mugs, and a plate of cookies. Not what I was expecting for what I assumed would be no less than the third degree.

"I liked you," she starts, her folded arms resting on the table. "Now I don't know if I should."

"I'm so—" She lifts a hand to stop me.

"I ain't done yet. This ain't about me, it's about my boys. You got one ass over teakettle for ya already, another gettin' there fast. You walk when this case you're working gets done, it won't be skin off my nose, but you sure as shit will answer to me if either o' those boys get hurt." I don't get a chance to respond before she does a complete one-eighty, lifts the teapot, and asks me sweet as punch, "What do you take in your tea?"

"Just tea," I manage, a little shell-shocked.

"Cookie?"

"No thanks."

"Baked them this afternoon."

"In that case…" I reach over and politely take a cookie from the plate. It seems the safe thing to do. "For the record," I confess. "Even if I probably should, I don't think I'll be able to walk away after all is said and done. I'm probably more than a little…ass over teakettle…myself."

Ten minutes later, I walk into the clubhouse, feeling like I've just gone ten rounds with a grizzly bear and somehow came away unscathed. At some point, Ahiga must've come over here because he's sitting on the couch playing on the game system, with an older boy. He throws me a cheeky grin.

Nosh is sitting at the bar, sipping a drink.

Kids, he tells me before I can ask the question. *Same kid he had a beef with this afternoon. Name's Shilah, been here for eight months.* He lifts the bottle off the bar with an eyebrow raised.

No thanks, I'm about ready for bed. Where's Ouray?

Office, probably. Unless he hit the sack already. He looks a little rough.

I smile my thanks and start heading toward the hallway in the back when I hear a bottle banging on the bar and I turn back. Nosh sets the bottle down and grins. *Night. Glad to see my Lettie left you intact.*

I bark out a laugh, but only the older boy on the couch lifts his head.

It was touch-and-go.

Nosh's raspy chuckle follows me down the hall.

The office is empty but the door to the bedroom is open. Ouray is already in bed, his arm folded behind his head and his eyes barely open.

"You okay, honey?" Nosh is right, he does look rough. "When did you have your last painkiller?"

"Before we left the hospital. Don't like 'em." His voice is scratchy and I sit down on the mattress beside him.

"Are you sure? You're clearly in pain." I stroke a hand through the beard he seems to have grown overnight.

He sighs deeply and flips open the cover. "I'll feel better if you get naked and in bed."

"Really? You can barely keep your eyes open."

"Just wanna hold you, Sprite. Wasn't sure I'd see you again after Momma got through with you." He chuckles at his own joke but right away grabs at his head and curses under his breath. "Fucking hell."

"She let me live—for now—provided I don't walk out and hurt her boys."

"Boys?"

I grin at him. "Yeah, Ahiga—and you."

"That so? What did you tell her?"

"The truth," I tease, dodging when he reaches for me.

"Luna," he growls threateningly.

"I just gotta brush my teeth real quick."

He glowers at me, but doesn't try to stop me when I duck into the bathroom. I brush half-heartedly, and quickly shed my clothes, hanging them on the back of the door before I turn off the lights, and dart back into the bedroom—buck naked.

Ouray's eyes shimmer in the dark room. He doesn't miss a thing as I walk over to the bed and crawl under the cover he's still holding open. I barely settle in before I find myself tucked with my back to his front. He may not be feeling well, but it's clear his dick didn't get that memo, I can feel it against my ass.

"Now tell me." I don't need an explanation: I know exactly what he wants to know.

"I told her I wouldn't be able to walk away."

"And why is that?"

"Because I'm head over teakettle for you too."

The arm around my stomach gets tighter and I feel his lips brush my shoulder.

"Damn right you are."

CHAPTER 23

Ouray

"Dylan just texted me."

Luna walks into my office and shuts the door behind her.

I've been holed up in here since breakfast, trying to make sense of the events of the past month or so, and in the process giving myself a whopping headache. I left Luna in the kitchen earlier. She offered to help Momma prepare a welcome home meal for the boys, which she grudgingly accepted. An attempt to get back in her good graces, I'm sure. It would appear I'm still on the outs, earning only an angry glare from the club's matriarch, as she slammed a plate of eggs in front of me this morning.

At least I got fed.

"And?" I pinch the bridge of my nose and squeeze my eyes shut, the sound of my own voice resulting in a hot stab to my brain. *Jesus*.

"And I think you should quit being stubborn and at least take some ibuprofen to try and cut through the pain. You go in to see the doc like this on Wednesday, your chances he'll give you an all-clear are slim to none."

Without waiting for an answer, she marches past me into the bedroom and appears a few seconds later with a glass of water and a handful of pills.

"Fuck, but you can be bossy," I grumble, accepting the meds and water all the same.

"Only when you need it."

Little smartass. If I wasn't feeling weak like a goddamn kitten, I'd drag her into the bedroom and show her who's in charge.

Who the fuck am I kidding? I've turned to putty in her hands. *Lovesick bastard*. Never thought I'd catch that particular disease, but here I am, gaining on fifty and drinking the Kool-aid, so to speak.

"What did he have to say?" I finally ask after obediently downing the pills.

Luna sits on the edge of my desk, smiling. "He's on his way back—with Paco."

"He got him off?"

She winces a little. "Sort of. It's more of a transfer of jurisdiction. Technically the aggravated robbery resulting in death that took place here in Durango trumps the aggravated robberies and assault in New Mexico, so Paco's being transported back to Durango as a prime suspect—in Dylan's custody."

"That's not gonna make him happy," I observe.

"No. But it is gonna keep him safe. He'll be handed off to Keith Blackfoot and taken straight to jail. Having whoever is behind this think they've succeeded casting the blame in the direction of Arrow's Edge, will buy us time."

It's true, but it brings me to another issue I've been racking my brain on. "But what about me? My guys'll be back sometime this afternoon, and we haven't exactly flown in under the radar. Other than the select few, everyone else thinks I'm still holed up in a cell in Ruidoso."

"For now," she answers. "Momma and Nosh will keep quiet about you being back, I'm sure, but we have to assume the boys will let something slip. We just need to buy enough time for a quick powwow with my team, Kaga, Nosh, and whoever else of your brothers you feel you can trust completely."

I snort. "I don't fucking know anymore. It makes me sick." It does. As much as I was relieved to find out Paco was only guilty of bad judgement but not betrayal—it doesn't change the likelihood there is still someone within this club playing for the other side.

"All the more reason to push forward and force their hand. The sooner we can solve this, the sooner your life can get back to normal. This is why I need you to take the damn pills, so you can stay sharp. You're gonna need it, because my guess is the moment they find out you've been released, there'll be a target on your back." She runs an impatient hand through hair that seems intent on escaping the elastic she wrapped around it. "I suggest we head over to your place, have Kaga and my team meet us there tonight."

"We could bring Ahiga," I suggest. "Reduce the chance something gets slipped before we want it to. Leave Momma to worry about the other boys."

"That's a great idea. I'm pretty sure he'd like that."

I sit back and take in the blush high on Luna's cheeks. She lives for this—the job, the case. The only other time I've seen her eyes this bright and her blood this hot, is right before she climaxes around me.

My headache almost forgotten, I reach out, pull her toward me, and guide her to straddle my lap, her legs fitting nicely under the arm rests.

"Got any idea how sexy you are? Confident and bossy—all fired up, all cylinders running?"

Her face shows a hint of calculation when she slowly grinds herself down on me, right before sliding off my lap onto her knees. My legs automatically make room for her. She holds my eyes, slides her hands up my thighs, and kneads my straining cock through my jeans. I grind my teeth and have to grab onto the chair to stay seated.

One by one she flips open the buttons on my fly, prolonging the torture. When she finally frees me, both hands on my dick, I hiss sharply.

She's not been this bold before, and when she opens her mouth over my crown, I make a mental note to compliment her more often, if only to remind her of her strength and the power she holds. There isn't a better reward than the sight of her hungry eyes as her plump lips stretch to accommodate me.

Any other time she's tried to go down on me, the gesture's been tentative—even a touch uncomfortable. My instinct was to interrupt her and take over, but not this time.

Perhaps lacking technical skill, she seems to rely entirely on instinct—which apparently is dead on—and giving me by far the best blowjob I've ever had.

LUNA

I can feel my cheeks burning every time my eyes catch the smirk on Ouray's face.

I'd been so caught up in the moment after making him come, I let him strip me out of my clothes and bend me over his desk, a hand between my shoulder blades to hold me down as he pistoned inside me. I was so wrapped up in the feel of him bare inside me— the first time since getting the all clear from the clinic on Friday—not even for a second had I considered the closed door was hardly an effective way to keep people out.

Mouth open, my hot cheek pressed to the cool surface of Ouray's desk, I was trapped when the door opened and a clueless Nosh stuck his head inside and looked right at me. The surprise on his face quickly morphed into amusement as he backed out, throwing me a jaunty wink in the process.

Mortifying.

To me anyway, Ouray seemed of the same mind as Nosh, and considered it amusing, which is probably why he's still wearing that damn smirk hours later.

"Are you good with that plan, Luna?"

Nothing like your boss's voice to work as a cold shower on your thoughts. "Sorry. I missed that." I try to ignore Ouray's low chuckle, throwing him as deadly a glare as I can muster, which doesn't do much to stem his mirth at my expense.

"You'll cover Ouray, spending the nights here, at his house. With his recovery as an excuse, you can explain he'll get more rest here than at the clubhouse. It'll also give us a place to meet quietly. The rest of the story is that Kaga's staying at the clubhouse until Ouray gets his feet back under him, and invited Dylan to stay with the club for a bit as well, in support of his *sister.* Between the two of them, they can keep an eye on everyone else," Damian repeats.

"I want Ahiga to stay with us." At the puzzled look on my boss's face I quickly explain, "The boy you saw when you came in. His name is Cody Washburn, he's the boy I've asked Jasper to look into. He's hearing-impaired and I'd feel a whole lot better if he stayed close to us."

Damian scratches his goatee, looking at me from under his heavy brows. "The boy means something to you?"

I nod and throw Ouray a grateful look when he adds, "To me as well. The boy stays."

"Good. That's settled then. Jas and I will coordinate with Blackfoot on the investigation and keep you updated on that front. Let's flush these bastards out."

When Ouray closes the door after the last person leaves, he walks straight to the stairs.

"I'm just going up to see how Ahiga is doing."

"Why don't you ask if he wants to come watch a movie with us? I can see what we have in the house and make some snacks."

Instead of heading upstairs, he stalks over to where I'm leaning over the back of the couch. He tucks his knuckle under my chin and lifts my face, only to confuse me when he says, "You said we."

"I said what?"

"You said 'what *we* have in the house.' I like it."

"Okay…" I'm still a little foggy.

"How attached to that little shack you call home are you?" he asks with an intense look in his eyes.

"My house?" He grunts, confirming. "It's been a good place to keep my things. A bed to sleep in. I don't know, I usually don't spend much time at home. I also move around a lot. I get restless when I stay somewhere long."

"Mmm. I say you ditch the place, and move in here with me."

That blush is creeping back up my cheeks, and I try to look away from his probing eyes, but his damn thumb keeps my chin trapped in place.

I'm literally stumped for words. Living here with him would be… I don't really know what it would be like. Or maybe I do. I've spent most of the past almost four weeks almost plastered to his side. Still, not even quite a month, surely… "Isn't that a little soon?" is what I finally manage to verbalize.

"That depends." He shrugs with a smile. "How much notice does your landlord want on that place? Or do you have a lease?"

"I never sign anything longer than a six-month lease and go month-to-month after that." I think for a minute. "I moved in the first of April, I believe."

"Perfect, that means your lease runs out in a few days anyway, and you shouldn't owe him more than a month's rent after that. Call him tomorrow."

"But we haven't even…I mean it hasn't even been a month." This time I manage to slip my chin from his hold and turn my head to the front door, maybe looking for an escape, but then his hands cup my face and he drops his forehead to mine.

"You said yourself you get restless, move around a lot. Just call this your next stop. You were expecting to be here with me for the immediate future anyway."

I look into his warm eyes and swallow. "But what if I get restless after a while?"

"That happens, Sprite, we'll deal. But one thing I do know, worry about *what-if* too much will only paralyze you." He rubs his nose along mine, and presses a soft kiss on my lips. "Trust me on this."

"How can you be so sure?"

His eyes take in my face as he brushes a curl from my forehead. "Because, Sprite…I've always been clear on what I don't want—so it doesn't take a lot for me to know when what's in front of me is exactly what I've been holding out for."

CHAPTER 24

"What the fuck?"

Yuma is just getting on his bike when we pull up in the rental. Of course with Luna behind the wheel, which still irks me. Since she won't let me drive—yet—one of the guys will have to go with her to drop off the rental today.

The moment the car comes to a stop, Ahiga—who was up at the goddamn butt crack of dawn this morning—is out and running into the clubhouse. Probably straight into the kitchen. We'd better get some more food over at the house if he's going to stay with us.

"Close your mouth, brother. Things could get lost in there," I snap at Yuma, immediately wondering if I should read more into his obvious shock. I fucking hate this shit.

"The hell are you doing back here? How'd you get out?"

"Cops managed to get their heads outta their asses, that's how."

"Well shit, I was just heading over to River's Edge. One of the tenants has some plumbing issues," he smirks and I almost groan out loud. Probably sniffing around that new tenant. "But now I kinda want to stick around, see the looks when that bunch of cranky gravediggers in there sees you come in. Talk about low morale, brother. That was the worst fucking ride this club's ever seen."

A little more encouraged, I clap him on the shoulder. "In that case, get on the horn and round the brothers up. My office at noon."

From what I can tell, the few brothers hanging around the bar are relieved to see me. Even Dylan, who apparently came straight here after leaving my place last night, puts on a good show of clapping me on the back. He clearly missed his calling on the stage, because he has my guys treating him like one of their own. After refusing a proper drink for the third time in a row—sticking to the bottle of water Luna shoved in my hand earlier—I've had enough, and as I'd been instructed, I quickly withdraw to my office.

The plan is for me to pretend I'm not doing that great yet, still recovering, making me an easier target. Gomez seems to think it may force the assholes who have it out for me to move quickly. I'm not about to argue with that. As far as I'm concerned, the sooner

I can look my brothers straight in the eye again, the better it is.

"Do you need anything from the store?" Luna sticks her head around the door. "I'm going to head out with Lea to pick up some last minute groceries for Momma, and I'll grab a few things for us as well." Since the boys got in late last night, Momma is putting on a welcome home meal tonight. Luna disappeared soon after we got here to help her and Leah in the kitchen.

"Where's Cody?"

"You mean Ahiga?" She grins as she slips into the room. "You gave him that name and now he won't answer to anything else, so the least you can do is use it."

"You giving me a hard time?" I tilt my head to the side. "I may just have to come up with one for you."

She shakes her head sharply. "No thanks, I like mine just fine. Anyway, he's in the garage with Lea's twins." She grins, looking at me from under her lashes. "Has them practicing sac squeeze 'n twists on each other."

I bark out a laugh. "Christ. Figures the kid would turn out to be a shit disturber."

"He'll fit right in."

Her eyes are bright when she smiles at me, and I'm smiling right back. *Jesus*, I'm turning into a fucking pussy. I'd be raked over the coals if my guys could see me now.

"We're gonna need a truckload of food for that

boy, Sprite," I tell her sternly, trying to find my balls as I pull out my wallet, and take out a stack of bills. "Stock up. I'll get Rowtag and Wapi to follow you in the van. They can help you carry."

"I can afford a few groceries, you know. You don't have to shove money at me." She flaps a hand at the money I hold out to her. The heated flush is back on the cheeks of my feisty little Sprite, and her back is ramrod straight. Fuck, I love that attitude of hers, however misplaced it is. I put the money on the edge of the desk and sit down, waiting for the next volley, because I know for a fact she's not nearly done yet. She doesn't keep me waiting long. "And sending a bunch of snot-nosed, ill-tempered, wanna-be men to babysit us is frankly insulting. I could take on both those punks with one hand tied behind my back and twirl a fucking baton with the other." She gestures wildly with her hands while she's talking, hair flopping in her face. When she's done, she plants her hands on her hips, and attempts to stare me down. I manage to hold back a grin until she purses her lips and attempts to blow a wayward blonde curl out of her pretty blue eyes, looking like more like an angry fairy than a lethal, pissed-off FBI agent. Then I bust out laughing.

"Hold on, hold on," I call out, scrambling out of my chair, and barely catching her at the door she's about to march out of. Blocking her path, I lean down so she has no choice but to look at me. "First of all, I'm sending those 'punks' with you so *you* can keep an eye on *them*, not the other way around. You heard me tell Yuma I'm expecting all brothers in my office? I don't want nosy cubs around for that."

"Oh."

"Oh is right. Secondly," I continue, leaning over to grab the money off the desk, and stuffing it in her jeans pocket. "The money. I take care of my family, there's no discussion there. The time comes you've moved in, and your new car is parked outside the house every night, we can talk and get finances sorted. But for now it's still my house, which means it's also my empty fridge, which will get filled with groceries bought with my money. Can you live with that?"

"I guess," she says, looking a little sheepish and pretty fucking adorable.

Before she has a chance to think up more objections, I take her face in my hands and kiss her thoroughly. By the time I lift my mouth from hers, I'm pretty sure I've left her temporarily incapable of speech. Just long enough to nudge her out the door and quietly close it behind her.

LUNA

"What's with that guy?"

I turn to Lea, who seems to be staring in her rearview mirror intently, and swing my head around. The club's white van is behind us, carrying Rowtag and Wapi.

"Who?"

"Rowtag. Do you know he was the most timid kid when he came to Arrow's Edge? Soft-spoken, surprisingly polite for a kid who'd seen too much hard life. I don't even recognize him anymore. Most kids arrive here with a chip on their shoulder, despair in their eyes, and anger in their hearts, but over time you see them gradually change. They settle in, start to learn about respect and trust, and eventually grow up into good, decent men. This one?" She cocks her thumb over her shoulder. "He's the only one I know who went the other way."

I can hardly identify the boy she describes with the foul-tempered punk I've encountered. "Soft-spoken and polite certainly aren't terms I would've associated with him. He definitely does not like me."

"He seems to have a problem with women in general. The only females he appears to be civil with are Momma and Britney. Besides, Kaga told me you kicked his ass in the ring." Her mouth twitches as she looks over at me. "So of course he doesn't like you. He doesn't like losing and certainly not to a five foot nothing, blue-eyed cherub with breasts. He's a bully among the cubs and the younger kids, and I'm sure you damaged his *street cred*."

I'm mentally filing every snippet of information, trying to figure out how it might fit into the puzzle—if at all.

When we turn into the parking lot of the City

Market and Lea pulls into an empty spot, I turn to her. "I meant to ask you, whatever happened to Britney? I haven't seen her since we went to the casino in Ruisodo."

"Took off. Probably found herself another biker to hook onto. That girl is bound and determined to get on the back of some poor sap's bike, claiming old lady status. You know she had her hopes set on your man, right?"

"She made that clear."

Lea snorts. "I'm sure she did. Anyway, she never showed Friday night, and Jill told me the next morning her stuff had been gone from the cabin when her and Hanshaw got back from the concert."

"No message? No note?"

"Nada. Apparently not the first time she's disappeared on Jill. She didn't seem too concerned. Said she'll probably float to the surface again at some point."

Wapi is waiting behind the car when we get out.

"Where's Rowtag?" I ask, looking around.

"He had to take a call. Says to go ahead."

I spot him sitting behind the wheel of the van, the next row over, eyes on me and talking into his phone. I'm torn. I'd like to keep my eye on him—and I'd really like to know who he's talking to, since I know the club is holed up in Ouray's office right about now—but I don't want to make unnecessary waves either. Turning away from him, I follow Lea's retreating back into the grocery store.

Two almost full carts later, I head over to the deli counter, leaving Lea to hit the freezer aisle. I've just placed my order when Wapi sidles up to me.

"Be careful," he says, under his breath.

"What do you mean?"

The cub looks around to make sure he can't be overheard before bending closer to me. "Rowtag. He has it out for you."

"That's not news, Wapi," I whisper back.

"Right. It's just that…I can tell he's up to something. Just watch your back."

Before I have a chance to ask what makes him think that he steps away, just as Lea walks up with her overflowing cart.

"You about ready?"

"Just waiting for my deli meats and I'm good to go."

I don't see Rowtag until we push the heavy carts, loaded with bags, onto the parking lot. He's waiting by the back of the van, the door already open. Wapi's words still echoing in my head, my training kicks in, and I quickly scan my surroundings. Other than a harried looking mom, trying to wrangle two little ones on her way into the grocery store, the parking lot is empty. Call me paranoid, but it feels like the air just got heavy.

"Wanna take my cart?" I ask Wapi who's a step behind me. "I forgot something."

"I have to grab something," I call out to Lea who is walking in front.

Without waiting for an answer, I turn and jog back toward the store, sharply aware of every kind of movement around me. I let out a big breath when I step inside, immediately turning to look behind me.

Nothing. Other than Rowtag standing in the same spot by the back of the van—while Lea and Wapi load the bags inside—his eyes on the store, no one is even paying attention to me.

Still, I quickly pull out my phone and dial Ouray's number. It rings a few times before going to voicemail. Guess he turned the sound off. So instead I send a short message, tuck my phone back in my pocket, and randomly grab some batteries and gum from the rack by the closest cash register.

While paying, I keep an eye on the van through the glass of the store front, watching Wapi close the back doors and pushing the carts out of the way. The moment I see Lea head over to her car and get in, I keep my fingers crossed. Sure enough, she backs out of the parking spot and drives toward the store. As soon as she pulls up outside the doors, I dart outside and get into the passenger side.

"What the heck is up with you?" she demands to know when the first thing I do is look over my shoulder at the van behind us.

"Just feel something's off, and I can't get hold of Ouray."

"It's because they turn their phones off when they congregate in the office," Lea explains.

Shit. I freeze when I see the van suddenly pull

around beside us, my hand sliding down to the ankle holster I've been taken to wearing. Wapi's window rolls down and before I can stop her, Lea lowers hers as well.

"What's the delay?" Rowtag leans toward the open window.

"Luna says—"

"I've got one more errand to run in town," I cut Lea off quickly. "Why don't you head over to the clubhouse. We won't be long."

"Chief says to stick with you. We stick with you," he says, looking at me sharply.

"Fine." I quickly adjust my hopes to ditch them. "You want to follow me all the way down to the Verizon store on South Camino Del Rio, be my guest."

"Is that where we're going?" Lea wants to know as she rolls up her window.

"Yup. We're shopping for a phone for Ahiga."

We've barely turned down Main and my phone rings.

"*Something's up…*what the hell kind of message is that?"

I ignore Ouray's irritation and dive right in. "Gut instinct. That, and a whispered warning from Wapi to watch my back with Rowtag, who's had laser eyes on me the whole time. Like I said, something's up."

"Stay put, I'm coming—"

"You're not supposed to be going anywhere," I stop him in his tracks. "Besides, it's not necessary. All you have to do is call him back to the clubhouse with the groceries. They're in the back of the van. Lea and I are on our way to the Verizon store, and he's stuck to our ass like glue. He gives me the creeps." The last I add for Lea's benefit. I'm not sure how much, if anything, Kaga shared with her, and I don't want her to freak out.

"He gives you the creeps?" I can hear the smile in his voice.

"That's what I said."

"I'll call him off, but I'm sending Honon out there, just in case. What are you doing at the Verizon store anyway?"

"We're buying Ahiga a phone."

"Sprite, you know the kid's deaf, right? What the fuck is he gonna do with a phone?" I don't even bother answering. I know the penny will drop eventually and he doesn't make me wait long.

"Fuck. Of course. Good plan."

I'm still grinning when I end the call and find Lea looking at me slack-mouthed.

"Man, I've known Kaga for over a decade, and I'd like to think I manage him well. You've known Ouray how long? And you handle that man with some serious skill."

"You heard him?" I ask her curiously.

"Every single word. I can feel that sexy deep rumble of his in my bones." She fans herself dramatically and I snicker at her antics. "But don't you go telling Kaga that."

"Wouldn't dream of it."

CHAPTER 25

OURAY

"Rowtag! My office."

The kid, who's been slinging drinks since he got back, swings his head around in my direction.

"Wapi can take over at the bar," I add before turning my back on him.

I'm already seated, my feet on my desk, when his lanky form follows me inside. My hands itch when I see stubborn defiance plastered all over his face.

"Chief?"

"Close the door, cub." I wait until he does what I ask, and then point him to a chair. "How long have you been with us now?"

My question seems to throw him off and he takes a moment before answering. "Five years, sir. I was fifteen."

"Right. And in that time, what have we taught

you?"

"How to be a man, Chief." He's starting to fidget in his chair, his eyes darting around the room like he's expecting something to jump out at him.

"What makes a real man, cub?"

Beads of sweat dot his forehead. "Loyalty, integrity, and respect." He mumbles the three core values we try to instill in the boys, but he can't fucking look at me.

"Ah, so you *do* remember?" He lifts his eyes briefly before going back to studying the floor. I suddenly sit up and drop my heavy boots on the floor, startling him. "So why the fuck is it when I tell you and Wapi to help with groceries, your ass sits in the van, jabbering on the phone? And why, when my old lady tells you to head back to the clubhouse, you disrespect her too? And it's not the first time you've done that either. How many times do I have to call you in here, kid? How many warnings does it take before you start to grasp those values you still seem able to recall? I have a fucking mind to take your vest right here, right now, but that's not all up to me. It'll take a vote, and it's fucking tragic that we'll be voting on whether or not your ass can stay, instead of voting to make you a full-fledged member. But that's on you. Now get the fuck outta my office!"

My voice has steadily been rising, especially when the little asshole's eyes turned mean at the mention of Luna. He gets up, knocking his chair over in the process, swings the door open violently so it hits the wall hard, and pounds out of my office. I rub the back of my hand over my eyes. Fucking cub.

Most of my anger is genuine, but it's also strategic. My gut tells me he's involved in whatever is going on, it wouldn't surprise me to learn he was part of at least some of those robberies. With the kind of temper he has, provoking him—calling him out—may trip him up.

A few minutes later, Kaga sticks his head around the door.

"Y'all right in here?"

"Done with the kid, brother. Dylan on him?"

"Rowtag went tearing out of here on his bike, but he wasn't far behind."

Surprisingly, Momma's welcome home dinner—for which some of the brothers pulled the folding tables and chairs out of the shed—is more subdued than I'd expected. I may well be to blame for that. Apparently most of the clubhouse was able to hear me tear a strip off Rowtag who, by the way, still hasn't returned.

Dylan got back right before we sat down, but only managed a shrug. I assume that means he lost him.

The younger ones are eyeing me cautiously, instead of their normal antics at the table, and even the brothers seem quiet. Although that may have something to do with our earlier powwow in my office.

I filled them in on the events of last Friday night. Told them the agreed upon story: part truth, part ruse. How the cops found stolen guns in the back of Paco's truck, with me in the driver's seat and took us both in, until they discovered my injuries were to the wrong side of my head to have been caused by a crash, and promptly released me. By the time I was done answering all the questions fired at me, my head was pounding, and I pulled out the bottle of pills. That quieted the room instantly. The guys aren't used to me being off my game—neither am I—but I played it up a notch, asking them to keep business running until I could get back on my feet.

I hate the deception, it goes against everything I stand for. It feels especially shitty since I just preached to Rowtag about the core values I'm breaking myself.

A deep sigh escapes me and I press my fingers against my eyes.

"Maybe we should get going?" Luna leans over, putting a hand on my chest. Something that clearly doesn't go unnoticed, since I suddenly find most of the focus on me.

Momma moves first, getting up and ordering the kids to clear dishes. The rest follow suit and in minutes the tables and chairs are folded and taken back to storage, and Luna is hustling Ahiga out the door.

I dive into my office to grab my smokes off the desk, when Yuma follows me inside, clapping me on the shoulder.

"You sure you're okay, Chief? Let me know if there's anything you need, I'm stickin' around here tonight anyway."

Christ. I must be giving the performance of my life if it's getting Yuma to voluntarily stick around when there's a whole world of untapped pussy to explore.

I grunt in response and hoof it out of there. I can't handle much more of this touchy feely shit.

"Chief, a minute?"

Dylan catches me right before getting into the Traverse—on the goddamn passenger side.

"What?" I snap.

"Update on the kid," he says, ignoring my foul mood. "Couldn't get too close with my bike, but I managed to follow him going south on the 160, then got stuck behind a slow truck. By the time I got around, he was gone. Drove through to the hospital, checked around that neighborhood for a bit before backtracking. He may have cut off on the 550, gone up through the mountains, or turned around and is somewhere in Durango, not sure. Wanted you to be aware."

"And now I am. I just want this over with," I grumble, climbing in the SUV so Luna can fucking chauffeur me around.

I can feel her eyes on me, but I keep mine straight out the windshield until she finally backs out of the spot, and drives us the two minutes it takes to get to my place.

"Feel like a movie?" she asks, when we walk inside.

"Heading to bed."

She turns to face me and tilts her head to the side. "You know what? You do that. But don't baby that miserable mood for too long—God forbid it sticks."

LUNA

I'm glad to get out of the house this afternoon.

The past forty-eight hours have been a barrel of laughs. Ouray is showing the strain, pacing around like an angry bear. Poor Ahiga is mostly hiding in Momma's kitchen or his bedroom at the house, and I'm tired of walking on eggshells around everyone.

Maybe this was a good test run on that cohabitation Ouray suggested, and I'm relieved I didn't give my landlord notice yet. If this is any indication of what living with the man would be like, I'll hang on to my little cottage, thank you very much.

Especially after this morning's visit to the doctor.

To say Ouray wasn't pleased with the man's assessment would be an understatement. I was pretty pissed myself, but mostly at Ouray. When the doc ran a simply eye test on him, it became obvious the knock had done more than just give him a cut on his head. He never mentioned any blurry vision to me, but apparently it's enough to impair his vision. Probably temporary, something the doctor assures us can clear up with proper rest. No work, no driving, at least not until his appointment next week.

I dropped both of my temporary roommates off at the clubhouse before coming here, where Dylan is left to keep an eye on things. I'll update him later.

"The prodigal daughter returns," Jasper jokes when I walk into the office.

"And you have no idea how happy I am to be here."

"Uh oh, trouble in paradise already?"

I plop down in my chair and smooth my hands over my desk. "Don't get me started. I have a scary matriarch breathing down my neck, waiting for me to cross some invisible line, while I'm helping her feed an army of locusts I'm supposed to be scrutinizing. My prime suspect has been on the lam since Monday, and we don't seem to be any closer to solving this clusterfuck. To top it off, I get to spend my nights with a troubled kid who's fast crawling back into his shell, while Mr. Congeniality grunts, scowls, and hides in his room. If this supposed to be domestic bliss, let me take a hard pass."

Jasper apparently finds this funny. "Ahhh, did you hear that?" he says to Damian, who is just sitting down at the large conference table. "Our little moon goddess is in love."

"I know," our leader confirms, not looking up from the file he has open.

I look from one to the other, my mouth open.

"You're both clearly nuts," I protest. "How on earth do you manage to conclude *that* from what I just described?"

"You wouldn't care so much if this was just an assignment, now would you?" Jasper points out.

"Was sich liebt das neckt sich" I look at Damian who shrugs his shoulders. "It's true," he adds.

"Since when do you speak German? And what is that even supposed to mean?"

"Same damn thing, Luna. If someone's worth fighting with—he's worth fighting for."

Since I have nothing sensible to say to that, I hold my tongue. The silence stretches on until Jasper finally caves. "Shall we get this show on the road?"

The briefing nets little. No one saw what happened to the truck or Ouray Friday night, according to law enforcement in Ruidoso. The description the sales clerk at the gun store gave was identical to previous witness accounts, nothing new there either. This time the clerk complied with the robbers, and was lucky to escape with only bad dreams. One is already dead and that poor old guy in Bloomfield was not so lucky either. Edward Burchfield still remains in a coma in an Albuquerque hospital.

The fingerprints found on the truck belonged to one Nathan Phillips—Paco, as I know him—and the others belonged to Britney Hughes. The only other fingerprints were Ouray's and those were just found on the steering wheel and nowhere else. No leads there.

Nothing on Britney either. Wherever she is, she never came back to her small apartment. Jasper mentioned her mailbox looked to be overflowing and none of her neighbors can recall seeing her since last week.

The only interesting bit of news was that the guns in the back of the truck didn't total up to the number actually taken. Whoever was trying to stick it to Ouray, obviously had a hard time leaving the entire haul for the cops to find.

I locate Ahiga in the kitchen at the clubhouse, where Momma is already preparing dinner. Nosh sits at the table with him, apparently working on math problems. It reminds me, we shouldn't wait too long to see if we can get him integrated into the school system here. As soon as things settle down. Of course we'll first have to get this case solved, because until then I don't feel comfortable letting him out of our sight.

"Need a hand?" I ask Momma after waving hello to the two at the table.

"Almost done here. But what would be welcome is if you can cheer up that pain in everyone's ass."

"Ouray?"

"That's who I'm talkin' bout. Never seen that man go an hour without a smile. At this rate, he'll have forgotten how to if he ever gets out of this funk."

"He's under a lot of stress," I find myself defending him. "The doctor's visit this morning didn't help."

"What'd he say? He didn't feel like sharin'."

Momma turns to me expectantly.

"Still grounded. At least until his next appointment in a week."

"Well shit. I ain't gonna survive one more week of this. Or maybe he won't. Folks are steering clear of him. Except Kaga, that man always liked taking risks."

"I'll go check in with him."

I walk out of the kitchen, ruffling Ahiga's too long mop of hair on the way, and trying to come up with a way to tell Ouray we're not much further in our investigation.

"I have an idea," I suggest, finding Ouray staring out the dirty window, not even turning when I walk in.

"What's that?" he asks, turning slowly, and it strikes me how tired he looks.

I slip behind the desk and force my way on his lap, running my hand along his beard. "Why don't we ask Momma if she can pack some food up for us, and head over to the house. We haven't had a chance to give Ahiga his phone yet. I had Jasper program a few things for him this afternoon. I can show him over dinner. It should lift his mood a bit."

"His mood? Sure you're not talking about me?"

"I wouldn't dare," I tease, jostling him a bit. "I mean the boy, he's been withdrawn, and I don't want him to go back where we can't reach him. This tension is starting to wear everyone down, but he's most vulnerable."

I know I've managed to reach him when he tilts his head back, closes his eyes, and lets loose a juicy curse under his breath. "I'm an ass. It's because of me, isn't it?"

Proceeding with caution, I first press a soft kiss on his mouth. "In part," I whisper, my lips against his before I straighten up. "But also because he's more in tune than most. His lack of hearing makes him more sensitive to the undercurrent. He picks up on facial expressions, body language, and—"

"And moods," Ouray finishes for me.

"Yeah. He was starting to feel safe here and now he can tell something's up. I can imagine it might make him feel less sure about his place here."

"And you think the phone will be a way to show him we're not looking to throw him out any time soon."

I grin into Ouray's blue eyes that look clear enough from where I'm sitting. "Something like that."

His arms snake around me tightly. "How'd you get so smart?"

"A degree in psychology helps."

"Yeah?" For the first time in days I see a tentative smile crack through his sullen mood. "What does your degree tell you about me?"

"That you're scared," I say immediately, not holding back. His body stiffens right away and his smile disappears. I put my hands on his cheeks and lean in, trying to soften my words. "Anyone would be in your situation, honey. You carry a lot of responsibility for a lot of people, you don't know who you can or can't trust, and to top it off your body is letting you down. It all piles on and there's nothing worse than feeling helpless against the wave of shit you know is coming."

It takes a few minutes but finally the tension leaves his face and his shoulders, and he looks up at me, his eyes glittering through his lashes.

"Like I said—smart."

I let out a sigh of relief before speaking. "You don't have to carry it all alone. I'm here. I want to help you shoulder the weight. I know you're not used to sharing—heck, neither am I—but we're stronger if we just hook our arms and hold onto each other to face the storm."

"Fuck, Sprite. I've tried hard to be a good man, and you still make me wanna be better. Not sure how I deserve you, but I ain't letting go."

CHAPTER 26

OURAY

Glad to see you managed to dislodge your head from your ass.

I drop in the chair across from Nosh, who is having his morning coffee in the kitchen.

Good fucking morning to you too, old man.

Momma slides a mug in front of me, and I throw her a smile.

"Now there's a sight for sore eyes. Have you eaten?" she asks.

"Yeah. We had breakfast at the house."

"So where did you leave Luna and the boy? Are they off to Aztec for his appointment?" She walks over to the large whiteboard on the wall that doubles as a calendar. Momma's way to keep track of everyone.

"Tomorrow. They're just heading over to Walmart to grab the boy a decent jacket and some boots for the winter."

"We probably have some stuff here," Momma suggests.

"She wants him to have his own things." I grin, I already had this discussion with her last night, which got a little heated and ended in bed, Luna riding me. Needless to say, I folded like a wet tissue on the shopping spree.

"She's really bonded with him, hasn't she?"

"Yeah. She gets the kid."

What if things don't work out with CPS? Nosh points out, referring to the meeting our lawyer set up in Monticello for the second week of October.

We have a good relationship with Child Protective Services in Durango. They pop in, every so often, to see how the younger boys are doing. That's a relationship we've been able to build on over the years, but we haven't dealt with the CPS in Monticello before, and it's always possible they won't like our setup. That's why we have Lawrence Brimley, he worked for the Colorado Office of the Child's Representative, the OCR, for years and has a stellar reputation. Our luck he retired and moved to Durango years ago.

It will. I assure Nosh, who always worries. *The boy is twelve, he gets to voice his wishes and you know he'll want to stay.*

I hope you're right.

Trust me, I assure him, *I'll make it so he won't ever want to leave.*

"And how do you propose on doing that?"

Momma wants to know.

I grin up at her. "I'm getting him a dog."

An hour later, I'm standing in front of the kennel of a mangy looking animal. A new arrival, the volunteer at the La Plata County Humane Society said.

"That's an ugly thing," Kaga comments.

I asked him to make a stop here on our way to check in on our businesses in town. I haven't stopped in for a few weeks, it's about time I show my face. Of course, since I still can't drive, Kaga gets to be my chauffeur for the day.

"Nothing a little food and a good home can't fix," I tell him, crouching down and sticking my hand through the bars, palm up.

The dog may not look its best and appears to be blind in one eye, but the other eye is clear and keen, and he seems to follow the conversation as if he can understand what we're saying. Cautiously he takes a step closer, his focus never leaving the hand I hold out. I let him sniff first, before curling my fingers and scratching him under his chin.

"How old is he?" I ask the volunteer.

"The vet estimates he's about three years old. He was brought in malnourished, was partially blind, had worms, and half his body was covered in ticks, but we cleaned him up, neutered him, and made sure he's had all his shots. He may not be the prettiest now, but I'm sure with proper care, he'll slowly put on some weight and his fur will start to look healthier."

"I'll take him," I announce, getting to my feet.

"You're not gonna get the boy a puppy?"

"Because a puppy is shiny and new?" I shake my head at Kaga. "No. I'd much rather show Ahiga that everyone's deserving of a good home. The boy and the dog have a lot in common."

We follow the woman into the small office where she pulls out a binder.

"If you'd just fill out the paperwork? We'll process it this afternoon and you should be able to pick him up tomorrow morning."

"What are you gonna call it?" Kaga asks when we get into his truck.

"Up to the boy to name his dog."

An hour later—the back of Kaga's truck filled with a dog bed, toys, leash, and bowls, and a food supply that'll last the mutt three months—we pull up to the clubhouse.

"You sure you have everything?" Sarcasm drips from his words.

"Fuck off, just hang onto it until tomorrow morning."

I get out and start walking to the clubhouse when Kaga calls out after me, "You realize if my kids see this, I'm gonna be in big shit, right?"

Without turning around I stick my hand up, flipping him the bird, but I'm grinning all the way to my office.

"What has you so happy?" Luna asks later that night. "Have you had good news I don't know about?"

"Come here."

I'm sitting with my back against the headboard and crook my finger at Luna, who's still putzing around, getting ready for bed.

"Just a few more things to put away."

She and the boy had come home, the back seat of the Traverse loaded with bags. Enough clothes for Ahiga to fill the small dresser in the spare bedroom, but also some sheets, new towels, and a few things for herself. I hadn't said anything earlier, just observed as she took the bags, ran everything she bought through the laundry, folded it, and put it away. The new undies, I happen to notice she bought, are the last thing she's stuffing in the dresser.

"Not sure why it all needs washing," I observe. "All that stuff comes out of the packaging clean. It hasn't had a chance to get dirty."

She shuts the drawer and stalks over to the bed, putting a knee in the mattress. "Have you ever slept on bedding straight out of the package?" she asks, as she slowly crawls up my body. I run my hands over the new sheets she put on the bed earlier. "It's like sleeping on packing paper. They're nice and soft now."

"Look at you…" I stroke the back of my fingers down her flushed cheek when she settles on top of me. "Big tough FBI agent, all domesticated. New sheets, new matching towels for the bathroom. Hot as fuck new little panties."

"Your sheets were threadbare, you had three towels in your linen closet, and I ran out of clean underwear," she sputters, lifting her head from my shoulder.

"I love you domesticated." I roll her under me, propping my head up on my hand and with the other I draw a line from her chin down between her breasts. "I love you making yourself at home here." I cup the handful in my palm and brush my thumb over the hard little tip. "I love how you probably don't think of yourself as nurturing, but you're a natural." Bending down, I close my mouth over her nipple and suck gently, her back arching into me right away. I let it go with a soft plop. "I love how responsive you are to my touch." I lift my eyes to her warm smiling ones.

"I love…"

Her eyebrows go up, waiting for me to finish.

"…you."

LUNA

I flick the light on and off and Ahiga lifts his head off the pillow.

Time to put that phone down and get your butt out of bed if you want to eat before we go. We leave in twenty.

"Is he up?" Ouray asks when I walk into the

kitchen where he's flipping French toast on the stove.

"He was up. Still in bed, though, playing on his phone—I may have created a monster."

Ouray's warm laugh washes over me as he snags me around the waist and tucks me close. "Nah, the phone was a good call. I think he sent me twelve texts while you were shopping yesterday alone. It's like a whole new world you've handed him."

"I guess. I just don't want him to get lost in there and forget about this world."

"Mmm."

I press my nose into his chest and inhale the familiar smell of laundry detergent and freshly showered Ouray. Fast becoming my favorite scent in the world.

"Kiss me good morning," he rumbles over my head and I lift my face to his.

A sharp rap of knuckles on the counter interrupts us, and I turn my head to find Ahiga—haphazardly dressed with hair sticking out every which way—scowling at us.

You're killing my appetite with the smooching.

"Get used to it, smartass," Ouray says chuckling, making sure the boy can read his lips.

I don't think his appetite sustained much damage when he scarfs down his fourth piece of French toast. I tap him on the shoulder and tilt my head to the door.

You may want to go ahead outside. There will be kissing in the next minute. When he snags up his phone, tears through the house, and out the front door,

I turn to Ouray. "I think we've discovered a sure way to light a fire under that boy." I step into his body and fit my arms around his waist, tilting my head back. "Now, where were we?"

Ouray doesn't waste time. I barely finish talking when his mouth slants over mine, his tongue stroking firmly between my lips to tangle with mine.

From the very first time he kissed me—even when it was just for show—this man unearthed emotions I thought were out of reach. Now, with every touch he shows me it was worth risking my heart.

"I should get going," I mumble through swollen lips when he lifts his head. "He's waiting outside."

"Drive safe," he says, pressing a last kiss on top of my head before letting me go.

I walk to the door and stop, turning around. "You know—I love…" I wait until I see his eyebrow pull up. "…you too."

The last thing I see before I dash out the door is the glow from his eyes as his face breaks open in a gratified smile.

Lost in my head, I leave Ahiga to fiddle with his phone all the way to Aztec. It gives me a chance to get my rambling thoughts sorted before I sit down with Gary. Other than my call to him when I was looking for a therapist for Ahiga, I haven't spoken to him since we had lunch at the beginning of September.

He's not going to believe the change in me. I was a mess last time, freaked out, scared, unsure how to take my next step and now look at me. Barely a month later and I've just bared the bottom of my soul to Ouray.

"I. Am. Hungry."

I turn to look at Ahiga, who loves the new app Jasper downloaded. It's perfect for him, he clearly never had the benefit of a speech therapist to help him gain the confidence to verbalize words, and this app gives him a voice. Albeit a mechanical one.

"You just had breakfast." I enunciate clearly, so the program doesn't bastardize my words into some garbled word soup text, like it's done a few times in the past three days when Ahiga was playing around with it. "Here." I reach into my purse and pull out a granola bar I stuffed in there God knows how long ago.

Garbage in the trash, please, I tell him when he threatens to dart from the vehicle, leaving his crumpled wrapper sitting in the cup holder. I swear he rolls his eyes when he snatches it up and tosses it basketball style in the trash can at the edge of the parking lot. I bite my cheek, holding back a smile. I'll take his eye rolls and deep sighs any day, as long as he engages.

It's a vast improvement on the withdrawn, almost skittish kid at the beginning of the week. As soon as Ouray's mood lifted, Ahiga started coming out of his shell. I'm not sure of the kind of male role models he's had in his life, but I venture to bet they weren't good ones.

See you in a bit, I'll be here.

The moment he disappears into his therapist's office, I turn and go down the flight of stairs to Gary's office.

"I think I'm in love," I announce the moment I sit down, figuring it's better to rip the bandage off.

Gary gives me an easy once over before he teases. "Thought I noticed something different. It looks good on you."

"Is that all you have to say? Aren't you surprised?" I'm actually a little peeved my news isn't received with a bit more fanfare.

He sits forward, elbows on his knees, and his joined hands dangling between. "Luna, this may come as news to you, but the only one convinced love would never be in the books for you…was *you*. You spent a long time hiding behind your view of the world, avoiding all emotion. I knew it was inevitable, at some point, someone would break through that barrier. Just as I knew once that first brick came down, and you got a glimpse at all that was on offer, that wall wouldn't be standing long. So in short, no—I'm not surprised in the least. I am, however, very happy for you."

By design, my appointment ends ten minutes before Ahiga will be done, and I'm about to head back upstairs to the waiting room when my phone rings. There's a strict no cell phone policy in the clinic and when I glance over to the receptionist catch her glaring already. With an apologetic wave I duck out the door instead, answering the call as I walk over to the Traverse.

"Hello?"

At first I just hear some rustling but then I hear faintly. "…Please…help me…hurt…"

"Hello? Who is this?" I'm trying to place the difficult to hear woman's voice. I pull out my keys, unlock the doors, and try to squeeze my way between the idiot who parked his van barely a foot from my driver's side.

I'm so focused on the disembodied voice on the phone, I'm too late recognizing the danger.

Even as the sliding door behind me opens and I'm hauled back—dropping my phone in the process—my mind goes straight to Ahiga. My eyes fly up to the first floor window, where I can just see his face and hands pressed up against the window.

I must've made a sound, because the next thing I know the door slams shut in front of me, and I hear a woman's voice.

"Fuck, it's the kid. Go grab him."

CHAPTER 27

OURAY

"That mutt's what you got the boy?"

I jab an elbow in Dylan's ribs. He volunteered to drive me this morning. Kaga dropped off the dog's stuff earlier, but is spending the weekend with his family.

"Fuck off."

"Excuse me?" The same volunteer who was here yesterday stops right inside the doorway, her mouth dropping open.

"Sorry," I mumble. "That wasn't meant for you." Dylan laughs heartily behind me—the asshole—I try to ignore him. "I'm here to pick him up." I indicate the dog.

"Right—Mr. Strongbow—I remember. Did you bring a collar and leash?" I hold them up and she takes them from me, opens the gate to the kennel, and puts them on the dog. "I need one more signature from you and you're all done." The phone in my pocket buzzes with a text just as she hands me the leash. "Just follow me."

A signature, a lengthy lesson in dog care, a stack of flyers with instructions, and almost twenty minutes later, we finally walk out of the shelter. The moment Dylan opens the door of his truck, the dog jumps in, taking a seat facing out the front window.

"Looks like the pooch has done this before," Dylan comments as he climbs behind the wheel. "Where to? Clubhouse or your place?"

"My place. They should be on their way back soon and will probably stop there first."

I let the dog off the leash when we get inside, and he starts sniffing around immediately. Doesn't take him long to locate the bowls of water and kibble I left by the back door.

"Beer?" I ask, tossing my keys on the counter and fishing my phone from my pocket. I check the screen as I walk to the fridge, Dylan following me into the kitchen.

"Sure."

"Damn kid sent me another message. At this rate we'll have to upgrade his damn plan. I think he's almost at his allotted texts for the month already." I swipe my thumb on the screen and it opens up to a picture. It takes me a second to register what I'm looking at. "What the actual fuck?"

"What is it?" he asks, looking over my shoulder at

an image of my vehicle in a parking lot. It's blurry, but I can still recognize Luna's blonde curls as someone looks to be forcing her into the dark van parked beside right beside it. "Do you know where that is?"

"It's a clinic in Aztec. The boy's therapist." I manage as cold fear crawls up my spine.

"Have an address?"

"I …no. Luna, she's taken him."

Dylan pulls his own phone out of his pocket. "Jas? It's Luna, she's been…"

It's all I register him saying before all I hear is the blood rushing to my head. I drop the phone on the counter and have to brace myself with my hands on the edge. All I see when I close my eyes are hers, wide open, over a dark hand covering half her face.

Aztec. I have to get to Aztec.

Before I realize what I'm doing, I'm already pulling open the front door, Dylan calling my name behind me.

"Hold up, where the fuck do you think you're going?" A strong arm swings me around. "Running off half-cocked is not gonna do Luna any good. You should be trying to call the kid back, not running off blindly."

Jesus, *Ahiga*.

Shaking off his hold, I stalk back into the kitchen, snatch my phone off the counter, and hit the speed dial for the boy. Five rings, and then the mechanical voicemail message comes on. I hit end and try again—same result.

"Nothing?" I shake my head at Dylan. "Okay, you hang tight here, Jasper is contacting local law enforcement and I'm heading out there. I'll keep you updated." He starts walking out the door and I snatch up my keys and follow him outside.

He's already getting behind the wheel of his truck when I pull the passenger side door open. "Like fuck you are. I'm coming with."

He doesn't argue and tears out of my driveway.

"Jas, you still there? We're on the road."

"Yup. Got the address for the clinic and a ping on both the boy's and Luna's phones for the same location. Sending it to you now." I can hear the ping even as Jasper's voice continues to flood in through the speakers. "Law enforcement is en route and Damian is too, but he's coming from home so you'll probably beat him there."

"Does that mean they're still there? Luna and Ahiga?" I ask, unable to keep the small spark of hope from my voice.

"Well, their phones are, I don't know about them." Jasper is the one who answers. "Ouray, can you shoot over that picture? I'm gonna see if I can get anything on that van."

I do as he asks, and with my phone still in my hand, I dial Kaga's number. He answers right away.

"Chief?"

I quickly explain the situation and tell him to head over to the clubhouse. Until we can figure out what the hell is going on, I need someone I can trust to keep an eye out, but I'd also like to know who the hell is missing. The moment Kaga says, "I'm on it," a little of the weight bearing on my shoulders lifts.

"Good call," Dylan says when I hang up.

I blindly stare out the window as he maneuvers his truck through Durango Saturday traffic. Faster than I thought possible, we leave the town behind us as we race down Highway 550.

Not ten miles south of town, my phone buzzes announcing a message. I look down and notice a number I don't recognize.

"What is it?" Dylan asks, noticing my hesitation.

"A text. Don't know the number."

"Open it." I startle at Jasper's disembodied voice, I'd almost forgotten he was there. "And forward it to me."

***Unknown:* 36.796567 - 107.990820**

Alone

"It's a bunch of fucking numbers." Even as I'm saying it, a photo pops up on my screen. "Jesus…"

"Talk to me," Jasper barks.

I struggle to get air in my lungs. "Both, they… they have them both."

"Shore it up, brother. This no fucking time to lose your shit. Now send those to me."

My hands shake trying to forward the information, while my mind spins out of control. The image of Luna duct-taped to a chair, her head hanging forward, and what's visible of her face and the front of her shirt covered in blood—and the boy sitting wide-eyed beside her on the floor with the barrel of a gun pressed to the back of his head—is indelibly burned into my brain.

A sharp hiss sounds over the hands-free. *"Christ."* I'm sure Jasper just got a glimpse. "She wouldn't have gone down without a fight." There's a soft sound of fingers on a keyboard, before his voice comes back. "The numbers are coordinates. Pulling it up on satellite now. Looks like some kind of container storage along the 550, just south of Aztec. I see about thirty or so containers in a yard east of the highway."

"Salinas," I blurt out, recognizing the description. "It's a container yard almost directly opposite the highway from the Amontinados' compound. It's fuckin' Salinas."

"Any back roads in?" Dylan asks.

"Yup. Take Legion Road east. It should have signs for the Aztec Speedway. Keep following for point nine miles until you hit an unmarked road, turn right—then at point three miles there's a dirt road on the south side leading into the yard. You'll pass a couple of buildings on your left that may provide some cover. The vegetation is not very thick. I'll shoot over images."

"Ouray," Dylan draws my attention away from my phone screen. "Reach behind your seat for a bag. My laptop's in there, I need you to pull up those images for me."

"And just so you know," Jasper brings up, "Damian is about seven minutes behind you. He's got

Blackfoot in the car."

"A little out of his jurisdiction, no?"

"Like he cares—you know how he feels about Luna. Damian picked him up."

In the meantime, I've got Dylan's laptop open on my knees. With my limited computer skills and two-fingered stabs at the keyboard, it takes all of my focus to follow Dylan's instructions. Still, it's a welcome distraction.

It feels better to be doing something.

LUNA

Fuck, that hurts.

I'm keeping my eyes closed and head down, continuing to let them think I'm out of commission.

Oh, I fought the moment I realized what was happening, but a well-aimed fist to my face knocked me out. Pretty sure they broke my fucking nose.

I could feel the van moving when I came to and heard a soft whimpering. Cracking a careful eyelid, I saw Ahiga's huddled shape just a few feet from me. His hands chained to a ring bolted in the floor of the van. I couldn't move. They'd duct-taped my hands behind my back, and my legs were wrapped tight from my ankles to my knees.

There'd been three of them. One in the back of the van with us, I could just see his boots from my peripheral vision. Biker boots. The other two I could hear occasionally talking in the front. I recognized the woman immediately.

Fucking Britney.

The man's voice I couldn't place—he spoke with a heavy Latin accent. The owner of the scuffed black boots stayed silent the short and uncomfortably bumpy ride.

I didn't want to risk letting on that I was awake, even as I was dragged out of the van and into what appears to be a metal container, the sounds bouncing in the confined space. I purposely kept my body limp as they trussed me up like a goddamn Christmas turkey to a straight-backed chair.

The moment I heard footsteps leave and the screech of a metal bar sliding in place, I opened my eyes. Pitch-fucking-dark. Just a tiny slit of light coming from the bottom of the doors. I blinked my eyes a few times, trying to adjust to the dark.

I didn't even realize Ahiga was in there with me until I heard a whimper right after the loud boom of a gunshot reverberated through the metal container. It came from the back of the container, directly behind me, and I tried to form the universal okay sign with my hands tied to the backrest of the chair, hoping he could see. I didn't want to risk making any sound, and he wouldn't have been able to hear me anyway.

It felt like hours, but has probably only been minutes before I hear the metal bar sliding back.

"The boy too."

Britney. I almost growl out loud at the sound of her voice. I've been trying to wrap my head around how she could be involved. I know she conned Paco into lending his truck, so she must've been aware of the robberies, but I didn't think of her as more of a pawn. A jealous bitch, presented with an opportunity to get her pound of flesh. But now I'm not so sure. She appears to have more clout than I would've given her credit for.

There's a sound of something sliding along the floor and a rustle of clothes, when I hear Ahiga whimper closer by.

"Put the gun to his head."

"Better not put me in the fucking picture, you dumb *puta*."

"Call me that again and Daddy will hear. That's not gonna end well for you, Dario. Remember who's in charge here."

Daddy?

I've heard some of the women refer to their men as *daddy*, it's supposed to be a term of endearment, but it just gives me the creeps.

She calls the guy Dario.

The only time I've heard that name in the past month was from Manny Salinas' mouth when he greeted a bunch of his men in the beer tent at the rally in Durango.

Salinas. It makes sense, with the Amontinados based in Aztec, but it all seems a little too convenient. Too obvious. Although I can see bitch Britney hooking up with the slime-bucket and calling him fucking *daddy*. And the guy has an ego the size of a small planet, so he could just be arrogant enough to think he could pull this off.

A bright flash goes off and I try not to flinch.

I may not know why, but I know what they're doing. I'd bet anything that picture is being sent to Ouray right this minute. *Jesus*. He'll be out of his mind, and I'm afraid he'll do whatever it is they ask of him. Including sacrificing himself.

My only hope is to leave my head down, lull them into believing I'm not a threat, and keep my wits about me.

I have to bide my time: I may only have one chance to get us all out of this.

CHAPTER 28

OURAY

"Stay down."

I duck back behind the tree at Dylan's whispered order and crouch down. He's up ahead, hiding behind a large boulder. The terrain doesn't provide much cover, just the occasional ridge or large rock, and some trees that are set a fair bit apart. It doesn't help that the midafternoon sun is beating down on us.

If Dylan hadn't held me back, I would've taken off on a dead run to the grouping of shipping containers I could see at a distance, through the sparse vegetation. As it is, we've been torturously slow in making our way toward them.

We left the truck on the other side of the ridge we just crossed. It was obvious, from the satellite images Jasper sent, we wouldn't be able to just drive up. It's all too fucking exposed.

On the plus side, we can easily keep track of any comings and goings in the container yard. I can see a couple of bikes and the same dark-colored van from the picture Ahiga sent, parked outside a small building on the far side of the yard. Earlier we saw a couple of men go in, but we were too far for me to recognize them, and there hasn't been movement since.

I thought I was in pretty decent condition, but running crouched from cover to cover, or belly-crawling across sections with no cover at all, is taking its toll. Dylan doesn't even appear to be winded.

He turns to face me, his back against the rock and waves me over. Give or take twenty yards and little to cover my ass. *Great.*

My chest is burning when I slide my ass down beside him. I really should quit smoking.

"Damian and Blackfoot are right behind us. We're gonna wait for them to catch up. Anything happens, we're close enough to act."

It's true, from here we're less than the length of a football field from the closest container. Unfortunately, I'm not a fucking receiver and there's zero cover.

"They'll get suspicious if I keep them waiting too long," I point out.

"You forget we were already on our way when you got the text. They won't be expecting you just yet and we can use that to our advantage, but it's a small window so let's be smart about it."

I'm surprised when maybe two minutes later, Keith Blackfoot comes darting from the same tree I was crouched behind. Damian is not far behind.

There's barely room for all four of us behind the damn rock, and I'm getting impatient while they're discussing strategy.

"You guys take any fucking longer, and I'm heading in on my own. My goddamn future is in one of those containers, and you're sitting here calmly discussing risk factors and variables. Can we get a fucking move on?"

"I assume you're armed?" Damian asks, ignoring my outburst.

"Yeah. Ankle holster."

"I assume you can shoot it?" I give him a dirty look. "Good, from here on in that gun is in your hand." I unholster the Glock and get a nod of approval from Damian. "Dylan has an earbud so he leads, you're right behind him. We'll cover you from here. Hoof it to the closest container. You stay right there, Dylan's going to try and get on top for a better vantage point." I look over at the yard where some containers are stacked two high. "Once he's in position, you two cover us. You stay put until Blackfoot and I take up position to cover the yard, and you both get Luna and the boy out."

"We're gonna have to find them first, it could take forever," I point out.

"No it won't," Blackfoot pipes up. "Look for tracks. The ground is sand and light gravel. The container will have evidence of heavier traffic in front."

"We're gonna try to get in and out without any engagement," Damian adds. "So move fast, but quietly."

Two minutes later I'm sucking in air, my back pressed against the ridged metal of the container, waiting for a sign when Dylan is in place. We made it this far undetected.

The moment I see Damian signal, I twist my head around the corner and focus on the building at the far end of the yard.

"*Stand down*," he whispers behind me, just seconds later.

It doesn't take long to find heavier tracks leading to one container. I already have my hand on the vertical bar locking the doors, ready to yank it open when Dylan stops me.

"*Not so fast. These suckers are noisy.*"

Right.

Despite sliding the bar as carefully as I can, it is far from quiet, and I flinch at the sound of metal scraping metal when I hit some resistance.

"*Incoming.*"

Dylan moves fast and pulls me around the other side of the container. I follow, squeezing myself through the narrow space between the containers to the backside. There I almost bump into Dylan who curses under his breath. In the dirt at his feet is the body of a young man I as recently as days ago ripped a new asshole in my office.

Jesus, fuck. Rowtag.

A mix of guilt, anger, and revulsion starts churning my stomach at the sight of a bullet hole right beside his eye and the large pool of blood he's lying in. Dead, quite obviously, as his vacant eyes stare up at the sky. Already flies are starting to buzz around him.

It makes me sick to my stomach to think what we might find inside the container. Are they even alive?

Then I hear it, the sound of a motorcycle approaching and I realize that's what Dylan was referring to. He's looking straight at me, a finger to his lips before pressing it to his earpiece. The sound of the engine dies suddenly. Then I hear someone say, "What the fuck is this?" before the loud slam of a door.

"Quick, quick," Dylan suddenly says, pushing me back into the narrow passage. "Get them out. Now."

He heads two containers down where he has a better view of the yard, while I unlock the doors, wincing at the noise I'm making. I've barely slipped inside, blinking against the dark, when I hear yelling followed by gunshots.

LUNA

I'm not sure how long we've been here.

Sweat is streaming down my face, stinging my eyes, from my efforts to loosen my binds. With the backs of my wrists strapped together, and my upper arms taped to the back of the chair, I have zero play. My shoulders already feel like they're being pulled from the sockets. My legs aren't much better. They're taped together and my ankles are secured to the first rung, leaving my feet inches off of the floor. I can't even fucking move myself closer to Ahiga, who I can occasionally hear moving behind me. I've thought about toppling the chair, but the way I'm trussed up, it won't gain me a thing. I'll just be more vulnerable.

I freeze when I pick up a rustling against the outside of the container, and my eyes immediately drop to the bottom of the doors, where a shadow interrupts the narrow strip of light. There's someone outside.

I wait with bated breath, trying to prepare for whoever or whatever is going to be coming in. A sliding sound, metal against metal, as someone seems to be taking great care opening the doors. And then it stops. More brushing, this time along the other side of the container, and I swear I can hear a whispered voice.

Hope blossoms in my chest, and I'm so focused on the small sounds outside the container, I almost miss the sound of an approaching motorcycle. Someone yells in the distance, a door slams, and then I can hear it loudly—right outside. "Quick, quick." I almost sob out loud at the sound of Dylan's voice.

Moments later the doors open, and a shape I would recognize in my sleep squeezes through the gap. But before I can make a sound, mayhem breaks loose outside.

"Hurry," I call out, and familiar hands find me.

"Can't see a fucking thing," Ouray grumbles.

"Flashlight on your cell phone."

"Shit. Hang on."

The light that suddenly floods the enclosed space is almost blinding.

"Oh fuck, Sprite," he mumbles dropping his phone on the ground and sinking on his knees before me. I'm so relieved to see his beautiful blue eyes, but it's short-lived, as another burst of gunfire sounds outside, the sharp ping of bullets hitting metal close by.

"Ahiga first," I urge him, when he pulls a folding knife out of his pocket and starts cutting at the tape. "Get the boy first." I can hear him behind me, talking softly to the boy, even though Ahiga can't hear him. "Is he okay?"

"He's fine. Aren't you, kid? You're a tough cookie."

More shots ring out, and this time I hear a yelp. Then the doors open wide and Manny Salinas stumbles inside clutching his leg, Britney right behind him.

"Stay right the fuck there!"

OURAY

I barely notice Britney, my gun is trained on fucking

Salinas as I step around Luna. He may be injured, but I know that won't do much to stop him.

He's using both his hands to put pressure on a wound that appears to be bleeding profusely, but that doesn't mean he doesn't have a gun in the back of his belt or strapped to his ankle.

"What the fuck is going on here?" He looks around confused, and I'm almost buying into it. Instead I step closer and press the gun to his head. "Are you out of your fucking mind?"

"Ouray!" Luna cries out and I swing my head around.

I was so focused on Manny, I didn't notice Britney moving. She already has her gun trained, pressed up against the side of Luna's head.

"Easy now," I caution, catching Luna's eyes, who is sending me a clear message.

Before her chair even hits the floor, I have my gun trained on Britney and pull the trigger. The next moment it's back on Manny, who is sitting there with his mouth wide open, his eyes trained on the crumpled form on the ground.

"I should fucking finish you too, you killed my cub."

"Jesus!" I look up to see Wheels standing right outside the container, Blackfoot right behind him. Manny moves when I'm momentarily distracted, knocking the gun from my hand. Even as I scramble to pick it up, I see Manny reach behind his back.

"Not gonna go down for something I didn't do, let

alone fucking understand!" he yells, as he points his weapon at me, at the same time my hand finds mine and raises it up.

"Wait," I hear Luna call out. "Please. Ahiga says Manny's not the man."

"Fucking right I'm not."

"Bullshit," this from Wheels, who I just now notice, is cuffed. "Salinas has had it in for you for fucking years."

"Hear the boy out," Luna urges and I turn to him.

Rowtag grabbed me when I ran out of the doctor's office to help Luna, but I almost got away. Then that man came and helped him drag me into the van.

Ahiga's finger is pointing straight at Wheels.

CHAPTER 29

LUNA

Wheels?

Out of all the possible suspects, he would've been at the very bottom of my list. His involvement messes up every possible scenario I'd considered. Yet, the look on his face when Ahiga stabbed an accusatory finger in his direction, easily confirmed it.

It's doing my head in trying to find the connective tissue between Britney and him. And Rowtag, how the hell did he get involved? Salinas, who I had at the top of my list, may not have been involved at all—or maybe he was in cahoots with Wheels?

My head is starting to hurt with the effort, but I can't seem to stop churning the puzzle pieces in my mind.

I'm in the back of an ambulance, on my way to San Juan Medical Center in Farmington, involuntarily

I might add. There's so much information to sort out, so many people to question—I should still be back at the scene.

"Jesus Christ, I'm fine," I announce for the third or fourth time. Of course it doesn't help my case that I sound like Gilbert Gottfried with a cold.

I try to sit up, but Ouray pushes me back down on the stretcher.

"Good, then this won't take long," he snaps. "You've got a cut the size of small fucking crater on your face, and your nose is pointing north when we're heading west."

I try to snort, but it sounds more like a steam whistle. Okay, so my face is a mess, but I hate not being there to finish the job I started. Especially with Dylan out of commission as well. He took a hit in the shoulder and was bleeding substantially. Damian was looking after him, and Keith had been busy taking down Wheels, which is why Britney was able to shove Salinas into the container. He claims she's the one who shot him.

Like the fucking O.K. Corral, bodies everywhere.

Despite probably having sold me out, I'm sad Rowtag lost his much too young life. He certainly was not the mastermind, and was probably an easy target to manipulate.

Britney was alive, lucky bitch. Her injuries were relatively minor, a good gouge just above her ear, apparently enough to knock her down. Dylan turned out to look the most serious and was airlifted to Durango, but the rest of us are on our way to Farmington by ambulance.

"Is Ahiga okay?"

"He's twelve years old, riding up front in an ambulance with lights going, what do you think?" he answers, a smirk on his face.

"Do you have your phone?"

I'm sitting on the edge of the hospital bed, waiting for the nurse to come back with some painkillers, should I need them. Ouray is pacing back and forth in front of the small window, like a caged animal.

"Yeah, why?"

"Because mine is still somewhere in the parking lot at the clinic, along with your ride, or in police custody, and I need to talk to Damian before I head in to question Britney."

"Not sure that's a good idea," Ouray grumbles. He looks as out of place in the clinical setting as I feel.

"My nose is set, the cut's stitched up, and both she and Manny are here. It's not like I have to go out of my way."

"Kaga's already here. He's in the waiting room with the boy, ready to take us home."

"I can't go home, Ouray. I still have a job to do."

His lips press together and he stares at the floor, taking in a deep breath that make his nostrils flare. My man is not happy.

"Fine," he bites off. "Don't mind me. I'll take the boy home. Here's the phone." He pulls it from his pocket and tosses it on the bed next to me before walking to the door.

"Wait." He stops with his back turned, hand on the doorknob. "Don't be like this, Ouray." That has him swing around to face me and the wrecked expression on his face is a shock.

"Be like this? Like what? Thought I lost you, Luna. Thought I lost the boy. My heart hasn't stopped squeezing yet, and all I can think about is gettin' you both home so I can fuckin' breathe again. But like you said, you got a job to do. Go do it."

This time he's out the door before I can respond, and I can feel my own heart squeeze.

"Ms. Roosberg?" The friendly young nurse walks in, holding a small bag. "Dr. Evans suggests to take as needed. I put a card in there with your follow-up appointment for next Friday."

I manage to nod and take the bag from her hand. She's already halfway down the hallway before I can get words from my mouth. "Two gunshot wounds were brought in around the same time I came in. Would you happen to know where I can find them?" The look on her face is one of suspicion, so I quickly clarify. "FBI, I'm Special Agent Luna Roosberg."

"Let me direct you to my supervisor."

It takes me twenty minutes and a phone call to Damian—who is able to get word to the officers guarding her at the hospital—to get me in to see

Britney.

Her wrists are strapped to the bed and she already looks fit to be tied. She becomes irate, struggling against her binds when I walk in.

"You!"

"Yes, it's me."

"I should've pulled the trigger when I could," she spits out.

"Probably." I stay calm, just shrugging my shoulders as I pull up a stool. I know I'm likely adding fuel to her fire by pretending to be unaffected, that's the idea. Angry people tend to say more than they intend to, which would serve me well.

"This is all on you. I had Ouray by the balls, it was just a matter of time for me to get that ring on my finger. That pimpled kid was an easy target, he caved at the first taste of my pussy and the promise of a patch. It would've been the perfect setup. And after all that work I put in—you show up—wrecking it all!" She screeches the last.

"Everything all right in here?" I turn to find the policeman standing guard outside poking his head in.

"Just ducky," I smile at him before swinging back around. "Sorry for the interruption." I lay it on thick to poke her some more. "You were saying?"

"Fuck off, you androgynous bitch." I raise one eyebrow, but otherwise keep my face blank.

"You were just explaining how you planned to fuck your way into Arrow's Edge, and I saw evidence of that with my own eyes." I feign a full body shiver.

"But I wonder; does your daddy know your favorite pastime is getting gang-banged on the pool table?"

I'm fishing, but luckily she bites. "He don't care, as long as the job gets done."

"You sound perfect for each other."

"Apple doesn't fall far from the tree," she snarls. "I do my daddy proud."

—

"She's what?"

I'm in the hospital cafeteria, scarfing down a stale bagel and some weak coffee to get something in my stomach, talking to Damian. Outside it's getting dark, and I haven't had a thing since breakfast, which seems like days ago.

"She's Wheels's daughter," I repeat, my mouth full.

"You're kidding me. How did we not catch that?"

"Probably not listed on her birth certificate. I don't know. She did say her 'daddy' always looked after her, so I assume he knew. Although what kind of father would order his daughter to whore herself out, I don't know."

"Any clues as to motive?"

"She mentioned something about merging clubs to control the region. Apparently she's been a busy girl, Salinas admitted he'd been banging her off and on until she started fishing for something permanent. Then he got cold feet."

"So you talked to him already."

"Yeah. I'm not a big fan of the guy, but I believe he had no clue what he was stepping into. He was surprised when she called out of the blue after disappearing, and told him she was in trouble, hiding out in a container across from his compound. He seems to think the objective was to lure both him and Ouray there and make it look like they took each other out, leaving both their clubs vulnerable."

"Did Salinas know one of his guys was part of the plot?"

"Nope. That was a shocker. I think they'd hoped to maybe get Paco on board as well, but his loyalty to Ouray is strong. Guess poor Rowtag was next, and a much easier target, although I'm not so sure Daddy Wheels was happy with that choice. I think maybe you should come in and question both of them, get some clearer answers, I'm not at my best."

"Right. You're hurt. Shit, I already got an earful from Blackfoot when I told him you seemed to be back in the saddle. I should be there shortly. I'm just finishing up with local law enforcement here. Why don't you go home?"

Go home. That'd be funny if it wasn't so sad.

I suddenly don't know where home is, and even if I did, I have no fucking way to get there.

OURAY

I walked out, a fire burning in my gut, and had every intention of taking the boy and heading back to Durango. If not for Kaga's suggestion we pick up the Traverse and leave it in the hospital parking lot for Luna, I would've been home already.

What changed my mind was the scent of her shampoo. A trace of it lingered inside the SUV, reminding me of this morning, when she stood in the door opening, her hair still wet from her shower, telling me she loves me.

That's not something you walk away from easily. That's something you fight for.

So I've sat here for the past hour and a half, in the parking lot of the hospital, with my eyes on the main doors, waiting for her to come outside. Unfortunately, without a phone. I gave mine to her, and hers was shoved in the purse that was left by police on the passenger seat, with a broken screen. I can't get the damn thing to work, and I don't want to risk missing her if I walk in there and start looking. So I sit and wait.

The moment I see her walking out, her shoulders slumped as she takes a seat on the bench right outside the entrance, I get out from behind the wheel. She must've heard the car door slam, because her head snaps to and she jumps up as soon as she spots me.

God she looks a mess, the nose splint they fitted her with looks ridiculously large on her small face, and dark bruising surrounds the cut on the bridge of her nose and around her eyes. But the eyes themselves are beautiful as ever, blue and shimmering like orbs of polished glass in her battered face.

She starts walking toward me and doesn't stop until her cheek is pressed against my chest, and her arms around my waist.

"I'm sorry," I mumble in her hair when I can feel her shoulders shaking.

"That's my line," she counters between sniffles. "I should've come after you. Explained."

"I shouldn't've walked out like that." I lift her chin with a finger and look into her now red-rimmed eyes. "Is it gonna hurt if I kiss you?"

Her mouth twitches. "Don't care if it does."

I'm gentle, or as gentle as I can remember to be, pulling away much faster than I want to. "Ready to come home or is there somewhere else you need to be first?" I'm a little confused when her eyes well up again.

"Home. I was just thinking I wasn't sure where that would be."

"Wherever you want, as long as it's with me."

With her lips pressed together she nods.

We're just walking to the SUV when a black Expedition pulls in, Damian behind the wheel.

"Taking her home?" he says to me, when he gets out of the car.

"Planning to."

"I'm right here, guys," Luna pipes up before peeking inside Damian's vehicle. "Where'd you leave Keith?"

"He's driving Dylan's truck back to Durango. I just got a call from Jasper, who's at Mercy. Dylan's out of surgery. The bullet did some damage to his shoulder, but they were able to patch it up and he should recover with some rehab."

"Shit. He'll be pissed he's benched."

"I've already put a call in to James. He's sending us a couple of his guys on loan since you'll both be out for a bit."

I feel Luna's shoulders snap back. "Me? Why would I be out? It's just my nose."

"Bureau rules, Roosberg, you know that. Only reason I let you follow up with Salinas and the woman is because this is your case, and I didn't have anyone else at the ready. You'll need medical clearance, which won't be until your follow-up appointment at best, and then it still has to be approved by HQ before I can put you back on rotation."

"Can I at least sit in on questioning?"

"Busting my balls here, Roosberg. How about listening in? It's the best I can do."

I have to bite my lip when she huffs dramatically at his suggestion.

"We should be off. There are a few people at the clubhouse I'm sure are eager to see you," I prompt her.

"Oh my God, Ahiga, how's he doing?"

"He should be fine, probably being pampered by Momma."

"On that note, I should get inside and see if I can

pry some more information loose from Daddy's little girl."

I let go of Luna and stick out my hand at Damian. The moment his palm hits mine, I pull him in for a one-armed hug. "Thanks for looking out for my girl, brother."

"Hey, she's ours too." He winks and, with a soft fist-tap to Luna's chin, walks into the hospital.

"What was that Daddy's little girl business?" I ask Luna, once we pull out on the road.

"Not sure if I should be telling you this when you're driving, but the daddy Britney was talking about is actually her father—Wheels."

"No fucking way."

"Oh yeah. It's a tangled web and we've not even gotten to the bottom of it, but let's save that for tomorrow. I need to get something off my chest first."

I reach over and take her hand in mine, slipping my fingers between hers and giving it a little squeeze. "Shoot."

"I want you to understand that my job has been the most important thing in my life since I joined the Bureau. Bar none."

"There's no need to—"

"Just let me get this out, okay?" she asks and I nod.

"But that wasn't the reason I was so focused on

it. I wanted to see this assignment through to the end as soon as possible, so that when I pack up my house and move in with you, you'll know you're my only motivation."

It's probably illegal, and the car behind me doesn't appear to appreciate it, but I pull off the road onto the shoulder, so I can properly kiss my old lady.

Ahiga abandons his PlayStation game the instant he spots Luna and barrels into her so hard, I have to brace her from behind.

"I'm okay, sweetheart," she automatically mumbles into his freshly washed hair. It doesn't seem to matter, he's not able to hear a word.

The clean hair is probably Momma's doing, she is standing in the door opening to the kitchen, dabbing at her eyes with a tea towel. I step away when I notice Kaga nudging his head to the office.

"Everything okay here?"

"Here, yes," he says with a grin. "At your house, not so much."

It takes me a minute before I realize what he's talking about.

"*Fuck*, the dog."

"Yeah man, I knew you were going to pick him up this morning, so I went to check right after I got back here with the boy. Figured you'd want to keep that a surprise. Shit, man, and I mean that literally:

shit all over the place. Took me fuckin' half an hour to clean that up. You're lucky you have tile and wood flooring, cleaning up carpet would've been a bitch. Which reminds me, you're out of paper towels."

"Thanks, brother."

"You'll owe me—I'm good with that," he grins. "He's walked, has fresh water, and I dumped some more of that food in his bowl, but I suggest not leaving him alone for too long."

Twenty minutes later, I open my front door and shove Ahiga ahead of me. The sound of galloping footsteps greets us, and the boy freezes in front of me as the big dog slides to a halt at his feet.

A soft "oh" comes from Luna, who is peeking around me to see what the holdup is.

I didn't know you had a dog, he says, when I step around him to help with introductions.

He's not mine, he's yours.

Fucking kills to see the disbelief on the kid's face morph into tears. *Goddammit*. Now I'm swallowing down a lump as I watch him drop to his knees and wrap his arms around the big mutt's neck, and turns his face to me.

"Taank-yew"

CHAPTER 30

LUNA

"Jack!"

I'm already five minutes late meeting Ouray at the clubhouse.

Standing in the back door, I can see the damn dog sit on a rock he seems to have claimed as his perch, overlooking the lake below, but he doesn't even acknowledge me. Maybe he needs more time to get used to the name the boy picked for him.

He knows how to listen to Ouray when he whistles on his fingers—a piercing sound that hurts my ears—and after practicing, for maybe an hour, Ahiga mastered the skill as well. I'm the only person in this household who cannot seem to do more than spray spit all over my hand.

I turn to Ahiga, who is shoveling down some cereal. *Can you call him? He's back on the rock.*

We've had him for just a week, but already he's made his preferences clear. Ahiga, then Ouray, and way at the bottom of his priority list is yours truly.

Ouray told Ahiga if he wants the dog, he's to feed it and clean up after it, which he's done so far. I hope it lasts once the newness wears off.

This whole sitting on a rock business started on Monday, when Ouray decided Jack didn't have to be put on a leash back here. There isn't any fencing, and I was worried the dog would run off, but Ouray was convinced he'd come back. He sniffed around, peed on a few blades of grass, and sat on that damn rock for an hour and a half before he came back to the house.

I flinch at the sharp sound of the boy's whistle, and immediately Jack comes trotting to the house.

Did you pack his food like I asked?

In my backpack.

Good, grab your stuff, and don't forget Jack's leash. We're late.

Today we're moving my stuff. There's really no rush, because I paid up to the end of October, but with a busy month ahead, it makes sense just to get it over with. Both Ouray and I received our all-clear so he can drive, and I hope to be back on the schedule as of Monday.

I was able to stand in the small viewing room at the police station while Damian and Keith questioned both Wheels and Dario, neither of whom were particularly forthcoming. Unfortunately, Britney hadn't been released from the hospital yet, there were some complications with an infection she incurred in the hospital and she's only now turning a corner. Damian says he hadn't been able to get much more from her than I had that first night, so we've all been waiting to put the thumbscrews on her.

Jill's husband, Hanshaw, was questioned as well, and he'd been able to offer some information on a possible motive, albeit under duress. He mentioned a meeting he'd accompanied Wheels to late July, in Corpus Christi in Texas. He'd met with a couple of 'businessmen' looking for protection for the transport of stolen arms through the Rockies.

The old man had been gung-ho—the money offered hard to refuse—but the organization wanted him to guarantee or force an alliance with other MCs on the route to ensure safe passage. It was clear that would be a problem.

Wheels returned to Shiprock and put the proposal on the table, but with the potential for violence between the historically friendly MCs—something few had the stomach for—the club voted him down. Hanshaw thought that would be the end of it.

Apparently not for Wheels.

Ouray is waiting outside when I drive up to the clubhouse. I've barely stopped and Ahiga is already out of the vehicle, Jack on his heels. Ouray ruffles the boy's hair when he passes him and disappears into the clubhouse.

"Move over," he says stalking up to the driver's side.

"Seriously? You can't even let me drive to my place? It's five minutes down the road."

"Spent almost two weeks being chauffeured around and it was torture. I'm driving."

I roll my eyes at the dramatics, but move over anyway. "Where are the guys?" A couple of the brothers had offered to help.

"At your place moving the big furniture outside."

"What? Already? I haven't even gone through my—"

"Sprite," he cuts me off, as he steers the Traverse onto the road. "They're not doing anything to your stuff. They're making you a staging area so it's easier to sort through."

I beg to differ, but I keep my mouth shut. After all, the guys are giving up their Saturday morning to help.

Sure enough, Kaga, Wapi, and Honon are toting what furniture I have out of the house when we come up my driveway.

"Whatever you don't want, one of the guys will drop off to the Salvation Army. The rest we'll load up and take to the other house. Then we go inside and tackle the small stuff."

I'm immediately overwhelmed. Having to pick and choose what stays and what goes suddenly seems more than I can handle. "I can't decide," I mumble.

Ironic, because if you'd asked me to describe the furniture in my place, I would've drawn a blank on at least half of it. But standing in front of it, I realize even that ugly dresser I picked up from a yard sale years back would be hard to let go of. These things…are the constant in my life. The reliable. The walls may have changed regularly, but my not exactly appealing furnishings have turned every new place into mine.

I hadn't realized agreeing to move in with Ouray wasn't really the risk—letting go of my stuff is.

"Look," Ouray says softly so only I can hear. "You don't have to decide now or even at all. There's room in the garage, and I bet we can get most of this in there and still have room for the bike and the Traverse in the winter. You can take your time."

I slip my arm around his waist and give it a squeeze. He's right, I don't have to make any decisions. But holding on to my security blanket of stuff like some kind of contingency plan, in case things don't work out, is not the message I want to send to a man who just now proves again he is very much worth it.

"The dresser can go," I point to the ugly thing. "The couch, it's almost falling apart and I like yours better." As I'm listing the things I can absolutely do without, the guys load them in Ouray's old pickup, while he moves behind me, his strong body at my back and his chin coming to rest on the top of my head.

It takes all of five minutes to reduce the pile to a few manageable pieces I actually like.

"Do you think we should keep my queen to replace the boy's twin-size?" I ask Ouray, tilting my head back.

He looks down at my face with a smile before

dropping a kiss on my nose. "He'll probably grow into it soon enough."

"Right. Guys? We're keeping the bed."

When one o'clock comes around, I pull the door to my cottage closed.

Wapi has done the drop off at the thrift store, the rest of my things have been carted to their new home, and this place is spic and span, ready for the next tenant.

"Ready to see what Momma has for lunch? Or do you want to get started on those boxes waiting for you?"

"Lunch first, pick up boy and dog, and then take us home."

"Good plan." Ouray throws me a wink before starting the engine.

As we drive away from my little house on the hill, I don't even look back once.

OURAY

"He was in love with her."

Every head turns in Wapi's direction.

I invited the cubs in for this powwow in my office and the room is packed. The meeting was two-fold. First of all to welcome Paco back into the fold—he was released earlier this week—and because I needed to clear the air. I still feel guilt over not being straight with my brothers—with the exception of Kaga—and feel responsibility for Rowtag's death.

I spelled it out in detail, the how and why of events leading up to and including the scene last week in Aztec, and the reactions are mixed. Yuma in particular seems angry, and I make a note to take him aside after.

I just described finding Rowtag dead behind the container where Luna and the boy were being held, when Wapi speaks up.

"With Britney," Paco confirms, his face haggard. It hadn't been easy for him to hear the truth about the woman he'd been carrying a torch for.

Wapi shoots a guilty glance at him. "Yes. He didn't care she was way older. Said she was showing him a whole new world. I thought at first he was talking about…well…sex, but then he mentioned doing a few 'jobs' for her and boasted about something big in the works. I never got what he was on about."

"Why'd you keep that to yourself?" Paco asks.

"I just thought it was Rowtag being Rowtag. He was always showing off and talking big. It wasn't until after your woman," he nods at me, "had her brakes messed with that I got worried. He never liked her, but was even more pissed at her after she had the accident. I asked him point-blank what crawled up his ass, and he admitted Britney had asked him to 'take care of the bitch' but she hadn't been happy with the results. After that I tried to warn her he was up to something."

"But you never brought it up with me, or with any one of your elders," I point out and he hangs his head.

"No. I thought maybe he'd snap out of it. The club was all the family he had, like it is for me. I was afraid he'd get tossed out, and maybe even me."

I look around at my brothers, trying to gauge the mood, but having a hard time of it. Some sport a damn good poker face.

Right. Time to put it in their hands, it's the only way.

I nod at Kaga, who's the only person who is prepared.

"You're gonna have to come with me, Wapi. Looks like we'll both be on the chopping block today." When he looks up at me confused, I clarify, "You and me, we need to earn back their trust. Come on, we'll grab a beer."

I sling an arm over the kid's shoulders and walk out, closing the door behind me. We're not even halfway down the hall when he suddenly dives into the bathroom, puking up his guts.

"Everything all right?" Luna asks, jumping up from the couch.

"What are you doing here? I thought you were unpacking boxes?"

"Momma called. Said something was up and you might need me here."

I throw a scowl at Momma, who is leaning unapologetically in the kitchen doorway, her arms crossed over her chest. "Had to be done, and you know it," I tell her.

"May well be. Still don't mean you've gotta take what's comin' on yer own."

"Okay, what are you two talking about? And what's wrong with Wapi?"

"I'll take care of the boy," Momma announces. "You two talk. I put your smokes on the bar."

Smartass. I've been trying to quit since I got knocked over the head. Without much success I have to admit, but at least I'm limiting my smoking to the clubhouse. No longer at the house.

I grab Luna's hand, snatch my pack up with the other, and head outside for the picnic table, where I light one up.

"I'm waiting," Luna says, bulging her eyes when I look at her.

"The brothers are deciding on Wapi's and my future with the club."

"Wait. What? Why?"

"The cub knew something was up with Rowtag and didn't share. As for me, I haven't been straight with them. Trust is our strongest bond, and not only have I betrayed their trust in me, I doubted my trust in them. Up to the brothers to decide how to move on from there."

"Could they kick you out altogether?"

"It's possible," I confirm, taking a long drag.

"But the club is your life—"

"Was. For thirty-two years. It's the only real family I've known until now. Now I have a boy, a dog, and my dream woman waiting at home."

"Who is she?" Luna teases with a smirk on her face.

I tag her behind the neck and touch my nose to hers.

"Love you, Special Agent Luna Roosberg."

"Love you right back, Mr. Mark Strongbow."

Then I kiss the sass right out of her.

—

Two fucking hours.

Luna just left to go check on Ahiga. She didn't want to leave him alone too long with just Jack for company at the house.

I saunter into the clubhouse, in search of another beer. I already had three. This takes any longer and I'm diving into the hard liquor.

Wapi is sitting on the couch, trying to distract himself with some action movie on TV, but every two seconds his eyes flit to the hallway at the back.

"Ready for a beer, cub?" I ask, but he shakes his head. He's still looking a little green around the gills.

I didn't think it was going to take hours. I can't imagine what they'd be discussing all this fucking time. Looking for distraction myself, I plop down on the couch next to the kid.

Ten minutes later, I can hear the office door open. Momma and Nosh must've been lying in wait as well, because both their heads pop out of the kitchen. Kaga comes walking toward us, a stern look on his face.

"You ready?"

That's enough to have Wapi running for the can again. While we wait for him, I try to read Kaga's expression but it tells me nothing.

Smoke billows out of my office when Kaga opens the door. The fuckers know better than to light up inside. Momma's going to have their hide.

"Probation for the cub," Kaga announces from behind my desk. That doesn't exactly bode well. "An additional six months, tacked on to the year he has left to go, before he's eligible to be patched in." The kid looks like he's about to cry. Hope he sucks it up, because that alone could have the brothers change their minds. "As for Chief, the vote was unanimous."

I wait for him to tell me the fucking verdict but he stays silent. Then Honon starts heading for the door, putting his hand on my shoulder in passing. "Chief." Next is Yuma, then Lusio, Nodin, as one by one my brothers file out the door, clapping my shoulder and calling me, "Chief."

Last is Kaga. "Chief," he says to me, a big grin on his face.

"Took you fucking long enough," I grumble, to hide the fact I'm moved by the gesture.

"Nah," he says, still smiling. "We were pretty much decided before you closed the damn door behind ya. Thought we'd make you sweat a little. Oh, and by the way, you need a better deck of cards and you're out of good scotch." His laughter follows him out of the office.

Bastards left my office trashed.

CHAPTER 31

LUNA

"Are you sure you want me to come?"

Ouray lifts his head from the sink where he's just spitting out a mouthful of toothpaste. He looks at me in the mirror.

"To Monticello? Of course you're coming." He says it so matter-of-factly, so confidently, I find myself nodding automatically.

"Okay."

But when I back out of the bathroom, my stomach is still in knots. I don't know why I got cold feet all of a sudden, but as I was putting on what I consider to be respectable clothes, I started worrying that maybe we wouldn't be coming home with Ahiga.

"Luna?" Ouray walks out behind me and stops me at the top of the stairs. "It'll be all

right," he says, his large hands tilting my face up.

"I promise."

Suddenly the tears are right there, threatening to fall, and I blink furiously to force them back. Ahiga is getting dressed and could walk out of his room any minute. He doesn't need to see me crying, he's nervous enough as it is.

"How can you be so sure?"

"Because I've never had to leave a kid behind, because I have a kick-ass lawyer—who is very good at what he does—and because with you there, my odds are better than they ever were." I roll my eyes at the last, but I do it smiling.

When Ahiga comes out of his room, I have myself well in control and slip from Ouray's arms.

Hungry? Ouray says he'll buy us breakfast at Durango Doughworks on the way. That gets me a raised eyebrow from Ouray—who never promised any such thing—but also a big grin and a thumbs-up from the boy. I call that a win.

An hour later, the dog is dropped off with Nosh, the box of donuts and the coffee from Doughworks are about done, and we're almost halfway to Monticello.

"There's something I've been wanting to talk to you about, but…well, shit just kept happening."

I look at him suspiciously. "What?"

"I spoke to Blackfoot, after you told me what happened to you." My head automatically turns to check on Ahiga, who is quietly playing on his phone, which he'd been happy to have returned to him. "He can't hear us, Sprite," Ouray says quietly, putting a hand on my knee, which I immediately brush aside.

"What gave you the right to—"

"Hear me out. You can be pissed all you want after but hear me out. When you told me, I felt both furious and helpless. I'm not sure why I called Blackfoot, but I needed to do something. I know you haven't talked to him about the incident since it happened, so you can't know that he got hold of Superman that same night and damaged him good."

That has me stumped. "Why wouldn't he have told me that?"

"I'm guessing he didn't want to open up any wounds. It really doesn't matter, because although that may have been about what was done to you, it was mostly about him feeling helpless and needing to find some justice."

"Did he know him? Keith? Did he know the guy?"

Funny, I've had the means and the resources to pursue this for many years now, but it was just easier to think of them as Superman and Freddy. More abstract and distant than an actual flesh and bone person with a name. Now I'm suddenly morbidly curious to find out.

"He didn't but he found out. It never let him go, Sprite, walking away from that. So he did some digging and found out Superman was a fullback with the college football team. His real name was Kyle Topping."

I've never heard of that name. Not that I hung out with the jocks or cheerleaders in college. I was a loner. "Wait, you said *was*. Does that mean?"

Ouray glances over and nods. "He died in 2006 of a brain tumor."

"Oh." I feel a little deflated. I'm not sure what I would've done with the information had he still been alive, but kicking at his gravestone isn't going to do me any good. "And the other one?"

"Blackfoot was able to give me a few possible names. I managed to pare it down to one: Skip Chafin."

That name sparks something. "I think I heard that name before."

"Could well be. He was Kyle Topping's teammate, and it turns out he was also a student advisor in your residence hall."

A picture pops up of a handsome boy who helped me find my room my first day at college. Athletic build, brown hair, a shy smile I remember being taken with as he carried my suitcase up to my floor. *Holy shit.*

"I remember him. I never would've thought...I mean, he never would've occurred to me."

Ouray's hand reaches out for my leg again, and this time I tuck my palm under it and slip my fingers between his.

"You're not mad?"

I think about that for a minute. I was, but now I don't even know what I'm feeling. "I don't think so." That makes him chuckle softly. "I'm going to have to process this."

"Well, I suggest you process fast, because I found

out where Skip Chafin lives."

"Where?" I ask the question, but the butterflies starting a riot in my stomach are evidence I already know the answer.

"He's in Monticello, Sprite. It's your call."

My first reaction is regret I didn't bring my weapon with me. I didn't think it would be an appropriate addition to the respectable impression I was hoping to make. I'm not at all feeling respectable now. Ouray stays quiet while I process every emotion imaginable.

What do I want to do with the information? It's not like I can—or even want to at this point—report the son of a bitch. Statute of limitations has long run out.

Exacting some revenge sounds appealing, but I've already let these men take so much of my life, do I really want to risk giving them more? I have too much to live for now.

I turn to check on Ahiga, who is still totally engrossed in whatever game he's playing on his phone, before I look at Ouray.

"What does he do?"

"He's a lawyer. A private family law practice."

The laugh, semi-hysterical, bursts from my lips without warning, and it takes me a minute to reel it in. "Married?"

"Are you sure you want to do this?" Ouray asks, throwing me a concerned look.

"Yes."

"Okay. Yes, he's married."

He would be. I may not have been sure what I was feeling earlier, but I'm pretty convinced this is anger.

"I want to look him in the eye," I announce, twisting in my seat as Ouray pulls in the parking lot outside the Child Services offices. "Skip Chafin—I want to look that rapist in the eye."

A strangled sound comes from the back seat, and the next moment the back door is open, and Ahiga is running full speed across the parking lot, about to disappear around the side of the building.

OURAY

Before I know what the fuck is going on, I'm alone in the vehicle. Luna running like the wind after Ahiga, who suddenly darted from the car. No fucking way I'll keep up with those two.

I reach over to pull Luna's door shut and then half climb into the back seat to do the same with Ahiga's door. As I'm climbing back behind the wheel, I notice his cell phone on the floor behind Luna's seat and snag it.

The screen is open on his speech-to-text app, displaying Luna's last words.

No fucking way.

I tear out of the parking lot, hoping I can intercept the boy before he goes to ground and we never find him again. Turning left behind the Child Services office, I scan up ahead and spot Luna diving through a hedge a block over. I drive by the spot and am able to see a park on the other side of the hedge. Whipping around the next right turn, I keep my fingers crossed I don't run into a cop.

They're sports fields, aside from a children's playground, the grounds are wide open, and I can see Luna catching up on the boy in the outfield of the baseball diamond. I turn into the far parking lot, slam the Traverse in park, and take off running myself.

By the time I catch up with them—out of breath—both are rolling on the grass. Luna is on her back, her limbs wrapped around the boy, who is grunting and struggling to escape.

"Ahiga!" I yell his name, but it doesn't register. "Luna, I'm gonna take him from you."

I ignore the punches and kicks he throws and manage to wrangle him off Luna. Sitting my ass on the grass, I pull his back against mine, wrap my arms around him, pinning his to his side, and trapping his legs under mine.

"Honey," Luna coos, now on hands and knees in front of him, trying to get his attention.

"He was listening in," I explain. "Had that app open on his phone. Something you said triggered him."

Surprise and then shock pales her face, but she holds it together and takes his face in her hands, forcing him to look at her. "Baby, you need to listen to me. Ahiga, settle down." She lets go of his face and starts signing furiously.

I was raped many years ago when I was in college. He starts shaking his head forcefully. She counters him by nodding. *Yes. I never knew who he was, but Ouray found him.*

"Meee..."

"No, honey," she sighs, dropping her hands to her lap.

Ahiga squirms in my arms, trying to pull his hands free. "Okay, buddy," I mumble next to his ear, releasing my hold just enough so he can slip them out.

Don't make me go back there. I can't go back there. Immediately his hands start repeating that sentence over and over again.

We would never send you back—never.

"Ask him if he knows that name, Luna," I urge her gently. Her eyes fly up to mine, almost pleading.

"But that's crazy. That's..."

"I know it is, baby—ask him anyway."

Her fingers shaking, she carefully forms the letters. *S k i p C h a f i n, do you know who that is?*

He nods his head.

It's him—my foster father.

—

It had taken a bit for Luna to convince Ahiga to get in the SUV with us. She had to promise she wouldn't go knock on Chafin's door today. Not yet. Not without Ahiga's permission.

Of course we were late for our appointment, but the counselor was able to see us anyway.

Two hours later, we walk out with all the necessary paperwork signed. For a moment it looked like the boy was going to bolt again when the subject of Skip Chafin came up, but when the counselor told us there had been several complaints and the man was now under investigation, he calmed down.

Luna is quiet and I occasionally throw a glance in her direction as I navigate my way back onto the road home. It's already been an exhausting day, and we're only halfway through.

"Tired?" I ask her, looking for her hand in her lap.

"I am, and kinda numb. That was a lot to take in."

"Sure as fuck was. I still can't get my head around it. The universe has a sick sense of humor."

"Hmmm. Is he listening?" she asks me, and I check the rearview mirror where I meet the boy's alert eyes.

"Yup, he is."

"Hey, Ahiga, are you hungry?"

"*Yesss.*"

"We're gonna need some burgers, honey," she says, scooting over and leaning her head on my shoulder.

By the time we get our order from the drive-thru, she's fast asleep beside me.

"Are. You. Mad?" Every time I hear that mechanical voice I startle.

"No. Why would I be?"

"Listening. In. Running. Away."

"The running away? If you promise never to do that again, then no. I almost had a heart attack just running half that baseball field, I don't wanna do that again." I throw him a wink in the rearview mirror and love hearing his monotone chuckle. "And I'm not mad about you listening in on our conversation, serves us right for talking in front of you."

"C.H.A.F.I.N. Are. You. Mad. Him?"

"Livid. I'd like to rip the bastard limb from limb, but I won't, 'cause it would piss Luna off and she can be scary." That has him laugh and I find myself liking his unique sound more and more.

It falls quiet for a few minutes and then I hear, "Sleep."

"Sure. You have a nap, kid. I'll get us all home."

CHAPTER 32

LUNA

"I'm gonna need the name."

Autumn's lips are pressed in an angry slash on her face, but her eyes are welling up.

It's been two weeks since I ended trussed up like a turkey in a cargo container, a week since I officially moved in with Ouray, and three days since our emotional trip to Monticello. It's been eventful to say the least. This morning Ouray insisted on driving us to Aztec. I didn't argue. I imagine this hasn't been an easy time for him either, so if it makes him feel better to hover over Ahiga and me for a while, I'm not going to make a fuss.

We've stuck to talking about mundane, day-to-day things the past couple of days, all needing some time to process I guess, but this morning I was able to purge in Gary's office and came out feeling much lighter. Even Ahiga seemed more interactive after his session. He'd been very quiet, sticking close to his bedroom and never far from Jack. Yesterday we caught that damn dog dragging his own bed from in front of the fireplace, all the way up the stairs, where he dropped it right outside the boy's door.

Like I said, a lot going on. Which is why when Autumn called me earlier to see if I was interested in drinks at The Irish, I jumped at the chance to get out of the house. A girls' night seemed like just the thing, but Ouray wasn't ready to let me out of his sight yet, and came along. That turned out okay, because some of the other guys are here too, including Dylan, who's been going stir-crazy being stuck in the office this past week. It'll be at least another six weeks before he'll even be considered to go back on the active roster. The guys are congregated around the bar, while us girls snagged a table.

I probably should've stopped at two beers, because my lips got loose after my fourth one. I ended up spilling my story all over the table, including Wednesday's discoveries.

"Not a chance," I tell Autumn firmly. "This is about Ahiga. He gets to call the shots. I had twenty-four years to do something and chose not to. Had I done things differently then, I could've spared that boy the trauma he'll have to live with for the rest of his life."

The guilt over this threatened to choke me these past few days. Catching myself playing the what-if game, imagining how many others there might have been because I chose to stick my head in the sand. But Gary reminded me that as much as I can't control some else's actions, I can't claim responsibility for them either.

I grab Autumn's hand over the table. "I'm angry too, but I owe that boy, which is why he gets to take the lead on this."

Bella promptly bursts out in tears, pregnancy hormones I guess, which has Jasper running to comfort her.

I feel a hand in my neck and tilt my head back to find Ouray looking down on me.

"You good?"

"I may have had a wee bit too much to drink." I squeeze my thumb and index finger together to illustrate, making him chuckle.

"Ya think? Are you playing nice?" He nudges his head at the still sniffling Bella.

"I may have overshared," I admit, wincing as I look around the table and see all eyes focused on me. "I should probably buy them a drink."

"I'll take care of it."

I watch Ouray make his way back to the bar, only to return moments later with a tray of refills for everyone.

"Well, when you decide to open up, you really don't hold back, do you?" Marya points out, taking a sip of her wine. "I thought I had a decent sob story to tell, but Jesus Hieronymus Christ, I'm just gonna take a number and hang at the back of the line."

Just like that the heavy feeling at the table evaporates as we all burst out laughing. Even Autumn.

The next hour or so the mood is light until the men come over and first Jasper, then Keith take their significant others home.

When Damian suggests he and Kerry call it a night, Marya grumbles and starts digging around her purse for her phone.

"You're drunk," Kerry states, pointing her finger in her friend's direction.

"I'm buzzed," Marya corrects her, finally unearthing her phone. "Which is exactly my objective. While you all get chauffeured home by your man candy, I can pretend the seventy-two-year-old Sikh driver who'll be Ubering me home is Jason Momoa."

"We'll drive you home," Kerry offers, and Damian quickly agrees.

"I'll take you," Dylan, who's mostly been a quiet observer, suddenly offers. "I may not be Jason Momoa, but I'm sure I can get you there."

Marya is far from subtle as she looks him over thoroughly, before getting up from her seat, a little wobbly. "Oh, honey—I'm sure you can get me there too."

I'm still snickering at the sight of Dylan blushing right to his roots, when Ouray pulls the Traverse in the garage.

"Did you see that?" I ask Ouray for what may be the tenth time. He just looks at me with one eyebrow raised, before getting out and coming around to offer me a stable arm. God knows I need it because my legs feel like Jell-O.

The house is oddly quiet, I'm getting used to Jack's excited greetings every time one of us comes home, but tonight he and Ahiga stayed over with Momma and Nosh.

"I don't wanna go to bed yet," I announce when Ouray guides me straight to the stairs.

"No?"

"No, I feel like watching a Jason Momoa move."

I'm laughing when he tosses me over his shoulder—growling—and carries me upstairs.

Oᴜʀᴀʏ

Minx.

I leave her giggling on the bed to quickly hop in the shower.

She's sexy as fuck, but I've tried to keep my distance—giving her some space since our trip to Monticello—and I sure as hell won't take advantage of her when she's drunk.

That's why I'm in the shower jacking off to the sound of her laughter.

She definitely had a good time tonight. Don't think she's ever had much of a posse—given her history—so it's nice to see her let loose with the girls.

Even surrounded by fucking cops, I managed to have a good time myself. It's rare I do anything without my brothers, but I guess it doesn't hurt every now and then.

I'm surprised to find Luna still awake, and the moment I crawl in beside her, she snuggles up.

"I wanna do this every week."

I grin. "We'll see. Maybe hold off any decisions until tomorrow morning."

She huffs, and with the next breath announces, "My stomach hurts."

"Already? That doesn't usually happen 'til the morning after." I receive a sharp little finger in my ribs. "Ouch."

"From laughing. I can't remember the last time I laughed so much."

"That's a good thing," I point out.

"Yeah…I didn't see you laughing much, though. You and Damian looked kinda serious there for a while."

Her fingers trail almost absently through my chest hair as she talks.

"He was telling me about the deal Britney made this past week, rolling over on her own father to catch a lesser charge."

I swallow down a hiss when she flicks my nipple with her nail. Slowly her hand moves down to the elastic of my boxer briefs.

"Always thought she was a nasty piece of work."

I have a hard time keeping my mind on the

conversation when she's slowly torturing me. So much for busting a nut in the shower.

"I was surprised you didn't tell me," I persist.

"I've decided I want to keep work and home separate," she announces, just as the tip of her finger brushes the crown of my cock, making the sweat break out on my forehead.

Sweet Jesus.

"Right," I start in a last-ditch effort to enforce restraint. "So what do you figure Britney will end up doing for time?"

Suddenly she surges up and straddles my legs, while shoving her hand down my boxers, wrapping it firmly around my cock. Leaning forward with her nose almost touching mine, she slurs, "You wanna talk about Britney or do you wanna have drunk sex? I hear it's the best"

I give up.

"You gotta ask?"

Drunk sex is the fucking best.

I let Luna wear herself out—wildly bouncing on my cock—before I took over and with slightly better-coordinated, deep, powering strokes drove both of us over the edge. She was asleep within seconds, softly snoring, while I lay beside her, panting like a lizard on a hot rock.

This morning she still hasn't moved and I carefully

slide out of bed. Downstairs I get coffee going before heading back up with a handful of ibuprofen and a bottle of water. Pretty sure she's going to feel it when she wakes up, so I leave those on the nightstand before hopping in the shower.

A few minutes later, the shower door slides open and a rough-looking Luna gets in, planting her face in my chest. Automatically my arms close around her, stroking a hand up and down her spine.

"Don't breathe so loud," she mumbles, and I have to bite the inside of my lip not to burst out laughing.

"I'll try," I whisper. "So I guess next week is out?"

"Ahhh," she moans dramatically. "Never again."

"Did you take the pills and down the bottle?"

"Yes, but I'm not sure they'll stay down."

"Just breathe in through your nose and you'll be fine."

She lets me wash her limp body and knotted hair, before I wrap her in one of the new towels, big enough to swallow her up.

"I feel a little better," she admits, sitting her butt down on the toilet as I hand her toothbrush to her.

"Good. Get dressed, I'll get going on some breakfast."

She groans, but ten minutes later she's sitting at the kitchen island, scarfing down bacon and scrambled eggs with cheese. Nothing like a greasy breakfast to settle the stomach after a wild night. I know that from experience.

Jack comes bounding up to the SUV when I pull up to the clubhouse. Ahiga is not far behind, wrapping his arms around Luna the moment she gets out, and she kisses the top of his head.

Something special happened between these two on that baseball field in Monticello. They'd already been tight, but their bond transformed that day into something much deeper. Watching them together, arms around each other as they walk into the clubhouse—it feels like a balloon inflating in my chest.

I close my eyes, feeling filled to the brim.

"Found yourself a family." I look up to see Momma leaning in the doorway, a soft smile on her face.

"Seems that way." My voice sounds a little gruff, so I clear my throat and walk up to her.

"My boy," she says, putting her cool hands on my cheeks. "I been prayin' every night since the day you walked into my kitchen—full of piss 'n vinegar but with a heart bigger than the sun—that there'd be a day I could read the happy off your face." She brushes a thumb under my eye. "And there it is."

EPILOGUE

Luna

Three months later . . .

It's like one-stop shopping.

We picked up our marriage license five minutes ago, and now I'm standing in the hallway outside a small room, watching as Momma slicks back the hair of a very nervous Ahiga.

This was a very last minute turn of events.

Today of all days, the region is hit with a major snowstorm. Luckily Nosh was up early and alerted us immediately when he saw conditions outside, and all five of us—Ahiga had asked Momma and Nosh to be here too—piled into the Traverse ten minutes later. It had been a stressful trip, with cars in ditches everywhere. Still, we made it to Monticello just in time for our first appointment with Ahiga's counselor at Child Services.

There we were hit with the next snag. Apparently common-law marriages aren't recognized in the state of Utah. They are in Colorado, one of the few states where common-law marriage is legally viewed the same as a traditional marriage. We clearly did not consider that, which is why after about two seconds of deliberation, we rushed over to the San Juan Court House on Main Street, paid thirty dollars for our marriage license, and were lucky enough the court clerk was willing to perform the ceremony right away.

I would've walked right into the small room with Nosh and Ouray, but the boy held me back.

Shouldn't your dad give you away? That's what they do in the movies.

Christ, I almost lost it.

Absolutely, but my dad isn't here. Could you give me away?

Instead of answering, he turned to Momma and asked her if he looked okay.

So here we stand, the snow still melting off our boots, hat hair for everyone, and big silly grins on our faces. Ouray shakes his head when he sees us walking toward him, but his smile is as big as ours.

The ceremony is so short, it takes no more time than going through the drive-thru at McDonald's. Of course we don't have any rings, so Nosh and Momma lend us theirs for the ceremony.

"Hold up," Ouray says when we start walking out of the room to get to our next appointment. "I haven't even kissed my new wife yet."

"We're gonna be la…mmmm." As often happens when Ouray kisses me, I forget where I am. This time is no exception. He kisses me like a starved man.

"Ahem, Cody Tyler Washburn?"

We collectively turn to a dusty-looking court officer, who looks older than Nosh and is about two sizes too small for his uniform.

"That's us," Ouray rumbles.

"Judge Winfield is waiting. If you would follow me?"

He leads us down the hall to a set of large double doors, which he opens and motions us through. The courtroom is pretty intimidating, as is the massive judge scowling at us when we walk in. The one friendly face in the room is that of Ahiga's counselor, who motions us over, and we slide in the bench beside her.

"Mr. Strongbow. Stand please."

"Yes, Your Honor."

"The original application to adopt Cody Tyler Washburn is in your name."

"Yes, Your Honor."

"However, Ms. Mangiane just informed me a second name has been added to the application." He shoves his reading glasses up his nose and studies the forms in front of him. "A Ms. Luna Roosberg?"

"Actually, that is Mrs. Luna Roosberg-Strongbow, Your Honor," Ouray corrects him, pointing at me.

"You're married?"

"Yes, Your Honor."

I've been biting my lip every time Ouray says *Your Honor*. Mostly nerves, but I can only imagine what it costs him to say it time and time again with a straight face.

Judge Winfield leans over his desk and glares at him over his readers. "And how long exactly have you been married, Mr. Strongbow?"

I actually snort when I see Ouray check his watch before answering that question. "About eight minutes and twelve seconds, Your Honor."

"Are you mocking me, Mr. Strongbow?"

"Wouldn't dream of it, Your Honor."

Twenty minutes later we walk out of the courtroom. Cody Tyler Washburn is now officially Ahiga Strongbow—our son.

"Wait one minute!"

We're almost to the SUV when the counselor, Ms. Mangiane, comes running down the steps after us.

"Things have been so crazy, I was going to mention this before, Skip Chafin was convicted on two counts of aggravated sexual abuse of a child. The verdict just came in yesterday afternoon. Twenty-five years. I thought you'd want to know."

I immediately turn to Ahiga who is looking at me questioningly.

He's in jail. Twenty-five years.

He looks around at everyone before his eyes return to me. Then he shrugs.

Good. Now can we get something to eat? I'm starving.

———

"Ouray! Have you seen my jacket?"

I've been looking for the damn thing for the past half hour. I planned to pair it with skintight black jeans and the pretty white tank Bella gave me for Christmas for the party tonight. It's kinda become my 'old lady' uniform.

The party tonight was Momma's brainchild. After the eventful day in Monticello earlier this week, and with Ahiga starting regular school in Durango on Monday, she felt a combined wedding, adoption, conviction, and back-to-school party was in order. I didn't have the heart to refuse her.

"What jacket?" I startle when I hear his voice right behind me.

"Jesus, you scared the crap out of me." I blow a strand of hair out of my eyes as I straighten up and step out of the closet. "That leather one you got me? I wanted to wear it."

He shrugs his shoulders. "Wouldn't know. Why don't you wear this one?" He holds up an old jean jacket I spilled paint on last month when I was redecorating Ahiga's room.

"It's got stains on it," I point out.

That results in another shoulder shrug. He doesn't care. Of course there was a time, not that long ago, that I wouldn't have cared either, but I'm afraid I've become a bit of a fashion snob lately. I blame it on

Bella, who insists on dragging me on her shopping sprees. Kerry is always a willing participant in those as well. Only Marya—who as a single mom has limited time or money—and Autumn, who claims to rather undergo dental surgery than hit up the mall with us, are the holdouts.

That reminds me…I dig through the closet until I find that gray woolen shrug I bought before winter hit. The tags are still on it.

"Ready?" Ouray asks when I come down the stairs. Ahiga's been at the clubhouse all afternoon, helping decorate.

"Yup. Did you let Jack out?" We're leaving him at home tonight. He gets too excited around a lot of people and starts marking every piece of furniture. We discovered that at Christmas. It wasn't pretty.

"I did. And he has fresh water and a bowl of food. He'll be fine."

I'm really appreciating having a laundry room that leads through to the garage with the way the snow is coming down.

Someone has plowed the driveway up to the clubhouse, and I'm surprised to find vehicles parked all over the yard, a lot of them familiar. When I left everything to Momma, I thought we were just doing something for the club, but clearly she had different ideas.

"Congratulations!"

Several voices call out the moment we come in, stomping the snow off our boots. I look up to see my fellow agents with their significant others, as well as Keith and Autumn, among all Ouray's brothers.

Yup, Momma went all out.

I barely have a chance to say hello to one before I'm passed to another set of arms hugging me.

"Girl, I can't believe you went off and got married without me," Autumn grumbles.

"She wasn't marrying you, Red," Keith points out, pulling me into a hug. "Fuck, I'm happy for you, Luna. He's a lucky man."

"And I know it." Ouray's deep voice comes from behind me as his arm slips around my waist. "Mind if I borrow my wife?"

"What are we doing?" I ask him when he leads me to the pool table, where Momma is standing beside a massive three-tier cake. "Oh my God. Did you make this?"

"Damn right I did. Not about to let some stranger bake a cake for my family."

"It's gorgeous. Thank you." I'm about to give her a hug when a sharp piercing whistle almost pops my eardrum.

"Everybody shut it!" Ouray bellows, and I punch his shoulder.

"You're so loud."

"Only way to get them to shut up, Sprite," he says with a grin, just as Ahiga comes walking up carrying a large flat box.

"What are you up to?" I ask Ouray suspiciously.

"You'll find out soon enough," he whispers,

before tucking me to his side and turning me so we face the bar. "I'm forty-eight," he addresses our friends, "Figured my life was pretty much what it was. Sure didn't expect a pint-sized sprite with a badge, a mean left hook, and a chip the size of a boulder on her shoulder, to come barging into my world." He turns his head to look at Ahiga, who's standing next to Momma. "And then I met a boy who reminds me so much of myself at that age, I felt instantly drawn, and I couldn't figure out what the universe was up to." Blinking back tears I slip an arm around his waist, as he takes a moment to clear his throat. "Four days ago, all the pieces fell into place. I came home with a wife and a son. Perfect—almost."

He steps around me, grabs the box Ahiga left on the pool table, and pulls my leather jacket out. He turns it around so I can see what's stitched on the back.

PROPERTY OF OURAY

"Property? Seriously?"

A collective chuckle goes up.

"Relax, Sprite," Ouray says, grinning. "I'm not done yet."

Ahiga hands him his cut and he shrugs it on. Then he points at the new stitching sitting right over his heart.

PROPERTY OF LUNA

"Better?" he asks, and I grin up at him.

"Much."

Put yours on, Ahiga signs, his face is excited as he helps me into my jacket.

"You may wanna check your pocket." My left pocket is empty, but on the right side I feel something and pull it out, staring at it dumbfounded. "I know normal people ask first and marry later, but we haven't done anything the conventional way yet, so why start now?" He takes my hand and plucks the diamond ring from my fingers. "I love you, Luna. Already put my name on your back—will you let me put my ring on your finger?"

Dammit. The tears win when he slips the diamond on my finger, and pulls me into his arms.

THE END

ACKNOWLEDGMENTS

Writing may be a solitary exercise, but there is an entire team of people needed to turn my scribbles into a novel.

The first person to clap eyes on my words is Joanne Thompson, who is with me from the moment my first chapter is written. She's also the last person to iron out any final wrinkles and has become indispensible to me.

The moment I type THE END, the book is off for two rounds of editing at the hands of someone else whom I absolutely cannot do without, Karen Hrdlicka.

I would be lost without both these amazing women. They make me look good.

I was blessed with a fabulous team of Beta readers for this book; Pam Buchanan, Deb Blake, Debbie Bishop, and Nancy Huddleston. They took time over the holidays to read HWY 550 and give me feedback in between rounds of editing.

Next the book is sent to formatting, and I'm so lucky to have found a spot on CP Smith's schedule. She turns my book into a thing of beauty!

My thanks and love to all of these incredible women.

Buoni Amici Press—Debra Presley and Drue Hoffman—thank you so much for your guidance, patience, and your invaluable set of marketing tools (since I lack those!).

SBR Media—my agent and at times guardian

angel Stephanie Phillips—thank you for your ongoing belief in me, your constant support, your awesome negotiating skills, and your steadfast encouragement in our almost daily chats and long phone calls. I absolutely adore you!

Thank you to all the bloggers who were willing to take a chance on me, and those who have stuck with me through the years.

And finally, a big thank you to all my readers—where would I be without you? There is nothing more gratifying to me than to hear I have somehow managed to brighten your day or touch your hearts

Love you all.

ABOUT THE AUTHOR

Freya Barker inspires with her stories about 'real' people, perhaps less than perfect, each struggling to find their own slice of happy, but just as deserving of romance, thrills and chills, and some hot, sizzling sex in their lives.

Recipient of the RomCon "Reader's Choice" Award for best first book, "Slim To None," Freya has hit the ground running. She loves nothing more than to meet and mingle with her readers, whether it be online or in person at one of the signings she attends.

Freya spins story after story with an endless supply of bruised and dented characters, vying for attention!

CONTACT FREYA@
freyabarker.writes@gmail.com